P Gerome

The shadow of the millionaire

P Gerome

The shadow of the millionaire

ISBN/EAN: 9783743372757

Manufactured in Europe, USA, Canada, Australia, Japa

Cover: Foto ©Andreas Hilbeck / pixelio.de

Manufactured and distributed by brebook publishing software (www.brebook.com)

P Gerome

The shadow of the millionaire

THE

SHADOW OF THE MILLIONAIRE

OR

THE NEW IDEAL

A NOVEL

BY

P. GEROME

" The mind of this country, taught to aim at low objects, eats upon itself. There is no work for any but the decorous and complaisant. Young men of the fairest promise, who begin life upon our shores, inflated by the northern winds, shined upon by all the stars of God, find the earth below not in unison with these,—but are hindered from action by the disgust which the principles on which business is managed inspire, and turn drudges, or die of disgust—some of them suicides."—EMERSON.

NEW YORK

BELFORD COMPANY, PUBLISHERS

18–22 EAST 18TH STREET

[Publishers of *Belford's Magazine*]

THE

SHADOW OF THE MILLIONAIRE.

PART I.

NEW ENGLAND.

CHAPTER I.

EXMOOR.

THERE are towns of New England that preserve the past; they lie like tranquil eddies in the rush of the flood of the continent's life; they are remainders-over, fast dissolving survivals of a by-gone time and a past civilization. New England, which conquered the South, is herself submitting to the spell of the new spirit whose wings she unloosened.

A stranger sauntering up the long main street of Exmoor, beneath the solid shade of the maples and the arch of the palm-like elms, is affected by the peace of the place and the severity of its aspect. He breathes an alien atmosphere, which clothes the town like a garment. A certain lofty modesty and grim Puritan beauty are manifest everywhere. Ambition and passionate sins have no place in this sombre soil; ostentation has no part in these plain houses, whose fronts remind one of the faces of Church elders; the fury of living casts no lurid gleam into the pale flame of these provincial existences.

The unfrequented street, wide, grass-grown to the ribbon of dust in its middle; the heavy shadows of the northern trees; the houses' pillared façades which front the streets with classic masks, Corinthian screens set before prosaic comfort—in all these features which make up Exmoor's countenance is a mournful and moral import, a serious beauty, Miltonic and solemn, like the melancholy of a psalm. Behind a darkened window the profile line of a woman's face is caught—a dim cameo, whose tracery is all spiritual and has, I know not what, of exaltation, steeped as it were in reverie, suffused and permeated with religion. Perhaps a timid gaze steals through the narrow panes upon you, furtive, curious, startled, like an encloistered nun's. The straggling figure which meets you on the wooden sidewalks throws a suspicious regard out of misty eyes, as a lotus-eater might look upon some bustling citizen of the world.

Winter accentuates these effects, bringing out the tones rigidly. Then the trees writhe their limbs into stiff grotesques, as if frozen at an instant of agony; then the cold doubles distance to the exterior world of activity and commerce, and thus tightens more tensely the concentration of each household upon itself; then the snow pads the footfalls on the street; then the mind is constrained to inward study, the morbid probe pries the conscience; then Nature ceases her distractions and the soul sinks into its own deeps.

To the American of this fast generation what of interest is there in Exmoor?—a hill village, where flashes no glint of conflict or of fashion,—"where nothing goes on and the inhabitants are dead!"

Remain many weeks and there is no change.

An empty street, weather-worn façades, drooping elms, a sad tranquillity; the first impression abides. It is the whole. Verily, the town is a Puritan and Protestant monastery.

Yet a lump from the quarry of this homely village between the great breasts of the hills yields a richer return to the psychologist or the student of subtleties than a mass of common ambitions, and hatreds, and bargains, and lusts, wrested from a city's upheaval. The buried men of Exmoor, for whom the sense-world is drowned, theologians and littérateurs, are chameleons of mood. Their brains are tissues delicate as the photographer's plate; their souls are voltaic piles of aspiration; behind their quenched countenances lurk miracles and metamorphoses. These rapt and morbid women, who trail like ghosts along the street, seldom seen, see with the revealing eyes of St. John of Patmos. Beside them, the hauteur of a rich woman's portrait wanes into stolidity.

These select of Exmoor inherit the religious posture from five generations of Congregational divines, while isolation and study have developed in them the intellectual temperament. Chaste sybarites of the spirit, exquisites of the soul; such is the final phase of Pilgrim stock, leavened and fermented by the modern yeast.

These professors and dilettanti, these pure women, cradled from birth in innocence and bathed in the culture of eclecticism, have never wandered from the summits of the ideal; agnostics of evil, for them the slagged valleys of the world do not exist; objective despairs and the brutal struggle for bread have not steeled their fibres. And that, perchance, is the reason that no original strength of literature or philosophy has come out of Exmoor—theirs is not the Samson honey secreted in the lion's carcass. They cultivate letters, but they produce none. Jugglers of

subtleties, refinements and elaborate conceits consume originality.   Yet so catholic is their critical culture that human
thought is become to them as a Capua to be revelled in.

These minds are drunk on Burgundy, disdaining the
heavy liquors, the gin of the sordid passions, the coarse
ecstasies of the solid and muscular animal, the massive
ambitions of the able or the blunt sensations of average
humanity.   They are not courageous and they shrink from
the world; for they are Platonists and not Berserkers.
The odor of the fight, the stench of the battle, the crunch
of the chariot-wheels of success on the faces of the failed
steam up to them faintly and but mantle their shoulders,
leaving their heads in light, as the summer's mist strands
on the foot-hills, while above, the heights soar into the
blue.   And if a reality, through mischance, intrude bodily,
it is but for a moment; just space enough to introduce an
articulate torture between the calm of Hellenic statues and
the glory of the Transfiguration, and so make complete the
Trinity of experience.

Such are the Brahmins of Exmoor.   There remain the
many.

Unless intellect single out a man, he sinks into the
vegetable kingdom, in this town.   Here is no stir of commerce or of gayety to blow upon his stagnant pool.   An in-
tenser apathy and a more entire emptiness of aim alone
distinguish him from the common provincial.   The presence of letters in his town has reinforced his natural lethargy; for they set up a standard as unattainable as absurd,
so it seems to him; and effort is deprived of logic before
this enthroned intellectual distinction.

About the stove of the grocery-store, squatted on barrels
whose contents are products like themselves, the idlers
drawl, gossip and turn their quids with lazy tongue.
The weather is a theme, a constant wonder, an inspiration
that invokes forecast.   The trivialities of life in a country

town absorb what wit they have. Occasionally the advent of some Brahmin customer enlivens the mental fog; a laugh, a tilt of politics, or a query in theology is exchanged over the purchase of tea or sugar.

What sluggish ooze slimes the veins of these barrel-warmers! Through nights and days they slide, without aspiration, and without its consequence—pain. But who shall despise them? Who vaunts as their superior? Their practical philosophy is negation, and towards that our wisest travel. Are they not tinctured with the divinity of India—nay, are they not a sort of unintellectual Rabelaisians, these loafers and time-consumers—these garrulous plants that sit in their flower-pots and note the climbing angle of the sun-rays through the years of many seasons, who are undisturbed, who have plain desires, who have caged happiness? Only the fool sneers at the oyster.

There are shores where drift of the sea strands; there are sheltered nooks in which broken stuff fastens. There are ships that stand and ships that fall asunder. There are ocean bottoms where the vessels of iron rust with wounds gaping in their hides; they were proud, and their death dramatic and entire. There are contemptible affairs, vain rafts and loose-built scows of poor men; insignificance lends such an escape, and so they shore in the mud.

There is a third class in Exmoor.

Those who are tired out, and those who are bereft, those to whom peace means more than honor, and to sleep the serenest heaven. Exmoor understands them and they divine her peculiar beauty. It might be written above the portals of this town, "Let no one without sorrow or its premonition entire here." One wonders at the number of widows and the men graphic with defeat. Those with gun-wounds in their sides gravitate hitherwards. Women who slip to the grave, old men without an interest, the broken and the inert—these leaven the town. The languid tides of Exmoor float silent sorrows, half-soluced disappointments, profound morbidities, elusive evils.

Dreamers, or idlers, or those who watch Time as a friend—such are her people. A cynic, or one seared with sensation, would call it "stupid and deuced slow." But a seer or a poet would gaze into that uniform life as into the ever-standing waters of the middle sea.

This is Exmoor.

At bottom a stagnate country village, platonized by the philosophic and literary spirit of its aristocracy and by the presence of a little college, its contempt of fact and its worship of the transcendentals have elevated its lassitude into a northern *"far niente."* Here emanates a subtle fluid that takes the zest out of action and ætherealizes the soul, that snaps the animating spring and refines the subjectivity, that makes a man a mirror and breaks the handle of his hammer.

CHAPTER II.

"THE CLYDES."

THE March evening was canopying the landscape of gaunt hills in a not unwelcome darkness. The long street was deserted, except by some shuffling figures hurrying to escape the sovereign dreariness of aged winter snow and dense leaden sky. Every minute deepened the cold vapors, through which objects looked as if plunged in clay-colored water. The hill bulks pressed in upon the town with their bony knees. Here and there a light glimmered wanly, like a drunkard's eye; but for the most part the growing gloom invaded the windows before the thrifty tradition of Exmoor permitted a match to be struck.

Julian Clyde, a tutor in Exmoor College, was walking with quick impatience, a stride unusual in that slow town. He had spent the afternoon (it was Saturday) with Mr. Keyes, the literary critic.

Along the silent street he scudded; his head well thrust forward, his long coat flapping at his heels. He did not like this weather; indeed, he felt he would like to beg to differ with all Exmoor to-night.

The long street ascended the slope, carrying its narrow road, its wide wooden sidewalks, its aisles of leafless maples and giant elms, straight up the south hill on which the college buildings stood. The tutor bent his back as the way steepened, but forged ahead at an equal speed. In his mood he was glad to pound the old hill vigorously, as if it were a trampled enemy.

Half way up to the first college hall is a square stone house, fendered with a high porch and beamy Doric pillars of wood supporting the projecting lip of the roof. Trees veil it in, as a silken gauze veils a woman; but as her eyes sparkle with the sights she still can see, so the windows of the house look down vistas out over Exmoor and northward along the extended hill-summits some twenty miles.

The tutor entered the yard through the hedge-opening. He burst along the path, oblivious of the signal-handkerchief waved in welcome from the parlor window. Once within the hall he flung his overcoat across one chair; his fur cap, aimed at another, fell on the floor; while his overshoes were kicked off with indiscriminate haste.

He made for the parlor, where he expected to find light, fire and Mrs. Lancaster. Instead, darkness, panelled with gray where the windows were, and a few pale flickers in the grate to cast vacillating gleams across the chimney-soot.

He shrugged his shoulders. "Why can't you have the lights lit? You always gloat in the black; you ought to have been a Puritan, instead of their descendant," he said, growling privilegedly to the indistinct figure seated near a window.

"You didn't see me wave, did you, Julian?"

"Light the lamps and I'll talk, but not before. One should be an owl to live a winter in Exmoor," he retorted.

"The Italian is uppermost to-night, isn't it, dear?" she said, giving him a soft pat as she rose to do his bidding.

The mild petroleum light suffused the room, leaving shadows to exist. It fell over the woman, burnishing the bronze ropes of hair that crowned the tall figure. Mrs. Lancaster turned on the young man with a benediction-smile which he tossed aside with a gesture of the head.

She came towards him. Her stateliness, was it not a little stiff, straightened with an unconscious pride, a patrician rigidity that bespoke the conversatism of respectability and the exclusiveness of fixed habit and selected familiarities, that could not brook a non-classical idea? It was all in her carriage. Are not these pure creatures who are pedestalled on Puritan character and patrician selection the supreme result of New England civilization? They possess the graciousness of the queens of society, but they have preserved the woman; theirs is the sanctity of saints without the prudery that tarnishes holiness; they have achieved the effects of nobility and of culture, without the limitations of the one or the toil-marks of the other: in a word, they are the consummate flower of their order. They have all the virtues, and what they lack is little esteemed by their world; for they are everything but passionate and witty and unwise.

"Don't you know you will wear yourself out with this continual friction, that you cannot afford to be always protesting? The world stood before you came and will go on after you. Let it wag its own way, then. What is it, Julian? Let me do something for you."

There was an entreaty in her eyes. Her sweet face

beneath the burnished hair rose above the black of her mourning, like Love from a grave. The young fellow's quick susceptibility caught the effect, the fair skin of the neck within the soft circle of ruching. He patted her check.

" How good-looking you are to-night, *ma belle tante!*" he said.

She flushed a little like a girl. " But tell me the trouble," she persisted. "Is Exmoor so tiresome ? What is it? Are there some disagreeables connected with your teaching ?"

" What makes you want to know ?" he asked.

He was surprised at her concern. Her affection had never shown any practical estimation of him or his circumstance. His childhood remembered her as a lovely beneficence which protected him and taught him beautiful things—the glory of a winter sunset, the sough of the north wind in the hemlocks; but she had in no sense been a consoler. At his blunt interrogation she looked up with wide, uncomprehending eyes, half in astonishment at such a question.

" Well, if you want to know," Julian went on, "the true inwardness is shortly this : I am sick of Exmoor and can't stand teaching a lot of freshmen and blockhead boys much longer. I want to get out and take a dive into the *real* world. I want to feel the actual pulse of things." He thrust the bare statement before her defiantly. Consternation rose into her face.

" You do not mean?—" she began.

" Yes I do," he interrupted; " I mean it exactly. I want to cut this town. I'm tired of plugging ideas into young numskulls. I am desperately weary of the name of literature and all it implies, its critics, its dilettanti, its literary women. Exmoor and its little conventions, its small unswervable dictates—I'm going to shake loose from its tyranny. You are shocked, of course."

Blasphemies against her life-ideals ! Mrs. Lancaster

looked at her nephew in a little horror. She had never suspected such deep-seated revolt.

"But you would not forsake books, Julian? You cannot mean to desert scholarship?" she gasped.

"Scholarship!" he cried. "Scholars! And if you mean by that plodders like Doctor Ponder, American editions of Faust's Wagner, or even such men as Mr. Keyes—no, I would not live their lives, either of them. Exmoor necessitates one or the other. Laborer or dilettante, the hod-heaver of learning who carries mortar for other men's bricks, or the elegant exquisite who prates over letters and has not vital passion enough to live what he praises, or to be what he goes into lyrics over—that is Exmoor's alternative."

Julian spoke the rebellion of a year in these words.

"You are so unjust, Julian, so unjust!" protested Mrs. Lancaster. "You don't present the possibilities rightly. It is feasible to be something other than plodding or dilettante, and you know it. Can't you be as real, as you phrase it, in Exmoor as anywhere? Can't there be real literature here? Emerson, I am sure, had no more in Concord than exists just here."

Her suggestion provoked him into rant again.

"Real literature, or any living actuality come out of this town of theology and connoisseurs! Humph! What do we know of the needs of the world in these hills? The professors and critics of Exmoor treat all these things as mere puppets of the imagination, delicate and airy illusions, with which to amuse the mind; they weave dialectic puzzles and sketch quaint designs. I, for one, am no longer content with shreds and patches. I wish to move down into the crowding world and have the facts of existence hammer me, and I myself push men and forces until experience reveals life and what it is. That is the only good in the world, the only way to truth; the other bridges to it rest on sloth and ease and good feeding. That is the only way true literature is born; or anything else true, for that matter."

He was smoking like a cannon which has just disgorged its bolt. Then a sense of emptiness came to him and he burst into laughter at himself. But his aunt had been too roughly dinted, and there was no humor in the thing for her.

" But your prospects, Julian," she said, " and your position in the college—you would not fling them to the winds! Not every young man of twenty-three holds such a position. Here you are known for your father's sake and your own merits. Your friends expect so much of your future. Mr. Keyes is so fond of you; he told me, himself, you were the one young man he cared to stand literally sponsor to. You are not material, and I know you have no vulgar ambition for money. Why will you persist in vague longings for the world, where other talents than yours are recognized, and such as yours are overlooked ? Can it be due to your Italian heritage, this unequal restlessness ?"

That foreign maternity Mrs. Lancaster made responsible for every discrepancy in Julian's usually well-ordered existence. The irregularity crossed her New England sense, touched even her instinct for rectitude. An Italian was altogether proper in painting or sculpture, and one should revere Dante; but, in a matter of birth, to have the blood of those dark distrustful southrons, those subtle Borgias, and those heated sons of licentiousness, mixed up with one's own clear, Puritan, righteous strain, in one's adopted nephew too ! Things were right and good in their places ; but, while passions in art are valuable, they should be labelled like them edicinal poisons; and it is not conducive to propriety to be indiscriminate.

Julian shrugged his shoulders impatiently and swept his hand out, as if to brush aside such absurdities.

" No, it is nothing but Exmoor that makes me want to get out. I don't ask for the things she can give; for I think them factitious. I always thought Taine hit it right in his comparison between Tennyson and DeMusset. It is pleasant and cultivated to be railed off from the Philistines, but to unwrap the affectations around you and go down into the ugly, difficult world and learn its lessons adequately, regardless of consequences to one's self, and out of such hard apprenticeship to speak—that is a task that never occurred to these leisurely spiritualists of Exmoor."

" Oh, don't talk so, don't talk so! You don't know what you say!" cried Mrs. Lancaster in a wounded tone.

After a moment she turned away. " I must go and see if supper is getting ready." She hesitated, and then came back to him. She put her hands on his shoulders. She was so tall, the stately woman, that she looked into his eyes on almost the same plane with them.

" My poor boy, be more at peace with yourself! You do not know that the world you think will help you, will only strangle you, and this Exmoor you recoil from now, will seem a blessed, blessed thing, compared with the real reality. Those men, those students whom you do not wish to imitate, they are cynical and comfort-loving, no doubt; but some day you will forget their superficial faults and the hollowness of Exmoor, in contemplation of their unprejudiced souls and of her peace and liberty. For you will not find freedom, nor justice, in that world to which you yearn to go."

After this long speech she kissed him and then went to her kitchen.

Bah! thought Julian, it was merely feminine reluctance to have him breast circumstance.

The supper-bell rang.

In the dining-room Professor Clyde sat at the end of the

supper-table. He looked about fifty. He had a white American beard and loose white hair. The head was high and nobly shaped, after the manner of the Plato busts. The features were regular and cold in repose, but continual laughters and little enthusiasms over trivial matters lighted up the face, as it turned to Mrs. Lancaster or to his son.

"What have you been doing this afternoon, Julian?" asked Professor Clyde.

"Reading for that Tuesday lecture," was the answer.

"What is the subject? Did you tell me? I think not; what is it?"

"Wilhelm Meister."

Supper, its illumination and social contact, mellowed the young man's crustiness. The genial table found an echo of impulsive speech in him, and before long he was talking about the proposed lecture with interest. Professor Clyde himself was always at his best at this hour, when the mind forgot to rattle in the scabbard of the flesh. The sop thrown the stomach, the gleam of the light and the harmony Mrs. Lancaster conspired to create under her sway, unlocked the human companionship in the man and drew from him the cream of his mature spirit, the old wine of his wisdom, the nectar of his happiest mood.

At the Clyde supper-table philosophy and criticism, the overflow of their lectures, gave the conversation a stilted and declamatory style, which would have only elicited an "Oh, hell!" from the average, unenthusiastic materialism of the man about town.

The Professor spoke in resonant voice:

"Is there a company in literature, outside of Plato, to which any author introduces us, as agreeable as that of Lothario and his friends? I shall have to go back to Socrates in the 'Phædo' to find their prototype, and even then the Athenians can hardly equal them. I think Goethe drew in 'Meister' a society of his dreams, an archetype of a cultured salon, so to speak. Lothario, Jarno, Therese, Natalia, the ever present influence of the dead uncle—these names call up beautiful and versatile personalities, informed and tolerant minds, whose perception matches their intention, and whose nobility is beaconed by clear intelligence. They seem incarnate sweetness and light. Goethe fills their lives with a high endeavor and a soft radiance."

"Yes," Julian answered, "as you say, it was an ideal. And if it was an ideal, even to Goethe, in Weimar, it's a regular seventh-heaven houri for us, with our shop practicality and that hard utilitarian sense, which despises pure intellect for its own sake."

"But then, you know, Julian, we have the same struggle. And it is the fight, not the attainment, that is worth while. Better than truth is the struggle after truth. That's Lessing."

"But I am not a Stoic like you. No miserable formula of sour-grape flavor, even if concocted by Lessing, shall cheat me," replied the younger man, almost sullenly. Mrs. Lancaster here interposed with the remark that Goethe was self-sufficient; that he spent his life scouring up to lustre his own marble soul, as a cook burnishes her copper pot. She expressed the idea partly because, like every woman, she believed it true, and partly for the pleasure "her men" would enjoy in combating the assertion. She possessed the virtuous feeling of a Roman ædile in providing an arena for gladiators, eager to fight. The two men rushed at the hated idea, full tilt, like two unrestrained boys. What a comedy for the never-surprised, always-contained, serenely inane people in such a scene !

"That's a miserable legend," Julian cried, "which has gathered about Goethe, as the legend Thiers created gathered about Napoleon. The poet was no more an egoist than the Emperor was *not* a cynical Machiavelli on horse-back. Because he was strong and did not cry out under the tortures of life like weaker men, he is removed from the humanness that is human because it is weak."

Professor Clyde chimed in, "'Meister' to my mind does not present the real Goethe. The book only shadows forth his practical solution of the equation of life. Faust is the real and innermost man. In him is seen the battle of the spirit, eaten with negations and stuffed with ennui, all desirous, but a Hamlet at bottom ; a sad man and a weary one. Yet he buried Self, and by sheer force drove his life into conformity with the intellectual conclusions of Meister ; despite doubt and defeat, to conquer, to attain, and to advance. It is as if he had said to himself, 'This illusive Maia of existence, this wheel of fire whose spokes are impossible yearnings, and whose tire drops tears, is, in truth, the actual world of my deepest consciousness ; yet I shall dare to do, despite waverings and despairs ; and over against agonies and bootless cries, I shall set up "Iphigenia" and "Tasso," like statues of pure beauty in the teeth of chaos.' How else shall we explain that this Phidian chiseller of marble tragedies can create Mephistopheles, and make Faust dream and speak? He unconsciously helped to form the legend which makes him a god, when, in reality, he was one of the great, unhappy souls, one who fought where most faint, and, in the dimness, groped for the knees of Truth."

Julian caught up the theme in turn. "If ever there was a good fight fought, he fought it. Because he smiled down the sentimentalists and sought truth and not martydom ; because there is no self-pitying in his case, and, because he *did* attain, and the pathetic disparity between most men's reach and grasp has no title in him,—signifies that his struggle was not the less but the greater. Of course he doesn't give his admirers a chance to play the Magdalen and break ointment over him; no tear-floods at his funeral, as for Burns or De Musset; but he is not therefore the less human, only stronger than the rest. Strength is not inevitably coupled with egoism."

Such were the table-talks of the Clydes. The dogmatic temper of the New England inheritance of theology appeared in these discussions, together with the long sentences and positivism of the lecture-room; but they aimed high, and helped the young man to "hitch his wagon to a star."

After a while, when calm had come, Mrs. Lancaster asked, "What day do you expect your millionaire?"

"Mr. Gay will probably be here on Wednesday. I expect a letter from him to-morrow. I only hope we shall be successful in gaining his support for the college—he gives so largely in charities," answered Professor Clyde.

Mr. Gay was a millionaire of New York and a devout Congregationalist. It was expected of him to stiffen the financial backing of the institution in Exmoor, for his religion's sake.

"Do you go out to-night?" asked Professor Clyde of his son.

"Yes; a whist-party at Jane Halding's."

"What an original that young girl is!"

"We must show her to Mr. Gay," suggested Mrs. Lancaster.

"Her independence won't consider his plutocracy, you know," said Julian.

"She and Mrs. Ballard are the two trump cards Exmoor always plays on strangers," laughed Mrs. Lancaster.

"Mr. Gay, I imagine, always plays and is never played on," Professor Clyde said, meaning to express a dark significance.

CHAPTER III.

A SUNDAY IN EXMOOR.

SUNDAY in Exmoor! As if the spirit of her Puritan people had a sensible emanation, the atmosphere of Sabbath wrapt the old town in a certain added tranquillity that the heart felt. A moral ether arose from her houses, as from a censer a fragrance is wafted.

But, under this respectable and orthodox cloak, certain strange existences were lived in Exmoor, certain unsuspected Sabbath moods were indulged. In this town of secluded women and hermited men, some few idiosyncrasies were developed, anomalies that flourished unseen ; as under the strewn leaves certain vines run and bloom. Puritans, theologians, bigoted Calvinists, narrowly intense religionists, served but to mask the emancipation of a spirit like the critic Keyes's. Their dark shadows, their sombre decay, gave him nourishment, and he drew from their dense protection a sap to animate the veins of absolutely different offspring. Their morbidities, their gloom, their Puritan passions were a sort of forest muck that clothed his spirit with heat and strength ; whence he put forth pagan ideas and untrammelled criticisms of literature, of religion, of men and the past. So it was that out of Exmoor came the clearest intellectual light, the most impartial mind, that New England knew at that time.

Upon the Sunday of Exmoor's majority this peculiar nature had foisted a new feast of the passover ; for the day in its peace lent him an exquisite intellectual sense, and he was aware that strange beauties and hidden griefs, grandeurs unknown and novel enlightenings of understanding broke in upon him with the advent of the Sabbath, as light pours in upon eyeballs heretofore blind. So he gathered together his week's research for the Sunday, and scanned the mass with the concentrated lamp the day gave him. Thus he was enabled to draw hair-lines, and weigh gold and dross to the minutest particle. He called Sunday his "Aladdin's Lamp." Or, if he had no definite work, he would devote the day to a Lucullean banquet of the intellect, musing upon many literatures and counting over a hundred gleaming wonders from the manifold coffers of his learning. He knew Sanscrit and Persian; he mumbled Greek like German; there was hardly a language under the sun, whose speakers had had wit enough to fashion a literature, that he had not mastered, or "dabbled in," as he himself expressed it.

Verily, a subtle spirit—so various, so profuse, so universal; entirely critical, never original, known only to itself and careless of the world. Its definition is a vast experience—and a barren one, some bore of a moralist will insist. But Keyes nursed his intellect as a miser hoards his gold; its panorama of pictures never sated his fine curiosity, and existence for him meant an infinity of mind-amusement, as a jockey's heaven is an eternity of exciting heats. He had no exclusive passion within his one passion for literature in the broadest sense; he was too impartial for attachments. Life was to him literally an endless Louvre, and himself a perception turned loose in an immense picture-gallery.

This was the man who had been, in large ways, an intellectual father to Julian Clyde; for the elder Clyde had stood aloof from the guidance of his son's life, and had been content to open the doors of his library, and occasionally to talk on some intellectual subject. Some note in Julian's character or some dangling sun-ray in his Venetian hair, perchance, had early attracted the critic, who became the boy's godfather, in a sense. When Julian was four years

old, Mr. Keyes was wont to climb the hill after him, from
whence he was carried off to the critic's study, or propped
up on two dictionaries at Mrs. Keyes's ceremonial dinner.
One of the critic's conceits at that time was to insist that
the soul of Walter Scott's Marjorie Fleming had reappeared
in his stout-legged, small friend.

Julian had passed his usual Sunday; a Sunday grown out
of his own tastes and Exmoor influence.   It was a day in-
doors, over books, a dip in Goethe, another in Bossuet, a
third in Leopardi; a tasting of poetry, of metaphysics, of
history—the leisure day of a man of letters.   He always
enjoyed it; but this last year a physical protest ran through
it all, its dilettanteism and epicurean intellectuality—a call
for activity and something done; something besides dawd-
ling over six or seven authors in four or five tongues of a
Sunday afternoon.

He sat in the library, and the deepening gloom en-
swathed him in thickening folds.   He was restless and re-
sentful.   He heard the sound of the church-bell, rising to
him from the valley, after filling its basin as water fills a
cup.   It summoned to the Sunday-evening prayer-meeting
held in the basement of the old Congregational church.
He determined to go; it was better than tossing in the
trough of his discontent and ennui, without steam enough
to ride steady.   Besides, Margaret would be there and he
could go home with her.

The church was traditional in Exmoor, a bodily projec-
tion of that dreary Puritan past into Exmoor's advanced
thought, a grim dogma of gray stone set in the midst of
her sweetness and light, even as the theology she adhered
to and taught, amid her literary and philosophical catholic-
ity, appeared like some Middle Age donjon frozen fast within the elegant magnificence of Renaissance porticoes and
columns.   The church was built of gray stone, a great, un-

speaking, square mass that loomed amid the trees above the low roofs of Exmoor.

Do you wish to see the worship your New England grandfathers poured out ? Go, then, into this Exmoor church, and you will behold that departed faith intact, unbroken by incursions of liturgy or free-thinking—in Exmoor it is to be found, alongside with Prof. Clyde and his veiled Hegelianism, and cheek by jowl with Alexander Keyes and his disciples. Strange that the footholds for freest thought in America should be under the shadow of an intolerant Calvinism, that intellect shuns the new cen-- tres which have no superstitions!

Within, a low-ceiled room, men and women in close ranks, stifled air, gaseous with human breath through which the oil-lamps shone like lights in a London fog—a fit tabernacle in which to display the morbidities of northern imagination, the sombre and grotesque dreams of a Calvinism, unenlightened and unsweetened by any ray of tolerant intellectuality.

A man rises to pray ; he is the embodiment of this old Exmoor. Watch him. A dark, spare man with abrupt body and great black head, with dark eyes and rugged exposed chin ; he prays in a monotonously impassioned voice —that is Doctor Ponder. He holds the chair of Eastern languages in Exmoor College. The gaunt bone of his farm inheritance stands in rocky relief after the waste of twenty years of excessive study. Doctor Ponder delivered a long prayer, old-fashioned and denunciatory, which impressed Julian he was not in salvation's boat. The assumption of Doctor Ponder that his creed was the discerning wand to separate the sheep and the goats irritated the young man. Nature, men, books, the ways of knowledge, were as open to him as to this man, or to any of the old dogmatizers of the past. It struck Julian as an insufferable piece of conceit to make a formula for humanity out of one's own bounded experience. This orthodoxy was another of the limitations Exmoor would fain impose on the free and reverent spirit.

After the meeting was over he joined Margaret, and the two walked homeward together.

She spoke of the devout spirit manifested in the meeting. The "beautiful prayer of Doctor Ponder's" won her peculiar veneration. This increased Julian's irritation—this praise and respect of hers for men whom he considered inferiors in some intellectual sense, this unquestioning acceptation of an iron creed that seemed to him not over-modern. She never understood his vague dreams, his grandiose aspirations. His ideals and his theories were eccentricities of his youth to her. Her calm gray eyes decomposed existence into the simple elements of father and child, duty and prayer, and a cheerful serenity ; she never comprehended that mysteries and terrible possibilities ranged round commonplace life, as around the clear disk of Homer's world fathomless mists and unshapen forms circled and watched. Intellect in youth is always more or less given to empty high soundings of speech, to theatricals and follies—it is measuring itself ; but to Margaret they were absurd.

The two reached her mother's house—that Mrs. Ballard, the widow, the Clydes had called one of the trump cards of Exmoor.

"Come in, Julian, it's very early," she said, as he opened the gate.

Within the hall, she directed : "There, sit on the stairs, while I go find mamma and light the lamps a little."

The Ballard house was always in gloom, except where Margaret herself was. The girl passed on through the dark doorways, until she found the dining-room. She closed the door behind her and spoke into the dark.

"I am here, mamma."

No answer. She groped her way until her hands touched a figure ; she wound her young arms about it.

"Why do you sit here in the dark, mamma ? You ought to have a light." There was no response. After a pause Margaret went on. "Come out into the hall; do come ! Julian's there, and it'll be so nice and cozy. You two like to talk. So come on. He says you understand him. Come, I won't leave you to the mopes here."

"No, no ! I should only sour the wine. I'll stay here where I'm best appreciated—by myself," answered the widow, at last. She probably smiled in a grim fashion in the darkness there.

But Margaret persisted, she would take no refusal. Finally Mrs. Ballard succumbed, and Julian beheld her stalking down upon him, Margaret in the rear, cutting off retreat.

"Here's mamma, Julian," the girl announced. "She was deep in the blues, so I brought her out to talk to you. You two can talk wisdom together, while I'll sit at your feet and humbly imbibe."

She put her mother in a big chair, she said the stairs were good enough for Julian's longitude, and finally she seated herself on a stool at her mother's feet.

"Now go ahead, you two," she proclaimed, with the air of a herald opening the lists. "I'm out. An ordinary mortal cannot hope to do anything but subside when De Staël and Goethe discourse together."

Her laugh stung Julian more than he was willing to confess to himself. The mockery of mediocrity is so easily available against a real or supposed superiority.

Julian and the mother exchanged an unconscious glance of sympathy, which shut out the daughter as an alien. These two were drawn to each other. There was a world beside the good and the practical, in which this sombre, rebellious, brilliant woman lived apart from her family, from her town; with exceptions, in a few instances, of those, like Professor Clyde and Mr. Keyes, who understood her.

Presently Mrs. Ballard asked abruptly, " Mr. Gay comes this week?"

Julian replied that his father so understood. " Wednesday, I believe. He is on his way to Boston, and his private secretary comes with him."

" I suppose we shall see a grand siege and regular assault, according to most approved methods, on him and his charity-money," said Mrs. Ballard with a bitter humor.

" If Mr. Gay is so rich, it will do him good to be persuaded into giving some for a good purpose. His money couldn't be put to a better use," Margaret broke in, a reproach in her tone.

Again the two exchanged a sympathetic look accompanied this time by a little depreciatory smile.

" No doubt of it," said Julian, dryly.

" So the faculty think, Margaret. Whatever they divert for the college will be saved from evil practices," replied Mrs. Ballard, mimicking the solemnity of Doctor Ponder when that divine laid down that so and such was the Lord's will. She changed her voice back into the scornful ring: "There will be a very magnificent scene, genuflections, and flatteries huge as Chinese bouquets. How President Pompes and Doctor Ponder will prate and pray ! the President with unction and suave compliments, the Doctor with earnest vehemence, in the same way he exhorts sinners to repentance."

" A regular Molière alive. I can see it, and Thackeray ought to be here himself to draw it. Bah! it'll be disgusting," cried the youth.

Margaret felt she must protest against such loose speech, but the two *would* enjoy themselves. Can a person of cyn-

ical habit find a greater pleasure than to secure a listener
who comprehends in a flash through intelligence, not by
grace of a bitter baptism,—one who takes such talk as a
mere elegance, and returns his debt in the equal coin of
banter?

Mrs. Ballard went on in her own inimitable way, pictur-
ing the bait the faculty would swish invitingly before this
enormous whale from New York; how they would make
ridiculous blunders, and heave all together in abortive ef-
forts to land him; how finally he would shake his big tail
good-naturedly, and leave them a few good things out of
pure amiability, before he made off. She sent stinging innuendoes out from her mouth, flings at those brooding
thinkers and their boorishness as over against the keen
decisiveness and man-of-the-world adaptability which such
a successful New Yorker as Mr. Gay would undoubtedly
possess. It was an amusing caricature, such a one as the
widow in her revolt, and Julian in his discontent, had often
summoned up between them.

"Julian," she said abruptly, "when Mr. Gay comes here,
why don't you make him like you? Such men take fancies
and have favorites. You might just as well be his favorite
as some other man. Here's your chance. He can make or
break a man, if he chooses—though, I suppose, he chooses
more frequently to break than otherwise. Besides, Exmoor's
no place for you. It's too small and the real forces of the
age are not here."

New York and her business men had always been one of
Mrs. Ballard's hobbies. She admired their clean vigor,
their swift intelligence, their style, and their verve. Our
attractions are dictated by our wants; so this moody, way-
ward, intense spirit entertained an admiration for those
superficial, lively, smart mechanisms. If her own son had
been only born with capacity, as was Julian, she would have

desired him to be able, rich, influential, generous, all alive, like successful New Yorkers.

As long as Mrs. Ballard talked before her audience—for she hardly conversed—she maintained the magnetic mien she wore for others. But, after bidding good-night, when she re-entered her dining-room, the mood of mastery fell from her, like an outer wrap. Her muscles grew lax; her nerves sank unbraced; in the dim light her figure seemed unshapen, to undulate; the tense cheeks fell into flabbiness, —just as if the bow-string which made rigid the bow were suddenly cut. She cast herself into a chair abjectly; she sat with staring eyes and brooded stupidly. Since her husband's death two years ago, this was her constant habit, when alone—a lethargy not concealed from her family, and only retired from when the world intruded.

Left alone, Margaret and Julian toyed with the hours. The evening of a day of peace, a beautiful girl with a Priscilla face and a haughty purity!—Julian was led to his confession. We all confess to some pedestalled creature when we are twenty-three, and ten years after think what geese we were—do we not? Ah! there are worse follies than sentimentalism. He gave utterance to some of those personal doubts of ability and opportunity which haunt young men. Margaret reassured him with a sweet, womanly sympathy. Here was a heart a strong man could find rest in, between the tremendous battles of a career—all of it given to sustain a youth with his womanish fancies and his callow misunderstandings of life. But when he half suggested those deeper conflicts between a man's success and his ideals, between his appetites and his intellectual wants, the girl had no patience. The ideas of Julian were too unsubstantial, too much in the air. Where did he get such funny notions, such absurd conceptions, anyway?

" Why do you make a mountain of the future? It's easy enough. If you go ahead and do your plain duty, you ought to be content. I'm sure if I were a man I could find a place in this world, I could earn my living in the practical world, as a lawyer or a business man, easily enough."

This was her answer to his imaginations! The path was straight to her, lighthoused by duty and common-sense. The noble, pale face flushed with an energy to do her work well, whatever it was. And let justice be done her. While the young man loafed through an easy life, and made himself cross with vain and silly fancies, this girl, this lovely Puritan, this high-spirited and true woman, bore the brunt of housekeeping and bore her mother on her shoulders through the widow's attacks of stupor and morbid misery. Surely her ringing words contrasted well with the wavering hypotheses and all-embracing speculations of the youthful egotist! Yet her practical solution to all things in existence seemed insufficient and contemptible to the youth. Passions, desires, renunciations, an infinity of emotions and imperative needs clashed together and dashed out a dust that filled his eyes.

"Yes," he cried scornfully, "you would be a success if you were a man. You know what you want, which is not much. You understand that to succeed needs so many blows a minute, and nothing in yourself would hinder you delivering them with precision. You don't dream nor desire too much."

He stopped a moment, then went on with added vehemence, "You are content with the ordinaries and have faith in God. Life is neither an emptiness nor a Sphinx to you; simply an army contract of groceries and dry-goods —production and consumption, like a problem in mathematics, solution foreordained and exact."

"So much rant, because I said I could earn my living!" answered Margaret, meekly. Julian was such a dear nonsensical boy! Then she went on, in the tone she used to her Sunday-school class: "Of course I could. There is nothing so very dreadful about it. You imagine too much. That is a bad habit. When you know more of it, it will simplify itself. Why do you torture yourself with these vain fancies? You had much better strike home, and do your plain duty."

Gospel of common-sense, which pricks the non-reliable balloon of the idealist; whose supporting gas is faith in his superiority over average humanity!

"Utility and prosaic duty, they're all you see," he blurted out. "As for me, I haven't submitted yet. There are other considerations. I don't expect you to understand. I'm going. Good-night."

She parted from him wistfully, as if her heart were willing to make amends for the failure of her head. But he would have none of it. Her marble regularity of beauty, expressive of a constant attitude of mind, exasperated him.

Once out, the cool air lowered his heat. The snow shone like silver under the diamond cold stars. The outlines of houses and fences were clear and clean-cut. Every twig of the trees showed entire, in silhouette against the frosty heavens. Julian walked rapidly home, crunching the dry snow. As his perturbation subsided, his mind gained a steady lucidity. In the firmament the solar scheme lay mapped out before him. He saw the planets wandering through space; and light, born of the impact of the sun's influence upon the fluid particles sheathing their spheres, escaped from them, as from electric globes of glass. Space stretched on and on, and deepened into space, and a million darts of flame flung through it, as gold slides through mercury. The dry air invigorated his brain, and his thought passed like lightning about every object, illuminating every hidden recess, and reproducing exactly every detail. He wondered at its swiftness.

The houses passed were seen through, as if their walls were glass. He comprehended all the life within their sides.

In an instant he understood it all. Actions of his neighbors, heretofore inexplicable, shone translucent. He went under a Pharisee's house, whose God was a mere infinite exaggeration of himself. Julian saw his holiness in bed, praying and self-congratulatory. He passed beneath the windows of a girl who had entered the portals of old-maidenhood, and her mortification and bitterness seemed natural to him, the direct and fatal consequences of causes he divined. Next door dwelt a young man and his lately married wife. He had known the bride when she was on sufferance in society; he had seen her take snubs with meekness, and pocket trivial insults. He understood her and her exultation in marrying a rich man; and the chagrin of her former patrons was sweet in his nostrils, just as if he were in her place. Thus a hundred relations of life in a country village arose in turn, and were understood.

This unusual divination possessed him with a sad earnestness. Life's variety and pleasure broke up before its sure glances. Yet it contained a victory of its own, and with its disenchantment was locked a sense of power and superiority. For the time he felt content. It was enough to imagine and discern, and he did not care for objective satisfactions. He decomposed ambition into its phenomena, and possession into its instincts. Applause was as tinsel to him, and acquirement as so much dead matter.

A light gleamed across his path. He stopped and considered. He looked up at the great house of Mr. Keyes and the one window in the wing whose illumination glistened on the snow crystals at his feet. Then he turned in and rapped upon the side door, which opened into the critic's study. A deep voice summoned a resonant "Come in."

The room Julian entered faced the street, and together with an adjoining room of equal dimensions, the two connecting by an arch, occupied the whole north wing of the house. The ceiling was gridironed with oak beams, the interstices between set with square blocks of stucco stained deep red. Black-walnut cases, handsomely carven, filled every inch of space, half-way up. On their tops, against the stained walls, rested a multitude of treasures; rare bronzes and exquisite bric-a-brac, fans, fragments of famous marbles from renowned quarries and old fanes, Roman lamps, Trojan obuli, Athenian coins, Middle Age crucifixes. A great flat desk stood in the room's centre; near it, a watery-green iron safe with its leaves thrown open, half displaying manuscripts. Close by was a shelf of books bound in yellowed or dingy brown parchment. This was that famous collection, some sixty volumes, originals, of monkish writings, which Harvard University desired, and over which Mr. Keyes was wont to run his index-finger carefully, and to say to visitors with a wistful half-glance, in the voice of the melancholy Jaques of "As You Like It,"—"This is all my life, all my life." It was usually heavy artillery on the ladies. Plaster casts of the Apollo Belvidere and the Venus di Milo were set on simple brackets; the Sistine Madonna hung from the wall; a Flanders clock hummed just beneath the gold chain of the Order of the Golden Fleece. An ivory statuette of Ariadne on the beast of Bacchus, capitalled a green marble plinth. Beneath this lavish display of curiosities and antiques were a simple carpet, somewhat worn, large and substantial chairs, a plain and rather meagrely furnished lounge—the wealth strewn about these walls was for the eye and the mind. No pamperings here.

The critic stood in the midst. He had a red skull-cap on his head, and he wore a silk robe lined with fur, like the one in the pictures of Henry the Eighth. His feet were slippered, and his thin ankles crept out from his curtailed trousers before plunging into his leathered extremities. He looked like Faust in the study-scene. He knew it. Yet he had much ground for vanity; for his was a real distinction. The profile was of that Tennysonian type found among æstheticians alone. The skin was an Italian brown, that had a glow underneath its aged dryness. The eyes were full and clear, like a deer's, and luminous as with an unceasing transport. Few heads have the beauty of this man's, and yet it was a beauty devoid of any sensuous charm. All its early physical glow had charred in the spiritual furnace.

Mr. Keyes stroked his long beard and eyed Julian askance. In one hand he held a volume of Shakespeare, his thumb thrust in the leaves for a bookmark. "Sit down," the critic began, in his high-tragedy voice, " sit down. I am glad you are come. I was just reading before my final retirement."

He had erratic modes of living. Ordinarily he retired at six to rise at ten and read or study for two hours, or as long as he pleased, before second sleep. He maintained midnight to be the " Delectable Mountains " for thought.

Julian sunk into a chair, after throwing open his coat. The Faust remained standing in his effective posture.

"I just came in for a moment, and I don't mean to detain you long. I hope I haven't disturbed you seriously. I was coming from the Ballards, and saw your light," said Julian, hurriedly.

"Humph! Come from the Medeia, eh! Why aren't you content to take your Euripides at home? Want it alive, I suppose. Well, she was grumbling as of yore, wasn't she?" ejaculated Keyes in short snatches.

At bottom the critic admired the gloomy woman. These masterful women magnetize men of his tremulous temperament. But he gave her superficial scorn because she never flattered him and always disdained his public readings from the poets. And she too, if she had been his wife, would have pedestalled and perhaps worshipped him ; as it was, he had surpassed her husband too completely. It is awkward for an aspiring professor of literature, as her husband had

been, to be overtopped by a resident citizen of wide reputation and altogether too loose views.

"Bah! Julian, boy, you are too young for love, and that
Margaret is a cold creature—no genial currents. She's so
unhesitatingly. pure. Pooh! she lacks color," the critic
muttered.

He did not half like Julian's friendship with the daughter
of that "Medeia-woman."

"I am glad you came in," he went on. "I was reading
Hamlet aloud to myself, and I felt as if an audience would
fit things. One needs a definite point towards which to
direct one's energy. You would like to hear me?"

He shut the book nervously on his fingers and glanced at
Julian with that appealing look women and literary men
use to beg sympathy with. It is charming in women; why
should it disgust when a delicately poised nature that basks in
approval, as the flowers in sun, yields to impulse and looks
it? Julian smiled assent. He always felt a little super-
cilious on these occasions, and despised his friend's weakness covertly, like all that brute world which licks a con-
queror's boots, but never was merciful to its saviours and
its children.

Mr. Keyes needed no more. He read the grave-scene in
Hamlet, the soliloquy of Richard of Gloucester, some rav-
ings of Lear, the Roman fighter's death and Egypt's royal
leave-taking, the frenzy of Constance in King John. At
little intervals he looked at Julian to catch his eye of appreciation, who felt compelled to evidence his pleasure.
The compulsion grated.

As the critic read, Julian turned upon him that intense
light of penetration which had been his since he left the
Ballards'. The recognized critic of literature, the elegant
scholar and dogmatic asserter of the spiritual, under the
mellow glow of the yellow light, his eager revealing face
flashing over Shakespeare, came apart before Julian, who

separated the flesh from the bone, the pretended from the real, as with the nitric acid of analysis. This passion over an author was half simulated, kindled from vanity born from the spectator's presence—a flash from flint and steel struck together, rather than the reflection of an immanent flame. Keyes had worn this affectation of heat so long that he became associated with it. It was analogous to the red skull-cap he always wore. Indeed, his voice habitually assumed a tragic pitch, as, they say, was the case with Mrs. Siddons. Julian felt, rather than saw, the dark semicircle of dirt underneath the critic's finger-nails. The dandruff in his hair seemed a long accumulation. The young man was repulsed; he shrunk from the physical Keyes, as from an "unclean" one. Keyes had always seemed somewhat unhuman; but never with this present emphasis.

The inordinate vanity of a man of genius, who admires his own moods and idiosyncrasies; the unhappy temper of a too sensitive spirit; the enormous waste of labor over literary curiosities and fantastic conceits which the man had expended—all these came up to Julian, while Keyes read. Julian marked what a sieve was the critic's soul. After all Keyes seemed to him no better than a dilettante, an elegant player with Art and its sacraments. He remembered a remark of his father's that Americans never devote themselves to pure Art as do foreigners, nor as they themselves do to business. At the moment, robust utilitarian motives that were honest and strove seriously, seemed preferable to this side-show rocketing, this appreciation and attempt of Art without its renunciation of vanity, of ease and self-gratulation.

At an hour's end Julian expressed fervid appreciation. Then he stepped thankfully into the night.

He paused on the slope up to his father's house and looked backwards. The pure night curved over the village, which stood gray in the bluish light reflected from the snow. What an evening! Exmoor prayer-meeting, Margaret, Mrs. Ballard, the critic Keyes—all quarters of the soul. Two strong disgusts filled him with nauseating fumes—disgust at utilitarian duty, the common-sensed, pietistic solution of life; but deeper, perhaps, disgust at the unreality of dilettanteism, the affectations of comfortable culture.

These disgusts were not generated in the crucible of Negation. He did not deny God and Beauty. He had not despaired like Faust and become a utilitarian, a builder of dikes and a helper in the common ways and needs. It was simply that his ideal was an unflecked marble; life was to him too supreme, too pregnant with meaning; culture, truth, the infinite, too serious, too crowded with import—that anything short of courageous effort and whole-hearted endeavor could answer. He glanced at the snow-laden roofs of the town between the blanketed heights. All of life that he had yet felt, its passions, its loves, its strainings, its ideals, lay within that little space between the hills.

And he felt it inadequate.

CHAPTER IV.

CHILDREN OF TWO ZONES.

THIS point of creative energy we know as Julian Clyde; how came its concentration into being? The chords, gathered from the four corners of the infinite and twisted into a knot, which serves for this human soul, as for every fragment of God, which we call a humanity, are twined into the entrails of creation, and we can only grope back along this length a beggarly inch. Yet that little distance may serve to render to us the direction, as two points in an eternal line dictate its trend. So if we set out the father and the mother of this puny ambitious pinch of wit, we shall be able to equate his birth with his education and thence deduce a result.

For a hundred years the Clydes of Exmoor had existed, generated, and duelled with nature in that hard, stale, but not unprofitable New England—which, in the mellow gloom of the minster mind of Hawthorne, has assumed a figure not all unlovely. A succession of lives, crowded with sordid works, flat with ennui as the prairies with loose grass; to be defined as continuous effort, stiffened into moral and perhaps heroic proportions by a repressive and manly piety —such were the chronicles of the Clydes from father to son. Oh! the colorless kaleidoscope of the old Yankee days, until death came in some harsh, Protestant way and substituted annihilation for vacuity! Chilly dawns and their gray forlornness; the chores doggedly done; the thin horses fed and harnessed in the cellar of the great barn, manure in heaps, pools of frozen water yellow on the earthen floor; the lugubrious breakfasts, where each sat silent and filled up; the naked house, lived in only in the rear, utterly without the warmth of human geniality; dead evenings of yawns and prayers; those ghoul Sundays when a dogmatic challenge was the minister's invocation and an argumentative combat his sermon, when the afternoons trailed dreariness—father in drones before the kitchen fire, and the overworked mother, querulous and sallow, in the angular chair, on her precise knees her Bible, whence she drank the fierce national poetry of the Old Testament, and extracted a bitter comfort to buoy her through a week's drudgery; thereby preserving in the otherwise complete ugliness of her life, by this acrid flame of a revengeful and sectarian Calvinism, the one point of non-utilitarian thought, the one glint of a poetic emotion. Oh, existence of the rugged past, from such strenuous loins were the best in America born !

Based upon such near ancestry, the miracle of American material progress explains itself. What system was ever devised so calculated to produce toilers ? Under such a régime elegance and art sink, and energy, restrained by the austere ethics from frittering its strength in the amiabilities, concentrates into power and crystallizes into tremendous acts. Men, born of this society, toil to drown time, and endure for love of hardihood. Muscle strained tense, will riding down the ranks of opposition as Sheridan rode down infantry, trampling and compelling nature—these are sensations potent and ponderous, so virile that a manly brute may feel them. The predetermined outcome of such a civilization is a nation built and buttressed in half a century, a continent sprung from the wilderness, Atlantis-like ; wealth massed into magnificent utilities, a so-called civil war which in reality was the surplus force of New England and her western colonies striking down an uncongenial and obtrusive community.

In 1840 a Clyde was sent to college, the first of his race —a long, lank, trailing Yankee boy with blue eyes and neutral strawy hair ; a face mild and inoffensive, yet in it a potential development, as if an under-countenance lay within the provincial mask.

In the years of college, the underneath emerged. The tall, thin, dignified figure that came out of Dartmouth, and the face fixed in reverence and a certain undefined strength which had there been born into it, was changed, as the form and features of Moses were transformed in his desert isolation before his return to populous Egypt. And yet the new spirit was identical with that of the country boy who entered college; for the hinge of his nature was shaped

upon his heritage, and these years had but extended its
range.

When Hiram Clyde went up to college, 'the German
thought-wave was smiting the coasts of the world. With
the same intensity of belief his mother lent to David and
John Knox, the son, sustained by the ethical gravitation
of his New England birth, turned to Fichte and Schelling,
and the new gospel of idealism. This indicated no molec-
ular change in the Clyde fibre. The same face that his
fathers directed to the old gods was here set towards the
new dawn, and to the novel formulas of existence from over
seas the young man carried the treasures of the persistence,
the faith and the exaltation of orthodox Puritan New England.

The parents were possessed of Enoch Arden's purpose
that their only son might tread in life a loftier plane than
theirs—a holy instinct, distinctly modern and democratic.
Hiram Clyde wrested the honors of his class,—one of those
stalwart Yankee peasants who once in a college generation
stride past the studious-lineaged. His father shared in the
joy of his triumph—the mother had fallen without this glory;
her sun gone down in the accustomed dreariness. They
both desired Hiram to enter the ministry; for the pulpit
was to them the veritable caster on the footstool of God.
When Hiram denied his father's wish, he felt it a blessing
his mother was no longer there with the infinite pathos of
beholding her son averse to what to her was highest—the
pathos of ignorance, whose love slights its superstition.
But Hiram had the cup of knowledge—of ethical speculation, to his lips, and with his long, thin, sprawling Yankee
fingers he clung to his goblet of life. He secured a scholarship and stayed in college.

In this outgrowth of agricultural Yankeedom had been
casketed a remarkable mind, and from his practical ancestry he had drawn all their religious temper as well as

the instinctive psychologic habit of Puritans and north-erners. So he came to the barriers of manhood a half thinker, and a half dreamer of inward things, who found in speculative ethics his native air. The old conduct-sense of his race, the profound instinct to formulate a moral code, so English and so Puritan, these governed him. Put the man in the great century of Scotch Protestantism, and with his youth in his veins he could have looked into the lovely eyes of Mary and denounced her lightness and French poetry as accursed before his stern abstraction of Jehovah. Place him in Germany and see him an enthusiast and an idealist, a devotee of some grand philosophic spirit, one of those famous bricks of pedantry, whose wall blocks in every magnificent mouth of truth—a dogmatist and confined, if you will; but with a well of belief and devotion in his cen-tral nature, like a water-spring in a waste lot. Fate set him in New England and his manifold destiny was a dreamer's, in a country where, unless coupled with genius, dreams are put by as stuff. His one possible lot was the pedagogue's, and his estimation with the world—a man who drags, a contribution to inertia.

But in 1845 his father died, and left his son a fortune of fifty thousand dollars. Thus at twenty-one, a year out of college, Hiram Clyde experienced that death is the great mathematician who solves the squaring of the circle. He was free to dispose of his life as he pleased. He went to the land that drew him, Germany.

His bereavement had reinforced his ethical purpose. His parents, Puritans and religious rhapsodists, had never over-stepped religious emotion, nor considered that it had appli-cation in the practical world in which they had toiled, and saved, and been mean, to the tune of a fifty-thousand-dollar accumulation. So the son was never moved into any object-ive philanthropy. He dwelt in his tower and scanned the heavens for the face of God, with no thought of the suffering

nests of wickedness at his feet.   In a manner there was no
renunciation for him as yet ; he simply acted out his nature
in seeking truth, as any common man obeys his inner law
in horse-trades, or money-changing, in sumptuous banquet-
ing, or attendance on society.

For two years Hiram Clyde haunted Jena and Berlin,
his spirit magnetized by those two towns where his
philosophical master had most suffered, where he had
taught and been tortured, where he had striven on, doughty
and true; the bravest, as Goethe pronounced him, preserving through all the awful mysteries and sombre subtleties
of a mighty intellect's speculation the peasant's sense of
duty, the Germanic passion for righteousness.   At the feet
of Fichte and where he once had trod, the emancipated
New Englander found his happiness ; here he slumbered
on in that modern monastery of thought, a German university ; here the world waned for him and he stood under
the immanent shadows of God, Creation, Truth.   Thus, as
in the New England college, he again sunk into a groove and
promised to slide easily down its hollow to that end which
was to him a yearned-for revelation.   But Fate jostled him
out with deft finger-touch, and tempted him over the Alps
with a fellow-philosopher.   He went first to Venice and got
no further.

Venice, rotting there on the Adriatic, like some gorgeous
fruit over-ripe, the glory of your garments stained with
rusts of time and hard handling of luscious conquerors—
we all come to you, and the least of us feel !   Your yellowed
marbles like the face of a waning and bilious belle, your
cracking palaces like the faded age of a man great in his
youth, your vanishing colors, your decaying bridges, your
more and more of tawdry modern flaunt—they invade the
heart; and Allemans from the North have wept sententiously, in wretched taste, over your dimmed façades ; even
that prig-ethical art-critic who wants to see some Christ-

woe-begoneness in the nudest magnificence of Titian's flesh —even he, in English such as no man now alive can stutter, even Ruskin, O Queen and Temple of color, has exalted you peerless, without a pretender to the insidious wistfulness of your charm! And those Scythians from the Northeast, barbarians at bottom, melancholy Tartars, feel something in you as of a wildly delicious and utterly sad dream of the senses let down into dimension and struck suddenly real. And we, the Americans, the commercial barbarians, shallow parrots of civilization, how we strain to mosaic our prosaics with detached memories from your canals and your houses, O City of a past wealth and a dead splendor, the pearl of the middle age in the flaccid oyster of modern existence, town of aristocratic voluptuousness and immoral art and doubtful character, with your pictures of magnificent worthless princes and divine soulless courtesans ! O City fallen away and gradually getting bizarre and flashy— Paris sets us on fire and Rome awes us by her years of massive past, but you feed us the lotus-fruit of your decay !

Was it that the physical plant was ripe for flowering in this year, the callow American's twenty-third on earth, so that the golden juices of youth were wrought by the chemistry of that magic city into a soft and deep glowing liquor, that bubbled, beaded, and shone with dark lustres like the crimsons of her painters ? Or was it that the joy of life suddenly woke in this offspring of stern-living, the blood of some distant forebear, who had loved and been passionate to excess, in times before the rugged Cromwell smote down the vigor of English renaissance—the strain of some sixteenth-century jolly yeoman reasserting itself in him, like a subterranean river springing into light again after devious wanderings ? Or was it that Art, alive, splendid, earthly, embodied for him some grand Germanic conception, shadowed forth, as a symbol and a sign, the high dreams of pure intellect, the sublime ecstasy of the elemental soul? Be it for what cause, Venice, her lights and shades, her sadness and her beauty, broke his northern austerity ; the lions of the senses snapped their guards and rolled and kicked and thundered with impunity, full in the court-yard of his heart.

He lay for hours on his back beneath the ceilings of the Ducal Palace, absorbing, as a dark cloth drinks up the sunrays, the symposiums of the great Venetians spread in profusion on the priceless plaster. Titian, Tintoretto, Veronese, became gods of beauty, and excluded the Trinity. At night, propped against a pillar, he watched the moon fill the square of St. Mark's. Like a golden beaker, jewelled around the rim, which holds Chian wine, so holds that square the moonlight, its one fit receptacle on earth. In the galleries, on the quays, in the Cathedral, tourists suddenly came up against his tall, thin figure with its scholar's stoop, the long, fair face in a trance of wonder, the cavernous eyes that shot blue fires. Seeing him, a man of the world would have laughed ; but a poet would have compared his face to a flower's, open for night's dew. One knows so many crooked-legged teachers of Greek, fanatical Hellenes, who, if they had shown their crumpled selves in Pericleian Athens, would have been hooted in the streets by those lovers of form. Ah ! the soul of the man was in tone with the jaspers and marbles; but the modern body, up against a stately citizen of Veronese's or backed by a blue sea and black gondola, is such a ragged affair.

It was the city of the present that laid the spell upon him. The golden stabs of the moon between two palaces in a narrow water-way ; the reflections on the water, dark and dark-billowed, like a metal mirror of old Rome ; the sheen on the pediments and capitals of a renaissance façade; a carved and statued doorway,—Venice was the name that expressed these effects, imminent, immediate, not distant, nor dim out of a past, not the historical town, whose remains these crumblings were. The Borghese Palace, on the Grand Canal, shone for him as a beautiful existence, not the elegant shell of a more interesting past. He never strove to realize that majestic pile aflare with the light of a sixteenth-century festival, the hum of the talk of the banqueters, the dark eyes of fair and evil women, the stealthy glances of ambitious intriguers, the elegant pose of proud nobles, artists and torturers at impulse. The arch of the Rialto needed no other associations than Shylock and Shakespeare, to round into meaning for him. The crowds of careless, trafficking humanity that once chattered there before the shops, were dead, and not raised up by any imaginings of his. All that fateful history that underlies the beauty of Venice, as the dungeons exist beneath the courtrooms of the Doge's state ; those real men and women who made Venice, refined in manner, tigers in desire ; that beautiful guilty City, where barter and pleasure and lovely sensuous art bloomed into the crown-flower of creation ; that humanity which knew neither morals nor an afterlife, which produced no poetry, nor even painted with pregnance of meaning—that City of the past, he did not comprehend, or even half divine. The limitations of his ethical imagination cut off suggestions of motives and forces, other than those which appeared in himself. The real Venice would have shocked him. Thus, even at this time, when he felt a Southern, a Catholic ; when he bathed himself in this civilization, so remote and so misunderstood by the Northerner, the moral man, the father of the family, —even here his inheritance protruded and set up barriers.

One evening he left the Cathedral square and plunged down a narrow alley to the left of the pile of St. Mark's. He reached the stone stairs that led down to the gondolas, on the canal. Gondoliers grouped about, some on the steps, some in landing-boats, some mooring their craft, all swearing those liquid Italian oaths that do not crush like solid English curses. They clamored round him, urging each his own gondola; eager, vivacious, with a multitude of courtesies and southern inflections. Just then a girl swung down the alley and stopped, speaking to one of the men. Clyde from the midst of his chattering crowd saw her, gesticulating, impatient, commanding her boat-men to move swiftly. That was all—but with a difference that turned the world another color. A gleam of ivory flesh, solid and smooth, graceful little sweeps of hands turning on firm-marbled wrists; swift motion of blue-black southern hair swinging in time with the audacious tongue; eyes of night that might be homes of a soul and might be but wells of vivid dark—only these ; but life and all its strains and cares, its sufferings and its visions, its bestial-ities and its glories, which had come to Hiram Clyde, were bound about the mincing ankles of that Italian work-girl, to be kicked into flinders, or to be gathered up and treasured, as her whim might veer. What are love and fate ? Two grand goddesses, or two dirty witches, full of spite ?

She descended to a gondola, entered, reclined back with a voluptuous ease, the great eyes joyous and shining with animal vigor. She tossed salutations here and there amid the throng upon the quay. Her gondola made off towards the Grand Canal.

"Follow that girl and keep close to her," Clyde said, in French, to the nearest gondolier.

Three months afterward "the rich American seignior" asked Francesca to marry him. He had wooed her with a southern passion, mixed with an austerity which the girl did not understand. "Why was he so long about it ?" she had often asked. But she put the delay down to "foreign madness."

To his declaration she made this frank reply :

"If I marry you, you will take me away to your cold

country ; and I will not go from Venice. What need of such trouble, if we love one another ?"

At another time such blunt immorality would have shocked him, but it may be doubted if he understood the total import of her words. He promised not to take her out of Italy, and so married her.

Ten grand months of pagan life, the glad old heathen days renewed ; sense and intellect, the two wheels of the chariot of existence, with no miserable brake of a conscience or a duty to grasp the flashing tires. She led him, with her eyes of Italy and her burnished hair of night, into gladness and into beauty. Never was his thought so quick, so sure, so faultless in its strides, so filled with verve. The abysmal chasms of northern imagination, the awful want of the infinite, all those Germanic convulsions of soul passed into thin air before the simple humanity of his Venetian existence. In this pure air and surrounded by these exact monuments, this objective beauty which draws the attention outwards, his mind became temperate and clear. He studied art and architecture, the finished thought of Greece, and the sublime practical genius of Rome. The vagueness of northern utterance seemed mere mutterings, and the grand dreams of his student-days mere vapor.

He drew on the capital of his little fortune; he crowded each day with sensations without thought of the future to come; he decked her in robes that garnished her beauty as with flame, and she looked a grande dame arisen out of the Past, even such a one as Paolo Veronese might have loved and painted. Such were these halcyon days.

But the novelty wore itself thin, as use frays the edges of a costly robe, and the old spirit reasserted itself at times, and yet more and more, with greater strength. His boy's birth introduced a duty, a responsibility. that demanded notice, and the moans of the mother in travail reminded him of pain and terror, that he could not banish.

The girl had loved him with passion, but without renunciation, after the manner of the Latins. He looked out for a soul to respond to his own and met an embrace. Like a fountain springing in a sea, buried so that it flings but white rings to the surface, so there lay a sombre intensity of emotion, born of gloom and the north, beneath his glad exterior. This gained on him and finally absorbed his frivolity, but it frightened Francesca, who believed him half mad at times.

Poor northern man with the moral genius, not content with the splendor of flesh, but must probe this Titian woman for soul and spirit; must discern, if possible, something Puritan and Christian in the rich passion of her love. Byron tried the same thing, seeking in that sensual city and its history of pleasure and beauty and assassination, an heroic and Teutonic Edda, a noble and manly lyric.

Behold him, gloomy and most subjective of men, attempting to demonstrate to English Phariseeism and to his own Gothic viking temper that an immoral civilization has its place, that morality is a matter of latitude and longitude, a cloak one leaves north of the Alps. The farce of it! Byron, the body, sunk in sensuality where Italians are but scented with elegancies; Byron, the spirit, meditating a liberty-war in Greece.

So this lesser man. Through the laughter of Venice he came to carry a grave face, and amid the gay jesters, the flippant and witty children of the sun, he wore a noble mien and tortured his wife to wring out her soul.

Under his treatment Francesca died two years after marriage; "frightened to death," her friends said. The end came unexpectedly upon him; he faltered like a man dealt a strong blow between the eyes. But afterwards, in America, he knew that it was well; for by it her memory became the poetry of his life, a revelation of the beauty youth hungers for and which belongs only to youth.   At first he looked to joining her after death, but years of thought and loneliness revealed many things; and at last he understood her and her people, his own cruelty and the cause of her death.   He had the remorse of one who shatters a costly vase.   He came to associate her with Greek statues and all lovely mortal things ; he felt she had her place, even as he had his, in this world's museum of grotesques and prettinesses, of butterflies and immortalities.

Ah, how admirably she had fulfilled herself, lived her fate, been true to her law! Puritans and Northerners, can we understand that fine and gay woman, whose death means swift chemical dissolution of her entirety ? Have laughter and bloom and lovely life for their selves' sake no place in this moral world ? Pass by without contempt, pale Northerners, gentlemen and respectable ; judge not that which is not, but has gone as a rose of last summer!

Hiram Clyde took his child and departed.   He came home to America and endeavored to find his place in her gigantic machinery.   But he seemed superfluous in a society of money-makers and virtuous mediocrities. Neither, indeed, did that democratic and commonplace culture, whose poet is Longfellow and whose philosopher is Emerson, offer a distinct post of duty to a man too profound for its metaphysical theatricals and too intense for its white waistcoat and clerical neck-dress respectability. He had fled the Old World; the New did not need him.

So he drifted back to Exmoor and planted himself in his father's house and swathed himself in ideas.   He thought over life and its meaning ; he came to know himself and to explain his past ; he trod the wine-press of his student years in Jena and extracted a mild and cordial vintage.   He made half beauties into whole divinities, and by dint of art and proudest spirituality he reconstructed from the jets of his Venetian life a poem and a glory.

That was his inner life.

A few years after his return Exmoor college offered him the chair of moral philosophy. He was twenty-seven at the time, when he thus entered upon his life-work, as outsiders would have said. At fifty he had acquired a European reputation in his specialty.

So, in that quiet renown, among a limited world, his life dropped towards its close. Exmoor never knew him. He moved, always a gentleman, but perfectly opaque among her people, who perhaps did not understand the world's consideration for the tall and meek old man who walked their streets, any more than they understood the reason of Mr. Keyes's celebrity. Hiram Clyde even became identified with Exmoor's theology, and people never dreamed that in that unpretentious cask dwelt a demon of speculation that in Germany had towered to the sky. Neither did those young men, veritable bottles of Christian creed, stoppered and pasted over with orthodox sealing-wax and labels, filled with the modern-Protestant-patent-medicine-ostensible-cure for every ill, hesitate to quote Dr. Clyde as a buttress to dogmatism.

He married a second time at thirty-three, a high lady of the land, a sister of Mrs. Lancaster. His wife died in two years, and he returned to himself.

He let his boy grow as nature willed. He had no faith in repression, and he felt it a fearful thing to shape a life.

Such was the cradle of Julian Clyde.

CHAPTER V.

THE COMING OF MILLIONAIRE GAY.

THE day was as if plucked out of midwinter. The cold condensed about the raw hills, and the shifting clouds rode low, volleying at intervals a whiff of snow in their flight up the valley.

The little railway-station was placed on the flank of the village. It stood by itself amid pieces of fence and railroad-tracks. The houses that looked on were shabby frame boxes, worn by the weather. The mud was crusted in the roads, and the pools of yesterday's thaw had turned to ice. The sky was leaden, the buildings were brown, the fields were bilious, streaked with stained snow-heaps.

This was the landscape Julian faced when he drove up to the station to wait for the late afternoon train.

Professor Clyde had gone to meet Mr. Gay in the neighboring city, to pilot him into Exmoor. The branch road which led to the town was badly appointed and difficult for a novice to discover.

Julian got out of the carriage. He drew out his watch after much fumbling with his gloved hand. The train was due in five minutes. Chesterfield, the horse, stamped as if to promote circulation in his slender legs. His master endorsed the action, walking from the carriage to the edge of the platform and jumping on his feet at every other minute.

Behind the dome of murk, the sun fell into the west,

and through cloud-interstices shot horizontal gleams of cold red. The frozen brilliance seemed, by contrast, to cast the landscape into a purpler hue. The wind scurried along the iron ground under the branches and surged up against the open places with their buildings, as the under-wave of a level sea sweeps up upon a sea-wall. The cold increased. The mists crystallized into ghosts, that might have stalked from the polar ocean.

It was that brief time, when day is transformed in a breath and a winter night falls unannounced upon the land. The red glows waned on the lips of the cloud-planes and the purple light sunk to blacker blue. The consciousness of a weird influence grew upon Julian. This is the mystery and poetry of the North, melancholy, desolate, grand and repelling, that drives the soul in on itself. This is the mother of sentiment and duty, of home and of sadness, of work and of heroism.

Suddenly a stir arose within the sealed building. Steps sounded and the door flew open. The station-master and his assistant came out and hurried about the platform. The boy attached the checks to the trunks. Julian counted them, as he watched the leather thongs slip through the boy's awkward mittens.

A whistle shrilled up the valley. It seemed to Julian like the shriek of the meagre day, driven out by the frost-whips of the impending night. The dark came down and the lights glimmered. A burst, a distant sweep of defiant steam into liberty, and round the curve flashed the terrible eye of the black being. It startled Chesterfield, so that Julian went to his head. He peered into the glare of the headlight—as if he could see anything!

There was a great rush, the rails rattled before the monster, steam escaped with a hiss, the ponderous wheels groaned along the steel, the engine disappeared behind the station-house and in a moment shot out again with a cloud of mist and careening vapor—a hurling impact of noise, trailing a black length behind.

The train was at standstill; Chesterfield, the good horse, shivered, and Julian looked intensely across the platform at the melée of human figures. He felt that something was about to happen.

Presently, out from the little tumult four figures emerged. Professor Clyde came forward hurriedly, with a nervous trepidation in his gait.

"Yes," he was saying to the expressman, "yes, take the baggage—all of it, both gentlemen—to my house." In his excitement he forgot to give over the checks, and when the baggage-man asked for them, he felt as if accused of carrying stolen property about with him.

"That is our carriage, I think," the Professor announced with no certainty in his voice. He ran out before his companions, calling out, "Julian, is that you?" In getting them into the carriage, he displayed the worry of an old woman.

They were all three in the carriage before Julian left Chesterfield's head. The good animal was a family affair, but the hoarse steam startled his meditative nerves for once.

"Hold the reins, father, until I get in," Julian called to Professor Clyde, who was on the front seat.

When Julian had driven out of the immediate presence of the hilarious engine, his father introduced him to a muffled figure—"Mr. Gay, my son," the accent on the "son," —and to another, indiscernible in the shadow,—"Mr. Mancutt, his private secretary."

It was six o'clock when the carriage unloaded before the Clyde house. Professor Clyde went before his guests, and opened the door. A fire burned in the great hall, where Mrs. Lancaster stood in her black robes to receive them. Her stately mien and gracious welcome did much to redeem

Professor Clyde's abruptness. Mr. Gay bowed to her, as he bowed to New York women. His secretary received just that touch of hauteur in her salute to him which is necessary to inspire respect in "arrived" plebeians. Mrs. Lancaster sent them to their rooms, herself standing by the massive newel-post and pointing out the way.

When Julian came in, he carried hot water and the satchels to the two gentlemen and announced dinner in half an hour.

Below, Professor Clyde was ill at ease. He crossed his legs a great many times and his fingers shook. Mrs. Lancaster had gone to the dining-room and kitchen to superintend the serving of dinner. Dinner at night was in vogue only on state occasions in Exmoor, except with the Keyeses, but then they were wealthy and were the importers of fashion into the town.

The disturbance of his ordered routine troubled the Professor. Gay was a new factor, and Professor Clyde, who had lived so long in Exmoor without a peep into the world, was unaccustomed to indeterminate forces. The placid man of old-time stately courtesy and unbroken reserve, as Exmoor knew him, before this representative of an alien world became literally unable to contain his uneasiness. When Julian came into the parlor, his father asked him a great many meaningless things. Did he think Mr. Gay a fine-looking man, and how soon would they be down? This waiting was intolerable. Did the President surely promise to come this evening? and perhaps Julian had better go and ask Mr. Keyes to call too.

"What can you be thinking of, father? Of course the President will come, and Dr. Ponder with him. That is what Mr. Gay is here for. As for Mr. Keyes, you never can tell, but I think he will be here."

Professor Clyde said he wished he had invited the President to dinner that night, it would be pleasanter for all around; but Mrs. Lancaster had said no, because it would be too hurried. Now, he wished he had obeyed his own impulse.

When Mrs. Lancaster came in, the Professor asked where she purposed seating Mr. Gay at the table. "What are you thinking of?" answered Mrs. Lancaster, surprised out of her placidity.

Upstairs, when Mancutt had opened his own satchel, swearing under his breath at country barbarism, and after quite finishing his dress for dinner, he knocked at Mr. Gay's door.

Once in, he laughed in a halting way, as if to suggest but not to set the pace to his patron. Mr. Gay smiled (he never did more), and with this permit the secretary chuckled at every breath.

"What a duffer the Professor is!" muttered Mr. Gay. It was his single comment and only those who knew the man understood the full content of the term.

"Didn't know exactly how to classify me, did he?" laughed the secretary,—"half took me for your valet. Good idea, by the way, you left *him* over in Springfield or you'd have overpowered them with that lackey's airs. I suppose he thought private secretary meant cross between valet and stenographer." Mancutt laughed a silent grin which had hardly any vertical extension, but drew the mouth into a wide slit and displayed the large teeth set together as in a bite.

"Humph!" he resumed, " I suppose I am a new variety, as it were, to the Doctor. Slang is evidently not one of his languages."

Thus the secretary ran on, a multitude of half-humorous suggestions, such as a thinking parrot might record of the peculiarities of his mistress. Gay was taciturn, and men often asked how he could endure his voluble secretary. But every great man has his " kitchen-cabinet."

These two men were both striking, and Gay was even typical. Mr. Gay was silent, combing his thin hair to conceal his bald crown. The millionaire was tall and dark. There was no superfluous flesh; the figure looked lean and potent, powerful, like a steel spring, with those flat, limber thighs that make the swiftness of the greyhound. The reflection of his face in the mirror showed a long oval, with thin subtle lips under a gray stubby mustache. The skin was slate-hued and the hair gray with a blue tone, which together suggested the impenetrability of a gray rock which fronts the ocean. The business shocks of twenty years had washed that face and had but sealed expression in it and left that unimpeachable look, like the polished dimness of steel. Like a limp curtain the cheeks hung upon the skull, but without a line and without a shade—a certain Napoleonic impassivity. A calm, subtle, acquisitive countenance that aroused neither fear nor liking, that was as impersonal as a law or force of Nature. One would, perhaps, overlook it in a crowd, ignorant that it belonged to one of the masters of events in these latter days of the nineteenth century. But the eyes, the eyes, wherein the potency dwelt, that revealed nothing and yet whose most indifferent glance startled one into curiosity or a half tremor! Blue shallows that drank in men and houses and relations, with the lined and interlined puffings just below the lower lids. Despite their light imperiousness, they bespoke the essential character of the man. Gaze into their cold flame and note the eyes of the schemer, that absorb and never flash; steady, treacherous, guileful, absolute self, insuperable calculation, infinite will.

The secretary leaned against the foot-board of the bed. He was elegantly dressed, boots of finest leather, light trousers of latest fashionable girth, dark coat and vest, and a cravat worth three dollars! Modern dress is calculated to cover the deficiencies of the mean frame, not to set off

the elegancies of the physical aristocrat. Attired, the secretary passed for a handsome man. He was blonde, and
taller than Mr. Gay. He had the powerful shoulders of a
coal-heaver and the solid limbs of the athlete. The head
was large and square-shaped, broad in the forehead and buttressed just over the eyes. He had eyes of the color of blue
china-ware; they were forever flitting in their sockets. He
wore a blonde mustache and English side-extensions of
hair. He looked "a swell" and decidedly English. He
was about thirty and unmarried. An accurate observer
would, nevertheless, have affirmed a certain unfinish in the
man. His manners were those of a man of the American
world, courteous, free, and altogether confident. Where
was the lack? In the square jaw, the straight promontorial
nose cut off at an improper angle, or simply in the whole
face? A man whom dress and appearance proclaimed a
gentleman, except that last evasive falling off, that last
flash of the plane across the board forgotten. Does he not
stand for many figures who tread the floors of American
society? And sometimes a half-faded, haunted look crept
into his eyes, remainder of the time when he was permitted; sometimes a humble note in his voice, remnant
of a more distant past, when he had fawned and quailed.

These were the two men, who got ready for dinner over
the heads of nervous literature and quaking philosophy.

The dinner that night was a singular affair. The cut-
glass finger-bowls and the solid silver were on the board.
The heavy damask table-cloth, reserved for occasions, hung
over the table with unaccustomed stiffness. The maid-
servant waited at table, much against her inclination, and
her mistress used adroit diplomacy in managing the irate
domestic. This Hibernian, who had emerged two years
ago from an Irish bog, rebelled at such menial service.
The single reason she could be induced to so perform at all,
was that it gave her an opportunity to see at close quarters

the famed operator. Mancutt took in all these slight jars,
and derived consolation from them; for, somehow, Mrs.
Lancaster impressed him with his own inferiority, despite
his scorn of rusticity, which products of New York like
himself hold over all the outer world.

Professor Clyde feared a pause in the conversation. He
talked of stocks, of which he was ignorant. He introduced
subjects he supposed interested Mr. Gay. He displayed
his own business stupidity, he exposed his innocence of the
world, he even ventured on horse-flesh. Mr. Gay was
rather taciturn, while the secretary would now and then
throw in a statement to draw the philosopher out. Politics were barred, for Mr. Gay had no notion of them.
What the State was he had never inquired, and his only
political maxim was, "Good business, good government."
Mrs. Lancaster officiated like a queen. She held the impudent secretary in hand; Gay deferred to her; he had the
feeling that she was a sort of superior product. She checked
some absurdities of Professor Clyde's, and finally with intuitive tact she introduced the Church, missions, to which
Gay had given largely, and the cause of religion. Gay and
the Professor charged at the subject full tilt. Both felt it
salvation. Mancutt sickened. He sank into silence and
enjoyed his dinner, though it was not too abundant for his
New York stomach.

The Professor beame more and more pious. He addressed
Gay as "Deacon." He spoke of the "power of Jesus Christ
abroad in this Christian land," in business, as manifested
in public charities and avoidance of war. Mr. Gay assumed his "pontifex maximus" air, the same he prayed in,
at the Wednesday night prayer-meeting, in the church on
Fifth Avenue and when he taught his Bible-class in Sunday-
school. They had manœuvred for positions ever since they
met in Springfield. They understood the right ground
was at last under their feet. At last they were mutually

comfortable and, as long as Gay stayed, the Professor played the priest, and the millionaire the Christian.

Mancutt smiled his horizontal dental grin. To him it appeared hypocrisy that Gay, the prince of business men, should take such interest in the Church. Still he thought there must be something in it, that engaged a man of Gay's capacity. At times in his recent career, when things were more dubious than now, he had thought of taking a try at it himself. But in itself religion seemed instituted non-sense. He had one time asked why a certain self-sacrific-ing minister did not "sell tea and get a living for him-self." Julian understood his father, and knew the pious fraud was often used to shutter an emancipated spirit from the "necessary superstitions," as Professor Clyde called them to those he regarded as initiates. Yet in the pres-ence of these men of the world, these able men, he experi-enced a slight shame for abstraction and culture.

After dinner the five returned to the parlor. A fire of soft coal burnt in the grate. The oil-lamps cast a mellow yellow light and left the shadows lurking in the corners. Plato looked from the wall; the luminous face in its intel-lectual beauty seemed discordant with this modern com-pany, and yet, with its companion-bust of Bismarck, repre-sentative of it, in some measure, as well, where Gays and Mancutts bow and converse with Clydes and Mrs. Lancas-ters.

Mr. Gay went to the fireplace and stood, resting one elbow upon the corner of the mantelpiece. His pose brought out to Julian the two characteristics of the man, subtlety and aggression. Julian thought him capable of half heaving, half sliding over obstacles; strong and elusive at once. This was the man that everybody knew, even Paddy in the ditch. The magnitude of his notoriety impressed Julian. He looked a great man. Was it not as if they entertained Richelieu or Oliver Cromwell? Success, mastery, force,

they are the apparent qualities.   Somehow Gay appealed to
Julian's imagination.   He was not that brutal coarseness
and obtrusive practicality the young man had supposed
to be the typical American millionaire.   He had none of
the qualities of Commodore Vanderbilt or Dean Richmond.
Rather he was clean-cut, very *distingué*, a Jesuit made a
Chancellor.   Julian compared him to the sixteenth-century
Italian princes, to Cæsar Borgia.

After Mr. Gay had got his cigar going well, he sat down
in a big comfortable chair.   Following the usual tendency
of after-dinner meditation, he grew reminiscent.   And that
reminiscence was complaisant.   He said he had made himself; he hinted at early hardships, he intimated, in his soft
suggestive manner, that he had received little education.
His early handicap at the start of life enhanced his great
success, and he had an unexpressed satisfaction that the
highest culture and aristocracy of New England, as represented in Professor Clyde and Mrs. Lancaster, were listening with overmuch attention to his description of what he
had been.   The man's passion was power for its own sake,
and his chief pleasure was in making superiority subservi-
ent.   He sought no good for himself from any contact.   He
would make great things bow; that is what they were for—
for a man to try his strength on.   To Gay the world was
merely a stupendous power-machine, such as are scattered
in railway waiting-rooms, and man's business on earth was
to see how much he could pull.

He went a step farther and insinuated that books did
little for a man's success after all.   "I never read much.
I have picked up most that I know.   Literary ideas im-
pair a man's practical vigor; at least, that has been my experience with many college men whom I have employed."
He spoke in his mellifluous tones, that might tell a man he
was a scoundrel, without conveying much offence.

"I suppose that is true," assented Professor Clyde.   Life

had taught the philosopher one lesson, at any rate—the inevitableness of temperament; so he seldom opposed—what was the use ?

" You understand I believe in college education,". the millionaire went on. " If I had sons instead of my two daughters, I should of course put them through college. But for business, for absolute coin, and where a man must make his way, he who has no theories and fights up from the bottom, conquering by downright toil, he is the man who can command business."

" I have often remarked that," said Dr. Clyde.

" The fundamental trouble is, that your college man is too metaphysical," said Gay. " I think it a wrong idea anyway, to educate any young fellow, whether he has anything or is as poor as a newspaper-reporter, to desires and tastes he cannot gratify for years. A fellow is destined for a drudge, and you educate him as if he were to be Lord High Chancellor of England. I know of college-graduates who are Sixth Avenue car-conductors, and glad to get two dollars a day at it, too."

Mrs. Lancaster descended into the conversation with—
" Success ! Ah, my dear sir, if that were all of life, how true would be your statement ! Education is valuable, is it not ? not for what it brings in the market, but for what it makes the man himself ?"

" Exactly my point, my dear madam, that education has made the man sensible to the pleasures of a drawing-room, only to plunge him into the odors of a laundry."

Mr. Gay was a bright man, he could coin a figure of speech on occasion. It is doubtful if Mrs. Lancaster understood him. The cloistered, ethereal woman knew no more of the crush of the world than of the atmosphere of Saturn. " Besides," Mr. Gay opened a third parallel—
" Besides, I should infinitely prefer a son of mine to be a success than an educated abstraction. I don't take stock

in a concern that refines the marrow out of the bones." Were these scholarly people who heard this concealed sneer so devoted to the ideal they were living for that it passed them scathless? Did Professor Clyde feel a secret contempt for this king-Philistine? Ah! there was a wince in his eyes. Americans who import Arnoldian disdain and the high superior feeling, sometimes have a secret hankering after what they cannot have, like Israel after the Baal of the idolaters. There is nothing so conducive to the literary worship as deprivation of the vanities.

The woman was the one who answered.

"But if a man must sacrifice to money-success all his highest, his culture, his capacity to feel and to understand, why, let success go by."

Perhaps Mr. Gay did not altogether understand her terms, man of stocks and schemes and hard finance that he was. He had recently been trapped into a philosophical critique, misled by the title, "Modern French Speculation," and had been much surprised when there was nothing on the first page about the "Bourse."

"What else can there be in life?" he ejaculated, fairly surprised.

Their eyes encountered, and only Professor Clyde divined the chasm between them. They did not understand themselves, and each spoke a distinct dialect.

The door-bell rang opportunely, and Julian went to answer it.

"We expect President Pompes and one or two of the professors this evening," said Professor Clyde. "Mr. Keyes, also—the literary critic, you know—expressed his great desire to meet you, and will probably call as well." Gay bowed. It was sweet incense to have these "literary fellows" dance attendance. He liked this sort of flattery better than any he had ever received.

The secretary had been none too comfortable. He had

attempted to talk with Mrs. Lancaster, but his little jokes evidently did not please her. Before her grave, gracious eyes the showy worldling broke down. He felt humiliated. His amiability, his hearty animal spirits, his mechanical cleverness, those factitious counters that pass current in the city, where life is too rapid to produce aught but froth, were of no avail with this bronze-haired stately matron. She looked him down unintentionally. His metallic laugh sounded like the dry rattle of dice in a box. The gay player of life's game, the superficial self-sufficient, was "rattled."

Julian relieved him immensely by proposing to go to a little party of young people. "I don't know whether you will enjoy it, Mr. Mancutt. It's a very simple affair, such as we have here in Exmoor. We just play cards and dance a little and talk—do as we please."

"I shall be delighted to go, Mr. Clyde. To tell you . the truth, I guess I shall feel better with a lot of young · people than in this literary crowd of professors, who are expected."

The two escaped into the library preparatory to their expedition.

"Gad!" said the secretary, "you've got a lot of books, haven't you?" viewing the array as he would a museum of bottled snakes.

"Why, do you like books?" asked Julian, for want of something better to say.

"Yes, I am very fond of them, dote on some of them," replied the supple secretary. "Got 'Lucile' here, have you? That's a thing I think extraordinary. Ah! I see, you have all of Dickens. What a lot that man did write! Made money by them, too. It must be rather nice to be able to just sit down and write out a fortune, don't you think so?"

Mancutt glanced over the shelves of unknown books

without comment. He never exposed his ignorance—except unconsciously to himself.

Like a young man, Julian felt prompted to air his familiarity with books. He took down a volume of Goethe, patting it with caressing fingers.

"Oh! that's Gayte, is it?" said the secretary, seizing his chance as he thought. "What do you think of him?".

"Me? Oh, Goethe is the greatest man of modern times," answered Julian with the solemnity of a priest to the multitude. The young man felt that such a primary truth would be gospel to Mancutt, who could not stand any stronger wine.

The corrected pronunciation did not irritate Mancutt. Next time to some "literary" lady of New York he would mention "Goethe" as the greatest of the moderns to his mind. He had the true adventurer's spirit. He had literally learned by mistakes, risen to higher things on the stepping-stones of his dead blunders. He never allowed himself to lose a lesson from any man. He never belittled men through envy, nor detracted an inch from another's height. He recovered so good-naturedly from every rebuff that his little humiliations were more valuable to him than some men's successes.

Julian introduced the secretary to the little company of Exmoor young people that had gathered that evening at Miss Halding's for talk and amusement. There were Miss Jane Halding herself, Margaret Ballard, Hester Harris, Edith and Elaine Browning—a circle of sweet girls, not very stylish, as Mancutt thought, but rather superior-looking. He did not know how to treat them. The formality of the city seemed out of place in their free presence and with their careless manners; and yet he could not bring himself to behave to them as to little girls, the only other manner in his repertoire. So he was distraught, stammered a little, when the eager group surrounded him, crying, "Oh, Mr. Mancutt, tell us about the latest in New York." They were so brilliant, so child-like in their unrestraint, so quick in their rejoinders, so old in their subjects of talk. Nowhere in the world save in towns like Exmoor could a company like this be gathered. Independent, each girl as lively, as forward, as swift to shaft wit and contradict as any Parisian; verging very near the improper, continually approaching delicate subjects with but a shell of laughter between allusion and danger; yet each so nicely poised, so delicately balanced by self-respect and innate purity, that no one fancied impropriety, or even supposed anything but perfect innocence. The young men were most of them tutors or such senior students as might enter this society. The "motif" of this company was unintelligible to the secretary: no effort at self-assertion or ostentation, no puny prides of possession or birth, no conscious display of mind or beauty—these Puritan girls dressed simply, almost plainly—these intellectual, high-bred young· men were acceptable for themselves alone, not for what they had.

They danced because they were filled with life and loved the rhythm of the movement. They laughed naturally at little things like children, and yet deep subjects were continually brought up. Politics, books, art, society, they bandied them about. They clustered about Mancutt because he was new. They pulled him here and there, and used him with indescribable abandon. They enjoyed his city jokes and slang. They were such curious minds! The secretary found himself quite the fad, although he was a little disturbed. He felt they had infinite scorn for ignorance, and he really became aware of his superficiality. Jane Halding danced him around, asking him a thousand questions, introducing him, telling him personalities—that Margaret was Hawthorne's Hilda, that Elaine Browning had been waiting for so long a time for a Launcelot, and suppose he himself were the knight, that Julian went by the name of " Beppo,"—" Byron's Beppo, you know, the fat Beppo—is that a satire on poor Byron or on Julian, which ?"

CHAPTER VI.

A DINNER OF STATE.

IT has been said the Keyeses were wealthy; that is, the critic had married a rich woman. Every summer Mrs. Alexander Keyes went to Newport, though she could not draw her husband after her by any persuasion. He hated an environment other than the pastoral one he had hollowed out of Exmoor for himself; so he rarely escaped her bounds. The nights his wife danced in the sumptuous Newport fêtes, he most likely, attired in a duster and shod with shabby slippers whose soles flapped against his heels, smoked in the moonlight, muttering the Greek of Theocritus.

Mr. Gay's arrival stirred the festival heart of Mrs. Keyes with sweet anticipations of hospitality to be extended. There were so few opportunities offered one to entertain in Exmoor, had been her social caption for years. Here was an occasion to match her zeal. She had gone to Mrs. Lancaster and stated her desire to give a dinner to Mr. Gay, if it would be acceptable to the faculty. She was assured of everybody's hearty endorsement; indeed, her project guaranteed a hospitality worthy the advent of the millionaire. Besides, she had known Mr. Gay at Newport.

Her spirits were high. Everything was moving smoothly and her ambition to achieve a dinner that would equal the town's expectations seemed prosperously embarked. The great colonial house was swept and garnished, the oil-lamps in the chandeliers glowed forth illumination from every window. The long mahogany table, which had been her grandmother's in the eighteenth century, glittered with glass and silver and old china. It was not blindly that Exmoor reposed confidence in Mrs. Keyes, who would show the great New Yorker that luxuries dwelt in the old town before the palaces of Manhattan were dreamed of. The hostess, too, was important with her past; and, lineaged as she was, her pride of birth urged her to justify the old New England order to this new noble of millionairedom.

Under its sombre hood of maples the house of Keyes gleamed brilliant. The great hall in the centre thrust out radiance and warm joyousness each time a new guest passed through the open door. They came afoot, over the new-fallen snow. They entered the hall, wide, dark-wainscoted, with heavy oaken stairs that shone under the lights. They passed into great, old-fashioned rooms which fashion had not overloaded nor the modern uphol-sterer "rococoed." They stood in little groups about a vivacious woman seated in one of the cumbrous comforta-ble chairs; or else they gathered before an antique on a bracket, or a picture lately imported. The half of Mrs. Keyes's income went to books and art-treasures for her hus-band's gratification.

The divinity presiding in these rooms was natural and serene. Before the wand of her authority affectation shrivelled to a wretched contemptibility, and hauteur grew a ridiculous mask. In the presence of these genial people, in these simple rooms in which beautiful things, old-world marbles and renaissance nudities, natural manners seemed the only possible thing, and postures and forms overmuch and out of taste.

Mrs. Keyes did the honors, while her husband insisted

on circulating like any other guest and having a good time. They all awaited Professor Clyde and his guests. The five came in together, Mrs. Lancaster and Mr. Gay first, the secretary and Professor Clyde behind, while Julian strayed in the rear. Mrs. Keyes had assumed the ponderous air of the society woman when the party first entered, and she received the millionaire with that grand manner which is stupid and absurd, since it is only one poor biped greeting another equally two-legged. As the New Yorkers advanced, a perceptible transformation came over the company; formality crept into their address, the women stiffened or simpered, while the men forgot their unconstraint and stood on one leg, or nudged their brothers in nervous trepidation. The critic himself recovered with a jerk and ambled at an indecisive pace up to his wife's bulky figure.

"We are very glad to welcome you to Exmoor, Mr. Gay. I had hardly thought I should ever see you here," smiled Mrs. Keyes, extending her welcoming hand.

Mr. Gay bowed and murmured some formal words of thanks and his unexpected pleasure in again meeting Mrs. Keyes and as his hostess.

"I hear they are giving you a very early idea of our town, Mr. Gay. They have taken you everywhere, I believe, over the campus and the buildings, and shown you views and just everything," she said vivaciously.

The millionaire assented, while Professor Clyde answered for him: "Oh, yes; we have shown Mr. Gay everything. We intend he shall carry back to New York a vivid picture of Exmoor and the college, so that he may know himself our peculiar advantages, and then may use a business man's sagacity in determining what should be done."

The implied importunity irritated the rich man. "You certainly have an admirable location for a college here ; and for me, I could see no flaw in the appointments, nor imperfection either of place or appropriateness," he answered, using the meaningless generality with which a man of great affairs covers his purposes.

The secretary, who followed his patron, was impressed by the blank distinction of his hostess's face and the volume of her figure. Mrs. Keyes received Julian with the formality they always preserved between them, to cover their non-affinity. Julian had never understood how his friend's fastidious sense and fine feeling for spiritual sympathies had borne with his partner's inane pretentiousness. Evidently their marriage savored of the contract and not of the sacrament; the consideration being her money for his celebrity; result felicitous, enabling him to build himself a "palace of art" and live removed from the sordid, while she basked in his name, and received the solicitous interest of society, foreign *distingués* and plebeian lion-hunters.

The secretary spoke some moments with the hostess. He managed better with her than in his passages with Mrs. Lancaster. Later in the evening he talked a space with her, and she took hold of his good things and understood his New York wit. She was the only matron of Exmoor who permitted him to indulge a self-satisfied feeling.

When he turned away from her, he steered for Gay, who stood at the head of the parlors, alone for the moment. The secretary neared him.

"Quite *recherché*, sir," the secretary began, in his quizzical impudent way.

"They'll never let me out of the trap without paying ransom," answered Gay, looking off, as if he had remarked a commonplace.

"I thought as much. I told you before we left Wall Street that, if you came, you'd have to plank. Dear racket, this," commented the secretary.

The millionaire had come to Exmoor with the preconceived notion of paying, but now it suited his humor to assume with his secretary that he paid with reluctance.

"'These professors are pluckers—hang on like leeches," he growled, looking down the room. He intended to give the college a new library.

The secretary moved away.

The assembly gradually dispersed into clusters of threes and fours, as before Mr. Gay's entrance, for general conversation is an impossibility out of France and we gravitate to the dialogue, as it were.

Meanwhile the millionaire stood at the head of the rooms, and one after another by twos the professors and ladies swept up to him or hit upon him in their circuit. Mrs. Keyes introduced them all, officiating with the solemnity of a high-priestess before the idol. He received them with low bows which obviated the necessity of overmuch speech, and he gave the profuse remarks of these loquacious students the flattering attention to which he had trained his intercourse with the world. Yet all the while he was involuntarily impelled to cut into their rambling talk with the curt "Make it short" he used to his clerks. He was bored. In that garrulous confusion Julian marked the tall, lean figure and the gray taciturn face. He thought of the Roman proconsul in the agora of Athens.

The President whelmed him over with attention; the President bowed and smiled and smoothed over millionaire Gay. The President was a blonde with a big square head and sandy side-whiskers. His features were inordinately prominent, from the knotty forehead impending over the huge ox-eyes, to the boot-heel chin clasped under the long, firm, mean mouth. The nose was heavily built out, as it were, buttressing the brows like the flying arch of a Gothic cathedral. Such was the man's forceful and incongruous head, and such as it was, set it on a column that circled out of the high-banded collar, like the bare neck of the vulture out of its feathers. The body was square and the arms grew out of its upper corners, over-long and ending in large white and tender hands, always clammy. The attenuated legs beneath the cask of the trunk looked like the dancing extremities of a puppet which is supported on a wire. Moreover, this anatomy was not strikingly ugly nor absurd. It was clad faultlessly. This man by dint of politic shrewdness and downright character had hewn a place for himself in the world, and exacted consideration from men. Even Mr. Gay, despite the faults of the President's manner and his almost fulsome obeisance, respected him in a way; for the millionaire recognized certain kindred qualities in him, those characteristics which had made him necessary to Exmoor College and which had conquered the community. The President's scholarship might be impeached, but he knew men and possessed executive ability, and so had seized the helm of a ship whose voyagers shirk responsibilities and demand a captain who will sail the craft without troubling their siestas. Yet strip the man of his manner and regard him as a physical specimen of the human plant, and Julian's verdict, borne out of his southern sense of form, was correct. Julian, who disliked him, always spoke of him as that "gargoyle." Mr. Keyes once said, "Oh, Pompes, he is our buskined Dogberry."

"Tell me, you know him," said the millionaire, abruptly breaking the rosary of the President's compliments,—"what sort of a young man is Professor Clyde's son? I think I never saw a handsomer fellow."

"Ah, yes, I think I may claim to know something about him. I have been his teacher in the past, when he was yet a student, and I hazard, yes, hazard the assumption that I may have contributed in some degree to his development and to the moulding of his character. Very important, exceedingly so, the first training. The early—the early ideals, I may say."

"Yes, but what is he?" interposed Gay's abrupt interrogation.

"What is he—what is he? Well, I—you know, myself—I am, perhaps, not the most competent judge. There can be no doubt, not the shadow of a doubt, and, indeed, I have absolutely no hesitation—not the least—in pronouncing him an estimable youth. However, you knew—him—of his mother," he added, in a guttural whisper—"you knew that his mother was a shop-girl of Venice—Italian, you understand, and a—"

"I knew his father married in Italy," said Gay, dryly. Then he went on in conclusive tones, "I intend doing something for that young man."

President Pompes threw a quick look, but Gay's ashen face was an unwritten tablet. Mr. Gay had divined the President's antagonism, and the knowledge had crystallized his undefined interest in Julian into settled purpose. The millionaire suspected the President's unctuousness veiled a contempt for a mere ignorant money-bags, and as he had no wish to cross his large plans of bounty to Exmoor College, he took it out on the inflated theologian in small ways.

When the President had pushed forward his two sons with amplest introduction, the New Yorker had looked over their heads, indifferent or absorbed.

President Pompes turned the conversation, but President Pompes was scarlet.

"Mr. Gay, are you an admirer of women, a devotee at the shrine of the ladies? You will permit me, I am sure, to draw your attention to the fact, which must be patent to you, that our Exmoor ladies may well occupy your astention. New England women are not the women of New York, of course; but then we shall not quarrel, for, as I take it, there is no rivalry. They are such different types, and I fancy I may invite you to admire our ladies without treason to your own city."

The millionaire alleged that every man should admire women.

"Ah, my dear sir, let me—kindly permit me to express my gratification at your gallant words. Of course, you who come here from New York and her fashion cannot expect us to vie in point of ornament or adornment, or, let me observe, of any of those charming accessories of beauty. But we have some old names here to-night, women whose great-grandmothers were leaders of society three generations ago. But I want you to know Mrs. Ballard, a grand—indeed a grand woman!—and will you not permit me, my dear sir, to take you to her? Her daughter is the young lady, a most charming girl, now talking—on your left, as we pass—to your young friend, Mr. Clyde." He had bent his back towards Gay and had passed his flabby hand through the millionaire's arm.

The New Yorker was undetermined whether the President's flowers of speech proceeded from his condescension to mankind, as to an inferior needing to be cajoled and led, or whether he was positively unaware of his own absurdity.

"He may think the world asinine, but why should he treat me as if I were one of the same kind?" Gay asked himself. At any rate, when it came to women, the President was —"one of those sentimentals." He afterwards said to his secretary, "That pompous goat is a soft old pudding."

The widow was dressed in black, without an ornament, without a jewel. Her black sleeves, edged with handsome lace, enhanced the ivory of her rounded wrists and beautiful hands. She stood with her back to the fireplace; she looked a grand woman there in her simple dress; her face had the cast of tragedy and greatness. Thus it was that she met Gay, the man who, pursuing his destiny, would illumine the sombre journeying of her life with one clear gleam of power and authority, ere Fate trod her into the mud, as the foot of the passer-by imbeds the pebble in the soft earth.

She interested the self-sufficient man at first sight. He felt drawn to this woman, whose soft fingers grasped his hand with a man's firmness.

When the President had retreated, she said in her sincere simple way, " We are all glad to see you in Exmoor, Mr. Gay. The advent of a man of affairs stirs up our stagnation."

Gay gave her the intuitive esteem of an able man for his equal. He answered her with direct phrases, such as he used in Wall Street about important matters. This woman made every one himself, so that people talked out their real selves to her.

Dinner was announced. The hostess requested Mr. Gay to take Mrs. Ballard out. She herself went out on the arm of the President, according to the tradition of Exmoor ; this perquisite of office was peculiarly pleasant to the incumbent head of the college. Exmoor had some ways of its own in doing things certainly, Gay thought.

The President said grace and the dinner was fairly begun. Mrs. Keyes diffused a radiant contentment and *bonhomie* from her massive person; the vacant amiability of her aristocratic countenance sheltered her neighbors, like the solidity of a Roman wall. The critic, however, was nervous and the servants irritated him. He hated these large entertainments. " Too much of the amphitheatre about them," he used to say. A hundred trifles demanded instant decision, and a nice dispute was always frustrated by a plate descending before one's argumentative nose.

Julian sat next Margaret Ballard—Italy cheek by jowl with Massachusetts. President Pompes had Mrs. Lancaster on one side and Mr. Mancutt on the other. Mr. Gay had the post of honor on the right of the host, while Mrs. Ballard supported the other flank. It was an Exmoor arrangement; people were supposed to be stationed agreeably and not for precedence' sake, the hostess delighting to honor no one over the heads of her other guests. Mrs. Keyes was said to possess an instinct for grouping people.

The President ventured to remark that men unconsciously acted out their character; that Mr. Gay was an absorber and compeller born; that, without intending to monopolize, he was certainly holding Mrs. Ballard from that market where her words sold above par and her smiles were esteemed coupons of gold. This elephantine humor brought down the table. Julian was impressed with its asininity. But it failed to divert Gay, who, after returning a polite response, resumed his conversation with the widow, only pausing now and then to answer a question from some one, or to throw in an aside to his host.

Mrs. Ballard was pleased. She lighted the seventy candlesticks of her charms for Gay. She revelled in the envy of that table of people, who had never understood her and who had persistently underestimated her.

The secretary sat next Miss Jane Halding, who greatly amused him. He got along with her much better than before. At first he had hardly known how to take her, as he told Julian afterwards; she seemed as elusive as mercury, and slipped away when he thought he had her tight. He had two thirds of a notion she was mocking him. Finally he dropped pretence and told her funny things, not thinking of himself. She enjoyed them with her whole soul, laughing in pure bell-notes, like a child. The irregular features and two little blue eyes, intense points of light, seemed charged with an electricity. Perhaps nothing she said was very brilliant, but the play of her face made it seem so, and the pouting mouth darted little silver arrows of speech that stung and sparkled.

In his droll way the secretary recited the tribulations of Mr. Gay and himself since they had come into Exmoor. He felt Miss Halding would forgive impudence, any irreverence, indeed, against Exmoor institutions, if he only made her laugh. Thus he revenged himself on these professors who treated him as a sort of annexed baggage-car to Gay's train ; he paraded their ridiculous points before this Mephistophelian chit of a girl with infinite gusto.

"Why, positively, poor Mr. Gay has nearly died of thirst since he came, let alone the Puritanical abundance of your 'high thinking' dinners. This is the first house in Exmoor where he has had enough to drink; I can see it by his expression. Between ourselves, if these reverend hermits only knew it, they'd serve up to him less flourishes and more fluid."

Jane Halding looked at the millionaire with pretended compassion. "The poor dear creature! What a shame to starve him so! But is he absolutely incapable of drinking water? How nice to have such a discerning throat!"

She turned her demure face to the secretary, who nearly exploded. They both thought it a huge joke. When the table asked the reason of their uproar, they concealed it together, entertaining a sense of joint-ownership.

"You know," said the secretary later on—"You know we landed in Springfield at five o'clock in the morning, and the train to your town doesn't get out of that beautiful hole until noon. Well, Professor Clyde met us and carted us over to one of your stuffy, quiet little hotels, such as you meet everywhere in the country, and slapped us down in the parlor. Two hours ahead before breakfast. We were enormously sleepy, but that old immortal had to be dealt with. I slipped off to bed; but what do you suppose?—that fussy old affair kept Gay there and talked Roman law to him until breakfast-time. Gay didn't even get a cup of coffee to revive himself with. You ought to have heard Gay swear afterwards—or rather you oughtn't,—wouldn't do at all! but you can take my word for it."

The secretary described the journey on the branch railroad up to Exmoor; how the Professor and the millionaire bungled over each other in supplying conversation; how Gay was uncomfortable and the philosopher seemed a fool. Jane Halding laughed and laughed. A professor's stupid wife near them picked up the drift of their talk and glared conscientiously at the blasphemers; but Mancutt did not see, and Jane Halding only felt like sticking out her tongue at the shocked thick-skull.

Modern life puts one coat on the back of the world and prescribes one style and a uniform manner of eating, but through the monotony of this warp runs a various woof made of strands drawn from every creed and colorings extracted from every ideal history has imposed on men or beaconed them by. The Puritan and the sensualist, the fanatic and the sceptic, the seer and the ordinary animal, were ranged at that table, speaking the courtesies of good breeding—all careless of the limitless gulfs between them, of the devils and angels embodied in those conventional diners. The century has been the cesspool of its predecessors, into which they have drained their ideas, their institutions, their laws, their love, their spirit, their sin. The modern man is a mass of a thousand elements crushed into cohesion; under the vulgar garb of the street beat passionate hearts and hearts dry as baked clay—Hamlets and Amiels, Iagos and Heines, melancholy harlequins and pompous heroes, Jews and Greeks and Romans, or all of them strangling each other in one single carcass.

There were men of large minds and rare natures about Mrs. Keyes's table, and women of spiritual type, with royal purity shining on their brows—for the select of Exmoor dined there. But the secretary, superficial skin of humanity that he was, thought he had never seen such a stupid set, and Gay himself was visibly bored, except with Mrs. Ballard. These recluses did not know how to be lightly agreeable. Their mirth was ruined by its ponderosity, as the Carthaginian elephants trod down the supporting footmen. They themselves took little pleasure in it, and it was, for the most part, but an ungraceful affectation. They told old stories current in town two years ago ; they laughed like schoolboys let loose.

Gradually, however, as the millionaire narrowed his attention to Mrs. Ballard and his immediate neighbors, the professors descended to their real exercise-ground ; points of theology and literature were unmasked and trained on the table. Keyes led off with Shelley, as usual ; St. Paul followed hard after. The women broached the " Carlyles." They had small mercy for the grim grand peasant and his genius that bluntly bore home to the truth. They were full of commiseration for the brilliant, egotistical, beautiful wife ; it never occurring to their feminine understanding that the egotism of a young woman who, loving another man, yet would appropriate a whole genius, merely as a comforter for herself, had something provincial and petty in it.

In the meantime Mrs. Ballard was reducing the millionaire. They talked everything, and every minute Mr. Gay got nearer to himself, his ambitions, his hopes. This woman understood him.

After dinner, in the parlors the two talked alone, apart from the others. They spoke of life, its aims, and that which best perpetuates a man.

" When a man has success in his hands, he asks what he shall do with it," said Mr. Gay. " I have money and place, but within two years after my death I shall be forgotten. I have no sons, and my daughters will but carry my wealth to other men."

The millionaire opened himself to this stranger, whose power made him confess what he had never said to another.

"Ah, but you who know the world so well must surely understand that a man's perpetuity lies in some work which affects men after he is dead," she answered, in her low voice. "And if you have the mind to occupy men's thoughts during your life, you can, if you wish, devise some means to be remembered." Her eyes challenged him to dare, to perform. "You are able, let me see if you are as able as I think."

"But how?" he asked. "Shall I found a hospital, or endow a college—here, in Exmoor, for instance?"

The widow swept round upon him with an enthusiasm, a conflagration lighting her face. "You do it! You do it! I never thought, but it is the thing. Back Exmoor—organize anew! Gay University shall be the name. It is your chance, your perpetuation!"

Her impetuosity shook even Gay, calculator that he was.

"I have thought of it," he admitted, with a trace of his old reluctance to show his hand. "But to tell you the truth"—he hesitated—"I hardly know how to handle these moles—I beg pardon! I mean I don't understand your Exmoor professors."

"I understand. They are hermits, recluses, impracticals—what Bonaparte styled 'ideologists.' So much the more for you; it makes your opportunity. There is no rival patron; there is not an able man to infringe upon your supremacy. The college needs money and ability behind her, and you are offered a monopoly of it all."

She would have made a splendid Madame Adam, the queen of a political salon. She was admirable in foreseeing the course of a conversation, in planting a stake ahead, to be led up to.

"Everything requires management and money, nowadays; even to be saved we need it," asserted the millionaire, resuscitating his dictatorial pride by the words; for at bottom he felt his individual inferiority before New England's patricianism. He had more brains than his secretary, and he could see that much.

"Well," he went on with the indifference of the powerful, "I suppose I could transform Exmoor into a great college, a main centre of education. I can spare ten millions just as well as not. I believe this is the right place for a college. It's the country, and I don't believe in city colleges. Why, with the backing I could put into it, we could just as well have a thousand students here as four hundred."

"There is the right tradition here too," Mrs. Ballard suggested. "The town has a fame of its own; Keyes and Professor Clyde and their coterie have made it so. That is a basement worthy building on. Take hold and work a reformation, and if you wish to be remembered you will have not only your own university but the prestige of Exmoor to aid. You will be associated together; you will stand as a sort of Mæcenas or Louis XIV. to the literary school here. It would be a gigantic memorial, a kind of modern Cheops, do you see? To do that is greater and more lasting than to leave an immense fortune your grandchildren will make fragments of; or to build a palace at which the next generation of clerks will ask, 'Who was the fellow, anyhow, who paid for it?'"

She went on. She pictured the new Exmoor; she painted in the enticing details, and by sheer imagination kindled the man. Electric lights, wide shop-windows, throngs of students in the streets, a rushing business, a new town born of the great college's demands, the royal buildings of Gay University seated on the hill and looking twenty miles northward down the valley—all the material effects which would appeal to a nature unaffected by spiritual forces. She used a business man's terms. She always dropped into other people's vocabularies; she spoke nonsense to women, slang and half-expressions frequently to Julian, classic periodics to Professor Clyde. She was so intellectually strong and of so free an imagination that she seized the position of others, as a skilful general grasps at the base of his foe. She paralleled her modes of thinking to another's, so that often she comprehended his intention more adequately than that person himself. She had seen the amorphous shape in Gay's mind and, through sheer inclination to lead and control, she was impelled to set his own ideas before him.

The enthusiasm of that powerful face, so calculated to impress even in repose; the ability and grasp upon the facts and the manner of her marshalling them to touch the self and the motives of his character; the appeal to his pride of power, his thirst for perpetuity; his unconscious purpose to offer redemption for the compromises of a successful career,—they all compelled Gay. That cold and skilful nature, struck through its one mode of sympathy— admiration of force, wherever seen—was dominated by the magnetism of the woman's thought and quickened by the vigor of her nerve-fluid.

Gay University!

Conquerors in the Middle Age endowed abbeys above their Senlacs.

CHAPTER VII.

A PROSE MEDEA.

JULIA BALLARD was a large woman of imponderable figure, the undulations of which were retained by corset-steel, as a reservoir is held in by a dam. Yet her entire effect was massive, and her walk bore her down upon her destination like a frigate on a foe. She always sat bolt upright, and in conversation, particularly when listening, her body swayed from the hips in rhythmic motion, while her hands lay in her lap, her beautiful wrists crossed like two prostrate columns, fallen one above the other.

She was a remarkable woman. That tragic face stands upon the memory like a headland on straight shores. The great head with the black bands of hair brushed smooth behind the ears, the dull deep eyes, the short Bismarckian nose and the blunt aggressive mouth—the elements of a countenance a master of men might not have disdained.

Yet even at this period of her life, when youth lay in the rear, masculinity did not dominate her appearance. True, she had no attractions for the mere man of the world, and too much of gloom and unregenerate power brooded in those sullen features to do aught but repel idle youth. But with a class of men she had always been an influence. Men of intellect sought her. To imperious wills like Gay she represented so much of their own force that, while they would marry a tenderer woman, they rushed to talk to her, to unfold their supreme ambitions, feeling that her great mind would comprehend their scope. To Mr. Keyes she had never burnt incense of adulation, and yet that delicate egotist, beneath the sputterings of his hurt vanity, had conceived an admiration and even awe of her, called her habitually the "Medea," and perhaps, if she had permitted him, would have clung to her resolute nature as intellectual minds of overmuch sensitiveness will fasten to a virile femininity. But she repulsed his faintest advances. What she held to be the tragedy of her life was too closely associated with him.

Are there not sufferings of the strong, paroxysms of rage and disappointment, gross stupors of lethargy, those attendants of excessive passions, that are crueller than any torture the feeble feel in this existence? Do not stunted powers and sealed capabilities revenge their defeat on the possessor and corrode the entrails?

She had been married when an unformed girl. When first the delicate-featured, blonde young clergyman had preached in her native village, the crude country girl fixed him as an ideal point in her realistic environment. Even then, plunged in the midst of the vulgarities and noxious details of small-farm existence, that potent brain dimly groped towards thought and progress for her after-life. Beside the agricultural boors of her acquaintance, beside her own somewhat uncouth family, the fineness of the Rev. John Ballard's grain appeared like the soft texture of his priestly broadcloth upon the usual background of overalls and high boots.

Mr. Ballard preached a summer at her town. He was just out from his theological seminary and was waiting for a settlement. He used to read Wordsworth to her during the August afternoons. She studied a little geology and French with him. These were their happiest days, a hyphen of joy between the unutterable griefs of youth and the stern sorrows of manhood and womanhood. By some crook he was offered a tutorship in literature at Exmoor College. There he went, and from thence he came to marry her and thither he took her. In time he succeeded to the full chair of belles-lettres; he had taste, but not enough to run away with his orthodoxy, and so was the man for the place in the Puritan institution. He worked a lifetime; he was universally beloved, his tender nature understood students' difficulties and old women's hysterias. He became a sort of lay-pastor for Exmoor's humble. When he died the town mourned.

In these years of his professorship, Julia Ballard had grown. She had studied some for herself, and she gathered knowledge and discipline from the simple process of living, as is characteristic of original natures. She had shot a great way on the tracks of thought and desire since she came to the college town as a bride, passionately proud of her young littérateur. A whisper gathered credence with the students that the rugged phrases, impact with force, tanged with a rude genius even, that here and there startled the decorous sterility of Professor Ballard's respectable lectures, owed their genesis to his wife. With the years, too, that face curtained into a sullen gloom, the eyes were dimmed, and the great promontories of the features emerged from the bloom of health and youth into solid relief. Her young beauty grew into a haughty Titanese effect, which the timid and the ordinary shrank from. Some of the town who had loved her dead husband shunned her very shadow.

She had two children, Margaret, the eldest, and John, named after his father. She had never been devoted to her daughter, who was like the father, and whom he had principally brought up, since the day her mother recognized whose child she was. Margaret was beautiful, an embodiment of that high, pure, marble-pale Christianity of her father's ideal and Tennyson's King Arthur. Exmoor adored her, raged over her, but the mother was unaffected.

When the boy came six years after, he was passionately

welcomed. The sombre, impassive face broke into storm and love over the little squaller. The mother caught it up in her rounded peasant-arms and hugged it to her face, while the great tears torrented forth. Over that weak baby mould all the repressed passion of the tumultuous soul was hurled out. Her husband with his sensitive face looked on, and the sharpness grew intense around his tremulous lips as he beheld the ardor in the mother which would no longer greet him in the wife. .

As the children grew up, she used to say, with a sad smile, that she had three children. The great maternity of her nature extended its protection over the husband. Her attitude to him became one of compassion—this woman whom Professor Clyde had once said might play Brunhild to a Siegfried. But the fierce love she lavished on her son ! And that huge body was put cheerfully into a hundred motions for his pettiest whims. She would steal into his sleeping-room and sit for hours over his trundle-bed, gaz-' ing into his face in an agony of worship, striving to detect the signs of coming strength, weaving image-pictures of his youth and manhood, deciphering, too, perhaps, the im- press of the father there.

The boy grew up very sturdy. He was dark and heavy like his mother, with her solid brows and indolent limbs. The mother read to him, studied with him, histories, liter- ature, languages, elementary science. She carried him through his primary lessons and went at even pace with him in his preparation for college. Gradually the sug- gestion deepened into the certainty of shadow on her face, and before John was fourteen the old sullenness had re- gained its throne, and the brooding habit settled upon her again with a deadlier weight, and for longer periods.

Oh, the stored hope in a child, a life-bark in which a mother heaps all her wealth—her visions of deeds achieved, the ambitions of her girlhood! When the hard fates swal-

low that last plank on her waste ocean of life, despair
steams up as a universal vapor and wraps all her skies. In
this boy she deemed herself re-born in a happier fortune.
He should run her career by proxy, in him she had stuffed
all her stifled powers, before him she knelt in renunciation
for herself, which might be accomplishment in him—this
culmination of her life, this essence of her passion and her
need, who should do and command, even as she might
have done with other sex or mated to a strong man—he,
her boy, her soul, was dormant, having the substratum of
her temperament, wretched amalgam of her physical stolidity and bovine health, and of the father's confined and
cribbed intelligence, that he was. Even Margaret, the
neglected, was a happier compound of chance. She cursed
her torpid body, from which her boy's slow solidity was
drawn. His vacant eyes made her hate herself, where before she but hated fortune. His big stupid forehead, she
had supposed to mask an intellect, irritated her. He became to her as a clod one stumbles on and damns.

She had put this final conclusion from her for years.
She was reluctant to accept its ultimatum. At times she
even wished to be deluded.   Something worthy of worship, something grand to be passionate over and to
sacrifice self to, something above prosaic duty, which to
her pagan sense had no appeal! Julia Ballard, like a
harassed animal that leaps from the fires to the spears,
sought illusion. For months she lavished a rekindled passion on her husband; she furnished him with dainties;
begged to hear his lectures; strove to regard his ideas as
more than ordinary. She burnt him incense by the bushel,
but the fumes could not transfigure him into a god. That
uncompromising intellect shone through to the facts, and
she could not but face reality. It is the peculiar torture of
intellectual power that the brain is emperor, whether or no;
and that it shifts the hated truth before the desired fiction,

as in a theatre the prison scenery of the next act is slid before the summer idyl we would clasp forever.

The tremendous tragedy of life always lies in its inadequate response to our supreme desires. The conscientious soul who is divided between love and duty, the man of pleasure who demands infinite voluptuousness, the being to whom passion is a necessity and who must remain cold, the enthusiast who must bury the ideal in the animal wants of four hungry children and a shrewish-tongued wife—these, as with the great capacity chained like a trotting-horse to a vulgar dray, find their sorrow in thwarted development, their debasing and deflowering rust, their mean and shabby tragedy, in the unanswering blank to their imperious necessities.

This woman, with the imperial powers of a Russian Catharine, with the need of command as a rod to conduct to safety the electricity of her temperament, was mired in a marriage to a good and limited nature, shackled by commonplace domesticities, drugged with sordid cares, made the mother of an ordinary family, and expected to cut a respectable figure in the community. As she said of herself, with her coarse characterization, she was "no cow" and did not mean to become one.

The night before he died, Professor Ballard seemed a well man. In the pitiful little room upstairs, over the hall, which he called his "den," his thin woman-sloping shoulders drooped over papers and books, as they had been doing in unfruitful toil for fifteen years. Under the dim yellow light of his desk-lamp the face looked haggard, and the hand whose lean fingers strayed amid the papers shook tremulously with a nervous affection.

For an hour his pen held on, sputtering drunken ink marks across fair sheets. At intervals he leaned back in his chair and clasped his hands behind his head, as if to support it. Finally, he dropped his pen. It was done.

He murmured to himself, "That is my best; I can do no more. It is not much, God knows. I wonder if God expects any more than the best I can do. I hope he is not like my wife."

A muffled continuous knock at the door, and before he could reply to its salutation, the door swung back and Mrs. Ballard swayed in !

"It is done," he said, not turning to her, but with his eyes on the desk.

"Let me hear it," she replied.

He read to her the address he was to deliver by invitation before a Boston society. She made some few suggestions, altering a word here and a phrase there, touching it up with swift strokes, as a master does the picture of a student. At the end she said nothing, but rose and seized his pen. She wrote a sentence at the bottom of the last page.

"Will that not be a better closing?"

"Yes," he answered involuntarily, inwardly prophetic of the hour to-morrow night when the Bostonese culture would thrill at that last clause of rugged power. The vanity of it—that applause from men of leisure, who take their literature as a sort of spiritual champagne! He, who could not convince his own wife of his importance—what was the prestige of a man of letters to him? He knew his little literary reputation was factitious, the result of management and chance; of his residence in Exmoor, and the fact that he never excited jealousies. Oh, to be sure, he had toiled, as only the few toil, winning by dogged tenacity and the rigid faith of a dull mind ! and the best world of America regarded him as an elegant and cultivated gentleman, perfectly harmless, perhaps. But beside that grand head and its undiscovered greatness, he felt himself a miserable insignificance. Was it not his wife who wrote those few sentences people selected to repeat and his critic-friends praised him for ?

Mrs. Ballard talked of other things; household cares; that John needed a new pair of trousers, and the sink in the kitchen leaked in the wrong place. All the while she was thinking, If she might go down to Boston, in this man's place, and lecture there before the intellect of America! The fires of a heart charged with suffering and thought would then break out in lightnings, and she tightened her hands as she felt that audience bowing before her freighted words. She longed to mould that assembly into tumult and into cheers, even as the wind feels the impulse to heave the ocean and hurl its floor into chaotic storm.

"John," she said, "you look tired and need unbracing before you go to bed. You had better go to see Mr. Keyes; he is always at full blast at this hour. You had better go."

She followed him down to the door and saw him put on his overcoat and round seal cap. When he was gone, she sank on the stairs. The moonlight came through the window and inlaid the blackness with a shaft of melancholy. She sat with her knees together, and her hands clasped strenuously about them. She swayed herself, and a moan came every little while. The night went on. At twelve she heard her husband's feet grind the porch, and she passed upstairs to her room, and so escaped him.

The next night at eleven o'clock she opened the telegram, knowing what lay within the envelope. She did not stagger. This new fact hurled upon her seemed of little significance. She was firm enough to write a return-dispatch. She went upstairs calmly, packed a satchel and caught a freight accommodation-train leaving Exmoor at six minutes after midnight. At Springfield she boarded the express. She could not sleep. She was aware of every station stopped at, and she almost counted the miles as they slipped under the thunderous feet of the train.

We, who live in time, enveloped in space, are for the

most part forbidden absolute sight. Only sketches of the
road are visible, and the hills of the immediate shut off the
mountains of the grand facts. But this night of travel un-
hinged Mrs. Ballard's life from the incidental. She was as
if hung between the two syllables of her past and future,
and the train bearing her from the old to the new allowed
her to view her former days as one surveys his planet from
a balloon. She felt like an actor between two scenes,
alone in the green-room, released from the imaginations of
the stage, in solitude with his own identity. She had no
sorrow, nor joy. It was the suspense of judgment. She
saw her life. She had finished the first heat of the race.
At forty-three she felt she had had one existence. She
had lived. And this strange change that had broken upon
her suddenly—what was it? She could not define it, so
strongly was she impressed with the fact that her old life
lay behind her; that overwhelmed the rest. That life of
hers, which was as a thing she had read about, she speculated over it as she had blamed and pitied, loved and hated
the lives of literature. That passionate, wilful, self-abne-
gating, burstingly proud, and altogether sombre personality,
which she now contemplated, apart from herself, inspired
an affection in her as for someone without. She did not
clearly recognize it for herself. She was so sorry for her!—
the powerful, poor woman—sorry for her, as she was for
Romola or for George Sand.

So she reached Boston.

When she saw him lying with the light brown curls
about his weak, idealistic face, a passion of grief came, as
for a child dead. That he was no more to make demands
upon her, no more to be her thought and trouble—that
smote her. She felt as if she had given birth to him. As
she looked longer upon the dead face and the immobility
of those once tremulous lips, with the little sad smile upon
them now which they had worn these latter years, a pity

seized upon her. She bent her head and drew him close in her arms. "Oh, my poor boy, my poor boy!" she said.

She took him back home. They buried him on those bulky hills which the north wind desolates in winter, and the tender spring pads with green, and the ripe autumn decorates with gold and russet and crimson. The genius of those cloudy places comfort him—him, so valiantly persistent, in his methodic, cabined way !

She missed him. We miss the most uncomfortable habits. That familiar figure whose coming in the afternoon about four o'clock she had listened for, for twenty-one years; that little desire expressed ten times a day—all these she awaited mechanically, and started when she remembered.

She had to clear up his "den" and go over his papers. A great compassion welled up. Here was the chair he had sat in and toiled in. This meagre little room—was it not the shell of a very meagre life ? She went over his books; and as she noted each, and the data of its acquisition, written in his thin, straggling hand on the blank page, the detached pieces of his career came before her. All the lonesomeness of the man, since she had fallen out of active co-operation with him ; all the daily struggle against hope that he might attain, and so please her; all his jealousy of Keyes, and all his eagerness after literary notoriety; all his petty shams and simulations of emotions he admired and of the eccentricities of great men,—they ranged themselves in front of her and dovetailed together to make complete the pitiful personality. Somehow they lifted his mediocrity to the pathetic. Was it true that he too had carried his tragedy around with him? The poignant griefs done his vanity, the dissatisfaction of unattainable ideals—what a poor starved soul it was ! She pictured him here, staggering night after night alone, without a real friend to share the secret of his sorrow, facing existence without a murmur and the denying fates without protest.   For the first time she conceived the sufferings of barren natures, of imprisoned souls, of spirits that have neither wings, nor legs, nor hands,—bodies without movement, life without voice. Was it true—had she, selfishly blind, walked over this tragedy of the commonplace ?   Of the two, him and herself, which paid the dearer, which suffered the deeper ?   She had cherished her own tragedy, she had anointed herself, in her own eyes, as a superior being bound to clogs like him; but which, after all, was the honester sufferer ?   The passionate strength rebelling and with an element of the poetic in its high-stepping dramatics, or the cribbed intelligence, aware of its mean measure, the aching vanity stabbed by her every day, and yet bravely silent—oh, which?

Mrs. Ballard repelled comforters.   To the commonplace condolence the marble of her face never relented.   Half Exmoor was furious that she should take so coldly the death of one so loved, so saintly, whose secret deeds of kindness had bound many hearts.

But his widow walked the streets in majestic mourning, and the rigid calm of her features was stone to the would-be wipers of tears.   Mrs. Morton, whose business in this world was to attend funerals and haunt the houses of mourning for a year thereafter, was repulsed summarily. The widow received her in a high manner, said not one word to her sympathetic tears, her sighs, her " reposings in the Lord's bosom," her " beautiful voyage in this evil world."   The widow was granite, and when opportunity offered, slipped in the interstices of Mrs. Morton's speech cool wedges of " fine weather "—" I am informed Dr. Ponder has finished his Syriac lectures "—" Professor Morton is conducting a new chemical experiment, is he not?" —" There is a report of the engagement of Miss Jane

Halding to a Mr. Gingham of Leeds, son of the great woollen magnate."

As Mrs. Morton afterwards affirmed, " The wicked iceberg talked as if she had just been entertaining pleasure instead of death in her house."

But alone, she had paroxysms of remorse, of despair, that left her moribund, so that she lay on her bed for days together, perfectly impassive, torpid, utterly drained of energy. Sometimes at night her dead husband's face stood written upon the dark with the poor wan smile and the suffering in his eyes. Then she would remember him as at first she knew him. She recalled his enthusiastic spirit, when first he came to Exmoor, and the blithe joy he had in his new duties. And the dark transition from that youth to the thing he died seemed due to her. This impression was vivid; she even nursed it, wearing it as a mental sackcloth.

When Mrs. Lancaster called, after the funeral, Margaret met her at the door.

" Mamma is upstairs, but I will call her. I'm so glad you came, dear Mrs. Lancaster. She has been depressed for the last two days, and I think seeing you will do her good." These two were elective affinities. They were but varieties of the same type. The tall girl with her sweet stateliness would develop into a blonde and majestic woman, with all of Mrs. Lancaster's air of selection. Mrs Lancaster loved her and encouraged Julian's admiration.

Mrs. Lancaster sat down in the dark parlor. As she waited, life seemed to her a theatre for religious joy, and the mysteries which border it were filled with beauties.

Above, Margaret pleaded in a darkened chamber. On the bed the widow's figure lay extended, the arms thrown out stiffly, and the head, with its masses of coarse black hair, half buried in the pillows.

" O mamma, do come down! Dear mamma, come,

please! I know it will do you good; you will feel better afterwards."

The girl stood in her pleading. She dared not go near her prostrate mother.

"Mrs. Lancaster is so good and lovely, and she knows how to comfort. Please come, there's a dear mamma! She helped me so, and when I felt rebellious, she showed me it was God's will, and how it was good; that everything that happens is really good. Please come, mamma!"

Still no movement. The girl persisted. At last there was a tremor of the pillows, and the bed creaked heavily. Margaret shrank back to the door at the resurrection caused by her incantation.

"Tell the neutrality down there I'll come," said Mrs. Ballard, rising from the bed and groping with her feet for her slippers underneath.

"O mamma!" gasped Margaret, at the blunt designation of Mrs. Lancaster. In a moment she resumed, "Will you let me help you? I can get you ready so much sooner." Still she did not advance from the door.

"No, go downstairs, and entertain her until I come. You two are enough alike, and I sha'n't hurry myself."

The daughter went, down-hearted. She did not understand this revolt. Her mother was a Christian, surely! Why then was she not resigned? This boisterous grief shocked Margaret's delicacy by its base vulgarity; it might have been a washerwoman's sorrow.

Mrs. Ballard entered the parlor abruptly, like a projectile. She extended her hand without a word. Margaret slipped out unseen; she wanted to leave them alone together.

The two women sat down opposite each other, Mrs. Ballard on the sofa with her arms folded, swaying her body. They were complete contrasts. Medea and the Madonna sat over against each other—one an exploding vessel of passion; the other, a steady tapering craft, anchored in the haven of secure love and well-considered habit. They had never been intimate, and Mrs. Lancaster had always secretly irritated the other.

In this presence Mrs. Ballard hardened. All the resentment against the tranquil and prosperous world, which years of hidden anger and disappointment had secreted, gathered to a head of hate against this gracious blonde woman, with her patrician mien and bronze hair. Mrs. Lancaster's soft, dulcet, inflected voice was a jagging spur to the other's envious contempt.

In her sympathy, Mrs. Lancaster leaned towards her "sister in sorrow." Her gentle eyes filled as she spoke compassionate sentences. She felt she did not comprehend this terrible grief, but she supposed it had the usual causes, and so she offered the usual ointments and oils convention deals out to the afflicted. She recounted the virtues of the dead, how he had lived life seriously and well, and had attempted to put into deed his highest conception. .

"How appropriate," she said, "that he should die in the service of literature, which he considered so helpful to man! It was the flower of his life, the final blossoming of his best hours and thought and faith—was it not?—that lecture upon Wordsworth, which he was delivering when he fell. You ought to be comforted that he left life at that precise moment, with words of reverence upon his lips, pointing men to beauty and to moral truth."

So Mrs. Lancaster went on, while the stern mask she addressed curtained a hundred bitter, cynical or remorseful thoughts. Yes, that lecture, Mrs. Ballard thought, the one she herself had primed him on!—she knew all the affectations and vanities and simulations stuffed into its tissue. How the Boston papers had praised it, when they published, on the first page in the middle of the sheet, how he had fallen down paralyzed, just as he closed with that last great striking phrase! Much source of consola-

tion she had, indeed—she, who had driven him to death
by work at that very lecture, and then let him go off
at last, without one word of approval for all his intense
labor!

Mrs. Lancaster trotted up the ambulance of religion.
But what had she, an unbeliever, a pagan, a hater of humility and acquiescence, to do with such milk-and-water
doctrines? They would do for Margaret, perhaps. This
passionless blonde, with mere milk in her veins, she could
be resigned! She could easily look back over her tranquil
life and contemplate it with serenity, as a calm sun looks
back down the valley he has illumined and suffuses its
length with a mellow light and a good-night kiss. This
gentle nature, what knew she of conflicts, of desire? To this
home-tender, who was respectable and aristocratic and refined, what were strains of strength tugging at the heart-
strings, ambition leaping like a vaulting battle-steed, jealousy, and hate and despair—what knew she of these, and
how could such as she console? Rich, with position, living
with people she loved and reverenced, without problems,
drifting along the slumberous tide of her lot, blessed with
the unquestioning devoted faith of a tender and limited
woman, she was happy in her very melancholy.

Suddenly Julia Ballard's veins grew swollen with hate.
Why should this woman have everything—this doll, this
waxen creature?

"I, that struggled and fought with beasts, that was
strenuous enough to desire greatly, and was passionate to
do much with my life, to make it avail much for men—I,
that had laboring ambitions and many talents, and whose
great longing was to use them for the best and highest—
lo! I am come to these—prostration, remorse, bitterness,
stultification!"

Mrs. Lancaster was saying, "There is comfort in res-
ignation. Be meek, my poor sister, even as your Saviour

was at Gethsemane. Bend like the reed, and the storm will blow over you."

"Stop!" Julia Ballard commanded. She rose, and the old, grand, pagan, unregenerate nature flamed from her countenance. She cried savagely, " I am tired of such babble. Tell it to babies and weaklings, and such as you are yourself ! You—weak inconsequential!—that may heal your wounds; but not mine. I am not tender, nor gentle, nor resigned. You, who have no iron in your thin blood, all that stuff is for you! Do you hear?—for you! But to attempt to console me with humilities and meekness! I'll have none of it. I will fight it out. Combat, dense and hard, that is what I prefer; and when I go, I'll break like a tower, not crumble into passivity and miserable Christian meekness."

Mrs. Lancaster had started from her seat in amazement. Now, she feared! The blasphemy was awful; she started back from it. Oh, it was dreadful, shocking! How could one conceive of it, much more give it utterance?

The fear and disgust on Mrs. Lancaster's face maddened Julia Ballard. She turned upon the stiff woman with these words:

" You have no passion and no despair. You do not know what it is to long for a great love and never receive it. You have no capacity, except for placidity and domestic things; in them, of course, you are admirable; you are respected, men admire the folds of the crape about your peachy neck, and your elegant figure, so erect and gracious. You pass for a lady and a good woman—for a cultivated personage, while I am hated because I'm sincere; called coarse because I'm able to define terms exactly; my intellect not even acknowledged, because I hammer people's prejudices."

These words were delivered standing, in low, stinging tones, repeated precisely, fired into Mrs. Lancaster, as a regiment at practice volleys into the targets. The woman chose to array against each other in absolute terms the distinctive qualities of her antagonist and of herself. But here her passions leaped the logic of her hate, and swept out in fierce ejaculations and vivid personalities. She advanced a stride towards Mrs. Lancaster, one arm thrust out, and rage distorting her countenance.

"You, you sweet innocence, you select child of God, you passive receptacle of peace!—you can afford to be good and generous; in fact, you can't help it, you are too neutral to be otherwise. You! do they call you refined, cultivated, the acme of womanhood? Humph! you are merely booted and gloved in kid—that's all. You haven't enough blood to understand what I mean, I suppose. Oh, I've heard you prate over Shakespeare and all his passionate heroines; I've seen your eyes moist over Gretchen praying to the Virgin hung on the wall; I've seen you sorry for poor Maggie Tulliver—you insufferable pretence! Don't you understand that those poor, unwise, gifted souls are out of your existence, totally foreign to your grave, religious, cistern peace? You wretched, sham-posturer in passions, you haven't enough purple heart-blood to feel! You impassivity, you righteous neutrality!"

Mrs. Ballard paused, all a-tremble, like one who has let loose a force too strong to be governed. The morbidities and revolt of years were in her imprecations, and Mrs. Lancaster was but the occasion, the wire that drew the lightning.

Mrs. Lancaster feared that a madwoman confronted her. These mingled defamations and despairs seemed insane. She moved quietly to the door. "I am going, Mrs. Ballard. I came with the best intentions; and I am sorry for this treatment, not for my sake, but for yours." She had forgotten her terror of insanity by this time. "But after this, you can hardly expect me to call again, or that I should care to see you in our house." After an interval, in which she looked at Mrs. Ballard, now limp and inert: "I am very sorry for you, so very sorry! I don't know that I can understand you, but believe me, I *am* sorry." She turned to go.

"Oh! wait a moment, an instant—forgive me!" Mrs. Ballard broke into tears. "I did not mean what I said— yes, I did, too! But it was not you—not you, so much as the world, the world! Forgive me! forgive me! Only say you will forget this and forgive me! I am utterly broken down. That head is ever before me, floating in the dark. It wavers, it lies in the corners and leers at my spoiled, maimed life. Oh, you will forgive me! will you not? and give me a little compassion—some of that sympathy, that human sympathy, I have never had, nor asked for before?"

Julia Ballard entreated with outstretched, beseeching arms. The proud face, but a moment ago instinct with hate and haughty pain, melted now, all the iron gone out of it. She felt a child's need of protection, and she threw herself blindly at the feet of the woman whom she had scorned into ladylike resentment.

"Of course, of course, Mrs. Ballard, I'll forgive you; but it was dreadful, it was awful! I hope this will never occur again. Of course you are forgiven. Don't cry any more about it."

The abused lady maintained her stiff post by the door, ready to go. She was a Christian, and she was glad her derider was humble before her God, repenting her blasphemies.

Julia Ballard on her knees buried her face on the sofa. The great sobs tore up through her throat and choked her. She was filled with self-pity and weakness. The superficial self, acquired through habit, was suddenly thrown off and for the time the real nature held sway. The imperious necessity for love, for absorption, for a grand passion, that was at bottom the sovereign motive in her character, quivered bare, like a nerve laid naked of flesh.

The patrician-bred woman surveyed the stooped head and the huddled shoulders. The colossal force of such passions was somewhat vulgar; she had not known they existed before; she was not fond of such vociferous displays. She had no tenderness for this woman who had insulted her, and though she a little pitied her and forgave her as a Christian forgives, she could not take the fallen head in her lap and wipe away the scalding tears. Mrs. Lancaster fulfilled her duty, she scattered platitudes of comfort, in the air, above the prostrate form.

After a while the sobs ceased. There was a long silence. Julia Ballard had time to feel shame for her outbreak. Without raising her head, she said in a low voice:—

"Go, please, dear Mrs. Lancaster. You forgive me and that is enough. Go! please go! and leave me alone. You are a good woman, and true, and deserve all you have. I know it. But go—go! You cannot understand, you cannot know."

Again she wept. The unreciprocated passion of a life, all the life-loneliness of a soul never yet understood, stood imaged in her request.

Mrs. Lancaster was glad to be gone. And, although she was a lady with a code of honor and never let mention of the scene pass her lips, she always regarded Mrs. Ballard henceforth as something of a monster.

Such was the woman who influenced Mr. Gay.

CHAPTER VIII.

"AND STRAIGHT WAS THE PATH OF GOLD FOR HIM."

THE company at Mrs. Keyes's broke up early, as was the custom in Exmoor.

In the room where the gentlemen's overcoats and hats littered the bed and draped the chairs and the towel-rack, the secretary addressed Julian in his light bantering way.

"What do you say to a smoke and a slow walk home, my handsome friend? A soporific cigar will just lay the wakeful spirit and allow me a good balmy sort of a sleep!"

"I'm with you," answered Julian. "Did Jane Halding so stir you up, you can't sleep? She is regular champagne, though—Mumm's Extra Dry!"

The young fellow had a consciousness that he was speaking like a man of the world. They stepped out of doors and stopped to "light up."

"But didn't I play the utterly-utter devoted?" lisped the secretary.

"Well, you did! I really am afraid for Miss Halding, who is a flirt, but not used to opposing her own tactics. Besides, she *is* susceptible—and then a New Yorker like you!"

Julian said these words jocosely and they seemed to him witty.

They laughed and walked out of the yard. After the preliminary puffs necessary to establish a firm fire, the secretary said, his cigar between his teeth,

"Did you ever deliberately set out to break a woman up—go at her with the fixed determination to get her in love with you—just to try your power and see if you could?"

He seemed to imply that such action in a man was fine and rather superior, evincing a kind of scientific curiosity, such as physicians have when they torture dogs, or Goethes when they play on Frederikas. His question, while suggesting a confidence as if from himself, was in reality sent out as a fathom-line to sound the young man.

"You mean without regarding the girl herself—in cold blood?" queried Julian.

"Exactly," answered the other, sententiously.

"I don't know that I have," answered Julian, reluctantly, as if he wished he could confess as much. "It must be quite a sensation," he added in a different tone.

"Ah! he's not such a prude," thought the secretary. "A little experience and diminution of ideality, and he'll do."

The worldling catalogued men into neat categories. There were swells, duffers and men of gumption. He had about made up his mind that Julian would fall under the last head. At all events, he was not a duffer.

"What made you think of that?" asked Julian, naïvely, "Miss Halding?"

"Not in particular," answered the secretary. "But she would make a scene, since you speak of her. She'd be worthy a man's best effort, she's so keen. I tell you it would be steel across steel with her. I should like nothing better than to get her gone on a man."

"She is attractive," admitted Julian.

"She is not beautiful. But such fire and nerve! She'd be immensely more interesting than lots of handsome women," said the secretary.

"'Sweet' describes her," thought Julian.

And all at once he became conscious of her winsome ways. She stood before his mind—the slim girl with the narrow hips and boy's bust! He remembered her little

airy graces and the peculiar *pechant* play of her thin arms.
He saw the gesturing movement of her slight shoulders,
and the child-dimples, and the wan, nervous little mouth,
and the innocent gayety and sadness of her blue-gray eyes.
He wished to protect her. In the darkness he felt the
vigorous animal at his side; the aggressive nose and the
blunt carnal lips of the man. Was this Mignon of Exmoor
to suffer by reason of this earthen one?

"The best way to enjoy a woman is to conquer her.
Passion has no proper reason for existing," the secretary's
dissertation broke coldly in. "Love is like the blinders of
a horse, it shuts out two-thirds of a woman from the poor
fool's sight. Besides, if you feel, you suffer; and the perfection of the whole thing is when she feels and you look
on."

The secretary recounted a few instances of his successes
with women. Nothing brings men together more quickly.
He caused Julian to finally admit his own invincible at-
tractiveness to females. Like men, the two experienced a
sense of rivalry and strove to overmatch the other's narra-
tive. Though the younger could not approach the older's
tale, yet he produced enough to excite a worldling's respect.

Youth and occasion were bringing one of those swift
intimacies, which are not friendships, and yet in which
men confess much.

They drifted on in their talk, remarking about this
thing and that, speaking of people the secretary had met
in Exmoor. They mentioned Keyes.

"What an old crank that celebrity of yours is, anyway!
I suppose to know him is about equal to having shaken paws
with Emerson. Won't I reap prestige in New York, now
I've been dined by the great—'critic,' isn't it? But after
all, I'd like to know his positive use, outside of any ornamentals."

" Why, literature," gasped Julian.

Mancutt, who never read and who had no idea of " The Function of Criticism," said bluntly: " He told me himself that he almost wished he had gone into active life and had a little money now in his old age to do as he pleased with. Why the deuce didn't he go into something and coin shekels anyway, instead of cultivating his hair ?"

" His wife is rich. He must have been talking to you, that is all—a way of his. He really thinks the sensible question would be, ' Why don't you business men shut up your ledgers and cultivate your minds, sense of beauty and that sort of thing ?' " answered Julian.

" He's a crank. Should think he'd cut his hair, whatever else he failed to do," muttered the secretary.

He had the American's aversion for peculiarity, or any individual differentiation from the uniform pattern of man, which democracy cuts out and measures every one by. Strange result!—the most individualistic civilization in history is as intolerant of originality as the Chinese. Public opinion, public decrees on manner and dress and speech, has grown a tyrant. Live within the limits and you are free, but what a restricted freedom, what a curtailed personality, allowed any one of us! " Crank"—it is the opprobrium the dominant average casts on all greatness that exceeds itself, as on all eccentricity that lies beneath it. New York, which makes a community a collection of unsympathetic units, resents all superiority, all departures from the respectable type. No wonder we lack great men.

Keyes, the long-haired eccentric, suggested his antithesis—smooth and average New York. The secretary said : " In New York friction rubs a man into civilized habits. There isn't enough elbow-room there to allow any growth of crankiness. You'd better come to New York, Mr. Clyde. You look as if you were built for it. Life is gloriously real there ; a day of it contains a month of Exmoor sensations. These literary fellows, who stand off and watch life, never get the true taste of it. Of course it takes nerve to go into the world, but the fight is beautiful. There are so many splendid men there, brainy fellows with big hearts, whose dress is irreproachable, and address to match. You people up here don't even know how to eat. You come down to New York, and I'll set you up a Delmonico dinner, such as you never saw in New England."

Julian listened to the panegyric of the secretary with a feeling that Exmoor was weighed and found wanting.

The two men had each a respect and a contempt for the other. Mancutt bowed to something called culture, which he felt was one of the many moonshines and, consequently, to be deferred to, but the naïveté of the young tutor amused him, and after all, the only thing the secretary really respected was " knowingness." Julian was impressed with his companion's world-knowledge ; but he had the contempt of a man of letters for the secretary's amazing fundamental ignorance. Knowledge of men and that adroit adaptability to new environment, which comes with a vast experience to one of native wit, goes far and veils much ; yet the secretary's very suppleness led him into exposures of his superficialness, of which he was altogether unaware. " One of the barbarians of New York," Keyes afterwards defined him to Julian.

Mancutt, indeed, had no more extended conception of society than a horse has of his stable. In society he fed and slept and fought and gained money and spent it. But why he was in it, or wherefore any established fact was so, and not otherwise, he had no more impulse to inquire than the mule, born in a mine, has of asking after the sun which he has never seen. Mancutt simply accepted things and made himself as comfortable as possible.

The morning after the reception Mr. Gay came down-stairs in a mood like his name. He felt well with himself; he was about to conquer this new world presented before him. He would swallow Exmoor at a gulp, institution, pro-fessors, the fame of the town and all, planking down the coin, placarding the whole with the dingy green of his bank-notes. He was strongly desirous of owning a college. Yes, they all let the drawbridge fall and heaved up the port-cullis before the battle-front of his stocks; even this last world of exclusive traditions, this Exmoor that boasted its literary and philosophic spirit and its standard of culture, succumbed at his nod. How the professors and unique-nesses had thronged to kiss the hand of this pious pillager, who rifled Wall Street and paid pastors' salaries by the score over all the country! At bottom of this masterly mechanism, concealed within the cogs and pistons of this embodied geometry of brokerage, smouldered a cold passion for mastery. Exmoor was a new land to be won, and her culture, that vaunted itself superior to mere commerce, was a new subject to be thrown or cajoled into subjection to that Napoleonic egoism, even as the stock-market, Knick-erbocker society, his obstreperous son-in-law, had in their turn been subdued.

Mr. Gay walked into the parlor. Julian was there read-ing. He replied to the millionaire's greeting by laying aside his book and looking ready for conversation. The two had not spoken together alone before.

"What are you to do with yourself, finally?" asked Mr. Gay. "Do you intend to follow your father's profession?"

"I don't know; I have not decided. And I'm tired of teaching."

Julian hardly knew how to respond to the rich man's query. He wished to please this powerful man, but he feared to venture.

"Would you like going to New York—a business life?"

asked Mr. Gay, standing over the young man and launching inquiries from his sinister eyes.

"I would go to-morrow if I could," cried Julian, impulsively. What if the great financier were to aid him!

"You are tired of doing nothing—here in Exmoor." Gay looked at the carpet reflectively. "Have you ever been in business?"

"No, sir."

"Humph!" ejaculated Gay, "you college geniuses are all alike. I suppose nothing less than a bank-presidency would compensate you for your tutorship in Exmoor College. Anything less would partake of the menial to one of you philosophers."

The jocularity evidently stung the young man. Gay watched him.

"Well, yes," said Julian, as if the admission were wrung from him. "It's the truth to a certain degree. But then, I suppose the average college fool gets it knocked out of him quick enough. I know absolutely nothing of business. I wish I had the chance, though."

The millionaire turned away. He never talked long. The young man pleased him. He admired his handsome face and liked his frank way. "He is thoroughbred, looks long-winded," reflected Gay. He desired to take this scion of transcendental Exmoor and "make a man of him." That it lay in his power to do so, somehow soothed Gay's pride, which the indefinable superiority of Exmoor culture had hurt.

After breakfast President Pompes's carriage drove up. The President, Dr. Ponder, and Professor Clyde took Gay over to the buildings. They flattered and flustered about him in the transparent serious manner of men unaccustomed to diplomatic usage. The gray heads inclined to him from a semicircle, they hung upon his words and applauded his shrewd practical suggestions. Gay liked their out-and-out obsequiousness, their up-and-down subserviency. He enjoyed the brutal vanity of humbling these betters of his. These professors gratified his love of evident triumph, of assertive power, even more than the world of exchange. He was a finger of that hand of Strength which in all history has lain heavily on Thought.

He got into so good a humor that he offered to manage some depreciated stock owned by the college. He promised to resurrect it into new value. The philosophers praised his disinterestedness and the next trustees' meeting consigned the stock in trust to him, relying on his blind promise. In the course of the summer Gay performed one of his most brilliant plays. He seized the railroad management by strategy, wrecked the road, bought in and bulled the shares. He sold out with profit. He emerged with three millions. Incidentally the college was benefited. Incidentally he trod some personages into the mud. As a corollary, the college built a new "Divinity" building, and poverty alighted on some few strangers' heads, so that an extra suicide occurred and there was one girl more on the streets.

In the afternoon Mr. Gay asked Julian to take him to call on Mrs. Ballard.

"If you don't object, I shall call on Mrs. Ballard and you on Miss Margaret," he said; "I shall only require you to amuse yourself, you see."

They walked down the hill. On the way, Gay entertained the youth with stories from his life. That was the one theme Gay was eloquent upon. If he did not talk business, the only continuous conversation he ever voluntarily indulged in was the history of himself. The man spent his leisure in gazing on his own portrait, as it were. He studied his own career with the enthusiasm of a boy following the campaigns of Napoleon. He related several incidents to Julian. Julian listened almost silently, overawed. The man inspired him with an immense respect. By the time they reached Mrs. Ballard's, Gay liked the young fellow even more than before.

Mrs. Ballard received them in the dim parlors and sat Gay down before her swaying body. As Julian went out to find Margaret he thought of an Indian snake-charmer, but " she'd got a whopper of a cobra this time."

They talked together as they had at Mrs. Keyes is, and the widow strengthened her impression on the New Yorker. She had such grasp on details that Gay, trained business-man that he was, found himself matched by this acute intelligence. The woman, by the multiplicity of her knowledge and the tremendous impact of her phrases, absolutely astonished him. She blew the kindling of his half-formed purpose into settled determination, she swept him along in the torrent of her persuasions.

" My dear madam, you should have been a man and you would have been my rival," he said, in conclusion.

Mrs. Ballard had never received praise so sweet to her. She wondered what was her purpose in arousing this stranger. She could not tell; she had no idea of the end, but had only followed a road whose signposts were incidents, each of which she desired to control; and she had conquered. They led to this—" Gay University." Well, she did not care, she had achieved a work few could have accomplished. She did not care; perhaps they might hang her picture in the Gay Memorial Chapel to be, along with the other worthies.

" Mrs. Ballard," he began, " I hope to be able to do something for your son some time. You have me so in your debt that I should feel it a favor to myself to do anything in my power for you or yours."

" I thank you sincerely; but John is too young now, and I even think him behind his age," said this truthful mother, who looked at facts like a man.

"Well, he'll grow, and then we will see to him," said Gay, in his conclusive manner. "But this young Clyde, Julian—what is he? Tell me about him."

Mrs. Ballard turned on him again in her intense way.

"You, Mr. Gay, you do something for Julian. I know him; he is cramped and bound in this pool of Exmoor. And he is a remarkable young man. This little community leaves him no space to breathe."

"I see; I thought myself he was restless. His mother was an Italian, I believe." After a pause,—"Well, does he want to go into business?"

Mrs. Ballard leaned forward. "I don't know if he has any concrete desire. This is what I know, he is a man of great powers and requires a proportionate place to exercise them. I don't think it would make much difference what it was—law, journalism, business or politics—something that is influential and absorbs him, that is all. Such latent capacity will corrode and corrupt him, if not drawn out on something worthy the man. Here, in Exmoor, he teaches, but that is a slight thing, and he is moody and angered. If some powerful hand would thrust him into the full combat, he would become a remarkable man." Again that appeal to Gay's pride of power, so alluring in that it came from her.

And Gay again accepted the vanity.

"I see what you mean," said Gay. "Business is the place for him. It is the only thing, nowadays. We business men run the country. Politics are side-show; and as for the statesmen, they are our servants. Then the cranks, geniuses and literary fellows—humph! they don't get much except the women."

"I have always felt it was so. The men of the age are the great business men, as in the Middle Age the fighters were. And a man wants to be of the greatest, at all odds. Julian has such powers, I know he has. I think you can understand it, how it is. You are a remarkable man, and surely you can imagine what it is to be immersed in a swamp of dilettanti and women-men, like he is in Exmoor. Oh ! he is filled with powers that demand an arena. All he needs is discipline and experience to become an honor to you—if you will take hold of him." She talked on until he became enthusiastic, in a cold way, to let down the obstructions before this youth and give him a clear field for honors.

When Gay arose, he said, " I go to-night, Mrs. Ballard. I shall broach my scheme by letter and shall consider you my agent. I shall tell them to come to you for particulars. And I will attend to young Clyde."

She had made sacrifices to the manes of her youth, to that old pain of hers. Margaret could get along; those meek creatures always did. It was the bird that dashed itself against the ruthless glass shutting her from the light, that suffered; not the one who slid before the storm-wind, whither it listed. No, Julian should not be tortured, if she could help it; and she pictured him as a tall proud man who respected himself, and to whom people were deferential. She thought she might have been such a man.

When she went into the dining-room, she found Margaret sitting in the gathering dusk. The girl was very still and her white hands were knotted together. The mother came behind her and stroked her hair; but the caresser thought, with a great pity in her heart for the girl, —" She would only try to regenerate him, and he could no more find understanding than did I."

There was early supper at the Clydes', in order to let Mr. Gay and his secretary catch the six-o'clock train for Boston.

It was after supper in the parlor that Mr. Gay bade good-by to a knot of professors. As an after-thought, he said casually, " By the way, gentlemen, I may as well tell you now, I intend to give a hundred thousand dollars towards that theological building."

" Princely munificence," bowed the President ; " Generous heart," echoed Doctor Ponder ; and Professor Clyde himself grasped the money-prince by the hand and stammered his acknowledgments. Julian saw them, saw the imperious figure erect amid the swaying scholars, the dark impassive face in the circle of nervous uncertain recluse-countenances. The man of the world—how his clothes, his bearing, his address, his confidence, his command, stood compact and admirable in contrast with the ill-fitting garments and the hesitating speech of the men whose apparent qualities were forever sacrificed to the intelligence and the spirit!

" Good-by, Mrs. Lancaster," said Mr. Gay. " We thank you for your hospitality and your gracious courtesies. I only hope we shall be able to repay you in kind in New York." He bowed deeply to the stately woman, whose blue blood and simple ladyhood impressed his plebeian breeding, Altogether his stay with the Clyde family had given him a higher opinion of them than of most people in this world he had found not over-genuine.

Julian and his father took the two New Yorkers to the train. The secretary sat on the front seat with Julian and plied the young man with city projects; how he would get into New York day after to-morrow, how he would go to his rooms and get rubbed down, do a little business during the day, go to the Hoffman House for dinner and to the theatre in the evening. For Julian the to-morrows seemed stuffed with *ennuis*, robed in the chill gray atmosphere of the winter twilight. Impulsively, he wanted that objective life of incident and color the New Yorker talked of. The pleasure-loving South revolted against the subjective existence in which he had buried his youth.

On the back seat Mr. Gay in low tones opened on Professor Clyde concerning Julian. He offered the young man a place in his office and promised to see him to success. He said he had a sudden admiration for Julian, and having no son of his own he intended to do much for the young fellow. Mr. Gay treated the matter as if it were already determined.

The train was already in, and Julian jumped for the checks.

"'Ta, ta, my handsome friend; I shall expect to see you in New York yet," said Mancutt.

"You are to enter business with me. Speak to your father," announced Gay, as he ascended the platform of the car.

The train shot out. The dreary evening beleaguered the heavens with gray intrenchments of cold cloud, the rutted mud of the roads looked hard and brown, Chesterfield stamped his chilly legs before the rickety family carriage. Ah, how flat and forlorn it all was! Julian looked at the travelling plume of smoke and wished he were rushing away from under this barren sky towards the city lights and gayety and lively throngs. He rode with his father along the uneventful streets back into his death-in-life existence of thought. But, through all the dreariness, like a bridge of bronze through a swamp Mr. Gay's last words built straight "the path of gold for him."

On the train Gay said to his secretary, "How did the plain living and high thinking strike you?"

"As high starvation and plain cranks," laughed Mancutt.

CHAPTER IX.

THE GRAVITATION OF THE GREATER BODY.

"I AM going to New York," said Julian in a tone anticipatory of opposition.

The young man stood with his back against the corner of the mantelpiece in the study of Mr. Keyes. The mild petroleum light fell over him, his Titian head and the long English frame. He looked the critic straight in the eyes.

"How long?" responded Mr. Keyes, from the depths of his leather chair. He evidently thought of a visit.

"For good." Keyes started. "Mr. Gay has offered me a place in his office. It is advantageous, and he told father he would see to my success."

Keyes was bolt upright, and his luminous eyes were fierce.

"What do you mean! Business, going into business! What, a broker of you?"

Julian smiled superiorly. "Not such a great matter. Simply that I mean to wrestle a fall with the world. A real fight, that is all."

"Do you mean it?" asked the critic in a low voice.

"Exactly," Julian answered, and his tone rasped, like the aspirate of the word.

"So you too have caught the infection; you feel the 'Zeitgeist,' as they clang it! You with the rest!" He said it mournfully. "Ah, you are of your generation, as I of mine, as every man is in compelled allegiance to his own. And the lodestone draws, does it?" Suddenly his meditation rang into exasperation. "Reality! the real world, the true facts, the serious struggle,—that is the nomenclature of the absurd cant, isn't it? Oh, yes, I've heard it before; you and your crowd of ambitious idiots sing it well. Dare to carry your ideals into the world and test them in the fires of reality, which, interpreted, means, scour your souls in the filth of the average conceptions, and see if then they hold color." He paused, a moment of indignation. " Will you young aspiring fools never understand that the great things are within you, not without. Environment, that's the word, the new standard coin, the word of your generation. It has ousted soul with you. Will you never understand that it is faith, and not knowledge, trust and aspiration, and never analysis and all the sensations the most fortunate circumstances can impose upon you—never those, that make greatness? Always the inner, the unseen, the unseen—" His voice died into a whisper.

After a short space Julian broke in with, "Well, which is worse, to be a money-gainer or a pedant? I don't think the 'average sensual man,' as you are so fond of phrasing it, any more utterly insufficient than the Exmoor edition of Doctor Dryasdust." Julian spoke hotly.

"You evade, you evade," smiled Keyes up in the young fellow's face. "You are neither, neither pedant nor shekel-changer. Do you want flattery? You are a thinker, and a thinker you will always be, whether in the monastery here in Exmoor, or in the market-place with Mr. Gay. And to you, to the thinker,"—the critic shook his lean forefinger in his earnestness,—"to the thinker, I say, seclude yourself, get into some secure eddy, stay in your hole, stay in your hole, and if this commercial age don't rout you out as the mediæval brutes smoked out Bruno and the men of Oxford, thank a fortunate fate. That's all that's left to us. Burly utilitarians and smug comfort-seekers shoulder the man of pure ideas with little enough respect. You should be grateful there yet exist in Amer-

ica a Concord and an Exmoor, where such people as you
and I and your father can burrow. Another generation
will sweep them out."

"All you say may be true ; indeed, perhaps I believe it
true.   Railroad brains, acquisitive instinct, executive intellect ; they command the times, I know. And ideas are
not salable." The young voice had a wistful note in it.
"But I am young and the heart's pulse overleaps the regu-
lations of the head. I still believe with my heart in the
world and its beneficence, that it holds for me place and
happiness. I obey gravitation and go."

" To return,"—caught up the critic,—" to return beaten,
with tail between legs. I foresee it, I foresee it! But it is
not a happy experience.   Let us preserve our upright
posture. Do you not believe with the Frenchman that no
experience and no success can compensate for a single
moment's loss of dignity ?"

" But I shall not return," retorted Julian.   Keyes
looked at the young man, his pride of beauty and manhood
and intellect. The critic shuddered, and then anger succeeded. He rose from his chair and strode the room, the
long robe trailing to his feet, his hands catching his beard,
in his eyes lightning.

" What do you expect of New York ?   You are no mere
money-getter. What do you want out of that Babylon of
commerce, that city of millionaires and groceries, that
dumping-ground of sixty railroads ?   Babylon ! it is the
old Euphrates city resurrected and transplanted, a capital
without letters, without art, without science, that has
cliques instead of society, and electioneering instead of
politics. You will find species of only one type there, the
money-maker ; and only two species at that, he who has
and he who hasn't.   A metropolis of clerks and ignorant
millionaires, of the average civilized and democracy's barbarians, Gays and Mancutts ; they're typical and there's

little else. It is neither old Rome, nor London, nor Paris, nor Vienna, nor even St. Petersburg. It is New Babylon—simply a hive." He stopped an instant and turned to Julian with a kindly bitterness. "And was it Edmund Burke you meant to play down there, or de Balzac, or even Dan Webster? Ah, my dear boy, Nebuchadnezzar is the only possible rôle—all they could comprehend. And you don't emulate financier Gay?"

He looked at Julian with a quizzical gaze, half expressive of scorn and half of pity. "Don't you understand that careers are out of date, since we sunk all our great questions in the Civil War? Don't you see that our system of federal government enmeshes every great personality, and seldom, except when a storm comes, allows a man full scope in the use of his powers? Our later leaders are not of the old stamp. New gods are sovereign. As for political speculation, and abstract ideas of government, and constitutional history, they don't concern this generation. Do you suppose a speaker could talk Cicero to a crowd of bald-headed sensation-seekers and superficial clerks? I'd rather have an audience of English laborers; they're serious and sincere and wish to learn. But you're no circus-manager, you couldn't amuse. Burke, humph! our wire-pullers and practical politicians would sneer at him as a hifalutin crank, who would lose every election and leave the legislature's pockets empty. Even Jefferson would be impossible now. Don't waste sky-rockets on moles." He glanced at Julian, whose set face had not changed, and then went on:

"And for literature, if you indulge any dreams of writing in New York, you are more foolish than I thought. They make a great fuss about what is to come in the future. It's stuff, pure stuff. A world of hucksters and bargainers, with women to match; you'd exhaust the types in two books. And then they don't want to learn; understanding's not their faith, though it may be their fad. Do you suppose a populace, which lives on its newspapers, wants an interpreter? Oh, there are no passions down there, except the money passions. It was different when I was your age, but now the tide has overcome us and we had better not rebel. A war might regenerate us. I sometimes wish we had an army-like Germany, or something, whatever it might be, to balance the tremendous preponderance of trade. Literature! you might as well try to write for ancient Carthage or Tyre." When the critic was fairly started on a theme, his ideas were poured forth in floods.

"Or do I mistake? is it that you indulge the notion you were born an able man? Have you imbibed that heresy from Mrs. Medeia Ballard? That is likely, I suppose. Well, you are mistaken; you are not able. You haven't a quality your generation puts into its ideal. Let me tell you, New York will discourage and break your spirit first, and then will make a drudge of you."

"I have no such hopes, no great ones," said Julian sharply. "I go to New York to find a solution of life that's not here for me. I want contentment in the place of the unrest Exmoor has for me. I don't ask much from the world, except peace. And what can they take from me?— not my ideals, surely."

The cynical lips of the critic curled. He broke out: "Boy, boy, what do you say? You do not know. You have never been battered against the wall of public opinion; you have never cooled enthusiasms beneath the dish-water of average common-sense, such as they throw out of window on high-necked idealists. Go down into the dominant commonplace crowd with your platonic conceptions and your Goethe philosophy, and see how you fare. You have never taken your soul in your hand, your quivering Ariel soul, and plunged it into the chill air of the world which beckons to you now seductively like the bare arms of a girl. This hollow of the infinite in which you dwell, this garment of God which nature seems to you, is to those who rule this time merely so much mud and liquid to make mud-pies with, though they call them manufactures. That dry air of mediocrity has rotted noble spirits before yours."

" But Exmoor! is Exmoor better?" Julian cut in.

" Exmoor!" exclaimed Keyes, and he swept out his arms as in an apostrophe,—" poor Puritan Yankee town, tucked away in the hills! In the deluge since the war, you have preserved, in scant measure it is true, but you have preserved the old New England spirit. One can have ideas here and no one sneers. One can be true and no pretence. One can bury himself in the beautiful and gather about himself thought. Julian, the crude, sweating world is not fashioned for you. It has an abundance of able men, strong, blind fellows, to do its work and its sacrifice valiantly. America has need of you in another manner, and desperate need at that. Even more than Europe, America needs her Brahmins, her idealists, her spiritualists, to keep alive the vestal fire of mind and soul, to carry over to the future the conceptions of the intellect, the idea of the soul, as distinct from institution and the millions. In the wild night of Cæsarism, of democratic imperium, of the barbarism of mediocrity, coming on, the few should hide in the catacombs the Promethean fire that a happier age may light its torches by."

Was not this an old man's anathema? Keyes had known Carlyle and he corresponded with Arnold.

" But is it not best to go with one's age?" asked Julian, sceptically.

" If you desire comfort, if you prize the puddings and sauce, yes; if freedom, no. That multitude, whose mass attracts you, what is it but an aggregate of individuals? It has no quantitative claim to your reverence, no more than its units may demand. The man individually, you would not budge for his opinion, you would not take his wisdom, you would hold him lower than yourself. What is this, then? You bunch a million of such together, and though they roar only what the one insignificance squeaked, you shape your life to the vociferous halloo; you submit your higher intuition to their arbitration and you value their applause." He paused.

"To be free, that is the birthright you squander for a mess of pottage. You can stand away from the world, its gusts of passion, its prejudices, its microscopic detailed sight. You need take no other system upon yourself, box yourself to no popularity, concentrate your intellect on no mean utilitarian temporal need. You can be free; it is permitted you to fathom the deeps, the causes and the hollow chasms of existence. You can stretch your soul to an infinite expansion, in which this earth-life is but a phase. You can take in all the breezes of creation. And yet you falter in the shadow of paltry gilded images, you desire to grasp the illusive flickering beams of worldly prosperity! If power were eternal, and fortune sure as death, I say it were nobler to stand out from under them and their tyranny, naked and free."

Julian was dumb before this flood of passionate hate and exhortation. Was this the sceptical intellectualist, the self-indulgent Epicurean, who passed by the sorrows of other men, whose only humanism was a strain of sentimentalism that peeped forth occasionally from his sarcasms and poetic conceits? Even to Julian, a familiar and pupil in a certain sense, this height of passion was inexplicable. The contorted lines of the old man's face, his flaming eyes and the deep ridges breaking round the cynical curved mouth, filled him with amazement, as if he had just discovered quivering fire leaping from ice. Keyes went on. He had lost his fierceness. He spoke with that intensity which is the conviction of despair.

"Boy, there are gifts in you too high to be appreciated in that ordinary world of average love, of every-day comfort, of mediocrity and uniformity, to which you turn. Wrap yourself in the pleasures of the flesh, riches and houses and men's good opinion, the envy of the unfortunate and approbation of the respectable, nay, even in woman's love and home and children—they will not balm your discontent; such pitiful rain can never gladden the naked summits of your intellectual soul. Power you will learn to be a lesser thing than understanding; love, a meaner thing than renunciation."

There was something fantastic in the critic's gestures, in his theatrical attitudes and the stage expression of his face, which would have amused the humorous man of the time. But the sardonic bitterness struck home to Julian, to whom this tragic habit was no novelty, and so forgotten before the impassioned protest. Yet, did he feel the full import of the critic's words? Probably not. The American is unprepared to behold himself a five-act tragedy with choruses. His own existence is so large a part purely droll, as presented to himself, that though he may discern the sorrow of another, he never altogether pities himself, or perceives the complete pathos of his own career. The trait makes for manliness and yet it brings its defects. It prevents us from descending to whining weakness, and it hinders us from attaining that distinction of personality which is founded on reverence for one's highest self. So with Julian. The tremendous seriousness of Keyes and his vociferous emphasis struck Julian as overdone in his own case. So much contained in his own carcass—to feel himself packed with such infinite alternatives, staggered his credulity. If it had been another man, Julian could have appreciated the critic's seriousness.

He was at a loss how to reply. He did not feel like

gulping down Keyes's speech as wholly applicable to himself. He muttered in reply :

" Well—but—you see, Mr. Keyes, that's laying it on a little thick. I—pardon me; you know I am no great-guns, like that. This is all : I want to do something, strike one or two strokes in the world's business and prove to myself that I am half-way a man—a thing I am in doubt of now."

" This damnable humility !" cried Keyes. " Your best impulses lead you into it. We are such young puppies and the world is wise and in the majority! We are docile too, quite removed from self-sufficient conceit, and the world contains much above us that we can rise by! We will go to the world and learn of her, like children flocking to the knees of their mother! The law of irony—that this beautiful faith, born out of tolerance and ability to learn adequately men's lesson, should beckon you to destruction! You believe the meanest person has points for you; you believe the world is your superior; you reverence other people more than yourself. That is the whole sin of America, which makes us smart and mountebanks, and deprives us of dignity and greatness. No doubt, now, to follow out another instance of the laws of irony, your father, who dwells with the universalities, prefers the world for you."

" He does. He told me to-day he was glad I was going, and he hoped I would show them we were not all dreamers yet, that the old hard stock produced fighters still."

" Quite so," sputtered the critic. " The angel tempts to sin, and the ass speaketh words of wisdom. You will find more good grown of evil and evil of good than the legitimate birth. Some ethical jackdaw, who plumes his feathers on the influence of his own good deeds that cannot but make for righteousness—if one could only open his ecstatic eyes, what visions of sin on the bushes of morality he would see ! Humph !"

Julian found it thus. Mr. Keyes and Mrs. Lancaster alone dissuaded him, while Mrs. Ballard and Margaret and his father urged him to go.

Professor Clyde seemed determined. New York was the grand theatre. Julian must go. "It is an opportunity of a lifetime. It offers you the chance to become one of the men whom your generation will respect, and that is much," said Hiram Clyde.

This New England recluse, this modern monk, this Puritan St. Augustine, this Exmoor Hegel, from whom life and its fires were so distant, but whose plummet had sounded the abysses of human philosophy—this man of thought, this irresolute and eternally suppressed nature, yet, in accordance with what Keyes had called the law of irony, yielded in his inmost soul to an admiration for action. He looked on the men of the world and he looked on Mr. Gay; for all that he classified him as a magnificent sense—as some poor poet, all fire and consumed flesh, looks on the mighty limbs and clean muscles and clear skin of some Olympian wrestler.

" I'm so glad you have the chance, Julian. Isn't it magnificent? You will make a success," were Margaret's words; and her thought was, " If only he will abandon his false notions and settle down to practical duty."

What we express is superficial. Beneath our passions, our consciousness, our appeals to human kind, our love of one another, lies the unconscious, ever-present self, which fulfils its destiny, whichever way our wills may waver, whether to accomplishment or negation. Deep beneath the wrappings of sense, beneath the categories of the understanding, beneath all those vibrations created in us by contacts with that exterior force we call the world, lies an inner core, never touched of time or space, silent and potent as the Sphinx, our real self, our true essence, not to be expressed to men. That it *is* which guides us; that it is which plunges us to our fate, even through and against the protest of our superficial nature, the reason and the will.

So, perhaps, Julian understood the whole matter before he left Exmoor, as years afterwards, when the determination of his life lay within the past. He was no blind enthusiast, no weakly sentimentalist, such as nowadays float art in the drawing-rooms. He had the sane brain to draw the measure of things pretty accurately. He knew what to expect. But the underneath held to a tendency and dictated his course. Whatever might be the billows of struggle and effort, the Gulf Stream of inner self, his unconscious self, bore on beneath and washed what shores it would, despite storms in opposition that smote the surface-waters.

I do not call this instinctive and compelling force which seized his shoulders and spun him round with his face to the world, Choice. He had no choice. Inheritance, the atmosphere of his time, the magnetism of numbers and swarms and great piles of buildings, which we call cities, made up his Fate, and he was swept to his destiny naturally, inevitably, eternally. He could no more contradict the determining impulse of his generation than a satellite of the solar system can contradict the law of gravitation. That impulse was the law of his being, the manner of his acting, and by it and of it he existed.

The gravitation of the greater body swung him into line with his age.

PART II.

NEW YORK.

CHAPTER I.

THE PALACE OF A MILLIONAIRE.

THE aristocracies of the old-world capitals seek the secluded quarters. They wall in their luxury and create an artificial solitude. Their palaces open on gardens and are screened with trees. The St. Germain of Paris fronts on narrow streets and presents to the plebeian world but monotonous ranges of blank stone. London secretes her exclusive, sheltering them in quiet squares and sequestered places, where, encircled by the rumble of the world's centre, they live withdrawn. Those old nobilities rest in the years and tradition, and they need not flaunt their ostentation in the eyes of a sceptical democracy.

But the plutocrats of the New Babylon thrust themselves upon the notice. They plant their piles on the great streets, and their housetops proclaim their rank. What other distinction, indeed, have they? Coin is the corner-stone of their supremacy, and the sole heraldry of selection belonging to the magnified Shylock or Cyclopean butcher, is his station on the central avenue, with arms akimbo, elbowing his brother-moneybags, challenging notoriety.

The rich men of New York build their palaces on land

no moderate wealth could hold; and ability to set their home walls against the pressure of commerce and maintain their bath-rooms upon golden yards of real estate is the seal of the coronet to this American nobility. To seat one's self in the midst of traffic, like a boulder in a torrent—that is the social test.

Indeed, in democratic America, in a mushroom society of a century's creation, what else shall constitute the optimate ? How can an optimate recognize a fellow-optimate out of that crush of mediocrity and barter ? Weighty questions, seeking, these some years, an adequate answer. Unfortunately, the optimate is not branded like a sentenced criminal; neither is he necessarily distinguished by any outward refinement, superiority of manners or grace of carriage. Plutocrats range in every size and mask in all shapes, of every complexion, of variety of noses ; they are Germans and Jews, Knickerbockers and inelegant Yankees; illiterate and learned; men who by some means, by any means, by worth, by toil, by villany, by stealth, have thrust their heads above the seething pool of every-day endeavor and sordid commonness. Such a heterogeneity requires an invented insignia, the old distinctions are misfits ; for this new order has no book of peers, from which to ascertain themselves, nor any fraternity of mind or belief to rally them together. Aristocracy, in the old sense, is obsolete. A new means of recognition has arisen ; locality stamps the rank, and the possessors of passive metal hasten to put their bullion under the mint-impress of a Fifth Avenue residence.

Those rich enough to crowd the great street are the optimates of this New Babylon. None other. And that is how the magnate of oil knows the magnate of sugar. Hence the potency of locality. "Place" has a new significance here.

There is a house on that imperial street of the New

World, ponderous even for Fifth Avenue, which stands out
an embodiment of wealth even on that street, paraded as it
is from end to end with miles of palaces and panelled with
naught that does not cost. The house sits on a corner and
rears its brown walls out of a stone moat. There is not a
blade of grass nor a streak of earth between its base and
the pavement of the street. It seems not to be built, not
put-together stones, but hewn out, as it were, of some
huge, immovable rock, whose foundations are the granite
of the avenue; indeed, so blended with the hard pavements seem its walls that one might suppose the street a
lava river cooled into flagging and granite and house-blocks.
The moat is dug like a trench in solid stone, and a stone
balustrade separates this ditch from the sidewalk flagging.
Out of that sink rises the house, immense, square, bilious-
colored, a sombre cube and grim, squatted heavily on the
avenue, like a grotesque dream, casting its gloom over the
vicinity, ominous, significant, implacable.

The main entrance is in the centre under an arch of great
stones that seem to brood over the doorway, a hanging
portcullis, a crushing lip about to be let down. The windows are high up, sunk in the masonry to a Gothic depth, the
glass in them half an inch thick. The stones of the walls
are all huge and even enormous. There are four stories
above the basement, and the castellated roof breaks into
abrupt edges. Above the whole sit eight short, thick chimneys. There is an eternity in the house's face, Roman and
imperial.

This mansion, so massive, so hideous, incarnates that
modern wealth which has superseded power. It is solid,
irresistible, impartially cruel as the laws of business, as
the imperative spirit of success. Eyeless, earless, unfeeling, this enormity outtops thought and sentiment, which
seem vapid under its weight. It is the monstrous idol
of America. Its opaque shades jaundice the clear face of

pure aspiration, the innocent content of simple love. There is nothing like it in history save Cæsarean Rome. It is sovereign.   To it our young men's faces are set, and round it our old men pray.   To women it is more than beauty ; to men it surpasses mind.   It is the Mecca of democracy.   It tinctures all souls, even the meekest.   It has embraced in its tentacles the common, the strong, the brave, the weak, the pure, the ignorant, the gifted, the great.   It has sucked out the nation's chances of an original Art, it has drained literature of genius, it has made politics a huckster's trade and shod the statesman with corruption.   It has even gilded religion and bought over Nature.   Our young girls aspire to be money-queens and relegate Motherhood to the superstitions.   Our young men forget peace, fame, knowledge, to wallow in the gutters of gain.   " A road for the talents ! "   hence a chance for the meanest in democracy's grand lottery.   They crowd to the drawing-booths, inflamed ; for some may draw the Presidency, but none shall draw worth.   That is not to be diced for.

This is the finale, then, the result of a century of politics and wisdom and toil—to establish a form of human society wherein each may buy a ticket in the Lottery of Possible Wealth.

Mr. Gay, who built that house, expressed his mastery in it.   The world he had fought with and thrown and gagged —the house was an Ætna monument enthroned on the prostrate Titan.   Mr. Gay loved its rugged masterfulness, its haughty supremacy, the grim way it looked upon the conquered world.

It was a crystalline day, such as November's repertoire contains.   Sunlight, the clear chilly autumn brilliance, flashed from a blue sky, down upon the Avenue.   Looking from the crest of Murray Hill towards Madison Square, a thousand diamond points struck out and flamed and flamed again. Carriages rolled solidly over the pavement; from silken cushions opulent idle women surveyed the humanity of the streets. The world of the Millionaires choked the groove of the Avenue with luxury and laziness and disdain.

The secretary and Julian lounged along in fashionable get-up. The secretary had introduced Julian to a Gotham tailor, who had done justice to the possibilities of the young man's lithe symmetry. The Roman-featured companion of Mr. Gay's secretary, with his southern tints and red-gold hair, excited the admiration of more than one group of romantic chits of sauntering girls, and drew the attention even of several carriages. The blood of some sixteenth-century Venetian noble, strangely mixed in his shop-girl mother, had reasserted its primal virtue, and the young man walked in the stately stride of those magnificent animals Veronese loved to plaster upon Ducal Palace walls.

"You attract attention," said the secretary. "I knew it, I prophesied it. Nothing like complexion and shape, wrapped into a New York suit. There! see that woman with the red plumage driving there ahead now, she looked you over. She's Mrs. Van Vooster; old family and shekels. Ah, my beauty! I tell you, stick to me and we'll cut diamonds."

"I'll stick, closer than a brother. A man needs a guide, philosopher, and friend in this menagerie," replied Julian, glibly.

"I'll tell you what we'll do to-night: we'll go to the Belshazzar, first night. I can get the tickets. All the fashionable women will be there. What do you say?" His tone had a touch of reverence on the words 'fashionable women,' as if they were to him something paradisaical.

The jovial secretary enjoyed piloting amid the shoals of the metropolis this young fellow, his inferior in worldly wisdom, his superior in birth and education, in all the gentlemanly points. Mr. Mancutt liked to associate with gentlemen. Then, too, Mr. Mancutt was of the unclassified; society had not yet accepted him unconditionally, though conscious of the fact that John Gay's confidential man was stuffed with possible futures. But he had no parallel sympathies with the "swells," by whom he was regarded as an industrious ant ; and those business men with whom he fought down town had neither his thirty-two years nor his keenness after life. Thus Julian was a windfall. The secretary was the young man's constant companion, his instructor in ways metropolitan. In return the rising secretary profited by Julian's entrée, and he used the handsome scion of New England Brahminism as a propeller to steer his own tramp-schooner into the wharves of fashion.

"There's Gay's house all open and newly swept and garnished," the secretary said, as they approached the brown bulk.

The hollands were gone from the windows and the huge pile seemed awake, like some monstrous animal with fifty eyes.

"The family got back from Europe two days ago," the secretary continued. "I went down to see them through the custom house. Miss Vivian, the unmarried one, wanted to know about her father's new find, as she called you, young man. I told her what a handsome cuss you were, and she is quite anxious to see you."

"Thanks," replied Julian, drily, "but you are a little too soon. Mr. Gay has not invited me to his house."

"And never will," laughed the secretary. "Damn it, young man, don't you know the American girl is a majority of the directors every time? If Vivian wants to see you, you will be forthcoming, right along ; Gay never notices." He had that familiarity with the family dispositions a lifelong servant displays. Indeed, he was attaché to the ladies, as well as kitchen-cabinet to the operator.

"O Lord, what divine luck ! There's Vivian now, coming down the steps. We'll pass her just as she gets into the carriage. When she has once seen you, she'll need no more persuasions. So come along and look handsome." Mr. Mancutt increased his pace.

Before the great circle of the entrance, backed by the dimness of its deep recess, upon the stone platform of the steps, she stood, one hand on the balustrade and one holding her saffron parasol—an instant's picture. Pedestalled on the stairs of a millionaire, staged by a palace, she looked the statue of a great Parisian doll; and when she moved her little feet daintily down the steps, her miniature proportions were revealed and lent semblance to the conceit her profusion of dress had suggested. Another, a larger woman, would have glared in her attire. Overloaded, furbelowed, beribboned, belaced, bejewelled, the tiny creature was not barbarous, but exquisite. Her innate artificialness chimed with her costume. The golden shade of her dress dazzled like a gleam of the footlights, her gilt boots stained the pavement with a burnished shadow.

Just as she reached the sidewalk, she caught sight of the secretary and his friend. She bowed to the sceretary—almost imperceptibly, more with her eyebrows than her head. A queen's head should not be a pendulum. But she shot a repeated glance at his friend over her shoulder, on her way across the sidewalk to her carriage. Those violet eyes, so large that they seemed to exclude the face, those scarlet lips that curved with alluring interrogations, that bloom of the rose-leaf's first powder on the delicate blonde cheeks; all that face that tapered to the chin, looked out from the gold-brown hair and the wide-drooping hat and seemed to say seductively to him, "How beautiful we two are!"

Julian had the nerves of genius; the slight variations of weather awakened new moods. This exquisite porcelain girl, this cunning manufacture, this charming blending of sensuous flesh and Parisian drapery, touched one man in him, as the severe spiritual beauty of Margaret Ballard's regular features had appealed to the Puritan and the aspirer, buried below his senses. His was that ductile temperament, that sweet nature, the god's gifts to poetic beings, which under Parnassus would have ripened and bloomed, which in America consumes its heart. Environment, is it not everything—that which fates a soul an artist or a drudge? Miss Gay placed a foot on the carriage-step, while the gilt heel of the other flung back the drapery of her skirt and for a moment exposed a golden ankle.

"She's a beauty, a thoroughbred!" cried Mr. Mancutt, enthusiastically, as the two watched her carriage roll onwards with the tide towards the Park. "You saw that ankle? Well, did you notice the curve of the hip, when she stepped into the carriage, as her dress drew close across? She's lovely," he added softly. Worship of women, even if nothing higher than that based on physical veneration, abides with the most material Americans.

"What do you think of her?" demanded the secretary, challenging his admiration.

"Miss Vivian is very vivid, certainly," said Julian demurely.

The other laughed, and added, "Seeing that I can't marry her myself, I expect you to, and—see that you remember me when you've got your hands in her father's pockets."

Julian had a shrewd idea that Mr. Mancutt engineered too much. He was no cat's-paw. The secretary underestimated, perhaps, the young New Englander's perceptions; for Julian's lack of commercial smartness and of that cheap humor which does duty for cynical insight implied to this New York floater a certain want of discernment. However, the secretary's good-nature was so contagious and his "putting on to the ropes" led to such good times that the

younger man was more than willing to reimburse his monitor for his pains by extending him a social towline. Yet
Julian's independence resented Mr. Mancutt's last suggestion, and he showed it.

"Come, don't sulk, my handsome friend," expostulated
the secretary. "I meant what I said, and I intend seriously
to help you to it. I am quite an ally there, let me tell you;
and I've had lots of fine fellows, bloods, request the 'courtesy' of my assistance. So wake up, go in and win, and
thank God that in these hard days there are heiresses to be
bridled."

Was the secretary serious? Mr. Mancutt had very clear
notions of things.

The afternoon of the next Sunday Julian lounged into
Mr. Mancutt's rooms by appointment.

Mr. Mancutt stood before a mirror, buttoning his collar.
"Hello, my crusher! Sit down; I've a great thing for you.
Darn the button—you're a regular two horse-team, a whole
English tandem, footman, dog underneath, and all."

"What's up?" cried Julian in amazement.

"A note from the vivid Vivian, and invites me and you
—you, as a collateral merely—to Sunday lunch."

"Sunday lunch! What's that? To-day?" ejaculated
Julian in bursts, the thrill of an exciting novelty coursing
his spine.

"Oh, it's informal; no classic distinction. They have
dinner there on Sundays at two and lunch at six; very light,
sit round and servants prance up to you. Awful cosey,
though."

Mancutt finished arraying his cravat and went across the
room for his coat, which hung over the back of a chair.

"Well, tell me about it. Whom shall we see? Mr. Gay?"
queried Julian.

"Just brush your collar a little and resume your overcoat. She wants us to come promptly, and it's a fifteen-

minutes walk up the Avenue. I'll tell you the family anuals as we trot."

The New York weather was on deck. The gray and vaporous clouds let down mists, as huge steamers lower boats from their steep sides. They trailed along the low sky, looking as if some celestial washerwoman might wring bucketfuls from their surcharged sheets. All was gray. The vista of the Avenue was spotted with gleams on watery surfaces, where the lights enlarged their circles with the growing night. The great houses masked their fronts in sable, and the cathedral, as they passed, loomed weirdly up through the thickening night, incongruous in this new-world line of power and palaces—the ghost of the Middle Age haunting the Babylon of nineteenth-century democracy.

The two men stepped briskly. With his vital temperament the secretary enjoyed the disagreeablenesses of the weather; for there would be a grateful contrast once inside the warmth and cuddled up to the luxury of the Gay sitting-room.

Julian moved as in a daze. This immensity of the world of money, which he had read of and had dimly conjectured about in Exmoor—how was it that its miracles impended over him? He felt numb. This young fellow who had declaimed Carlyle and believed with Plato, who had always associated aristocracy with letters and intellect, quailed before the stupendous imminence of the money-power, of this gigantic materialism, through whose main artery he was now walking to the palace of one of the richest men on the planet. He was abashed. A shame of himself, of his birthplace, of his father's celebrity, even, choked his manly independence. What were culture, education, literature, ideals, before this buttressed massiveness of wealth?—mere mists of the mind, hallucinations of needy vanity; windy fabrics with which the naked clothed themselves, swathed

their pennilessness in; a moonshine-robe in which the impecunious proud might strut and fool themselves, nursing
a phantom superiority.

When the two came beneath the Gay mansion, Julian had
the sensations an Athenian must have experienced, circled
by the colossal arches of Vespasian's imperial circus. Force
crushed out soul; and what the legions of Rome were to
Hellenic civilization, that, was this stone house to him. As
they passed within the entrance, Julian involuntarily measured with his eye the enormous blocks of the arch; their
silent solidity mocked his fitful ideals and the intermission
of his moods.

An imported English flunkey swept back the door with a
snap. The sharp secretary watched the servant's reception
of Julian. The Englishman, with the air of assisting a lord,
removed the young man's coat. The secretary was satisfied;
if Julian passed muster with Mr. Gay's door-keeper, Mr.
Gay's daughter would not criticise his air.

A spacious hall, half filled with a grand staircase, pierced
deep into the body of the house. Its size, its sumptuous
appointment, the wide sweep of the great stairs, ornamented
with figures of bronze, dazzled Julian. They were shown
into the sitting-room, a square little space, fringed with
divans, and crowded with cushioned furniture, suffocated,
as it were, with comfort. It was next the Avenue, and the
shrill tenor of the uptown streets, so unlike the heavy sustained rumble that fills the lower city, rattled feebly through
the walls. Julian's latent luxury, his Italian voluptuousness, repressed so long in Puritan Exmoor, burst out in the
presence of this profusion. The situation excited him, the
colors stirred his art-sense; the fragrance that wandered in
and out the curtains, the black lustre of the silver-bound
Spanish cabinet,—all acted upon him and made him a
beautiful creature; his nostrils fanned like a panther's, and
his eyes grew liquid flame. He sat just in front of a portière

of deep red, an admirable background. Even Mancutt
became alive to the sudden glory of this young manhood,
thus opportunely magnified, as Athena on occasion oblig-
ingly improved Ulysses.

A peal of soprano laughter, tinkling down corridors, and
preceded by a curly dog, Miss Vivian Gay floated between
the hangings and stopped just clear of the curtains. Mancutt was on the watch.

In all young love there is much that is physical, and
even the most exalted passions have a secret physical
affinity, the suggestion of which is spurned, but whose
potency is fact. Vivian carried with her a physical con-
tagion which caught our country scholar just when his
senses were most tuned to receive impressions. And then,
she was his physical complement—blonde to his olive, petite
to his height, plump to his slender, artificially lovely, like
a wax flower, to the magnificence of his natural strength.

She came forward at Mancutt's introduction in her pretty
gracious way, inviting admiration and appealing to you, as
it were, if she were not a ravishing bit. She held out her
small jewelled hand with exquisite coquetry which flattered
and allured. The siren lifted her rose-leaf lids timidly,
and let the violet eyes swim over his face in one glance,
frankly, like a child; the young man felt their hue suffuse
him, as a purple mist might do. She was such a miniature
of a woman, every piece of her perfect, but turned out on
a reduced scale.

"I am so glad to know you, Mr. Clyde. Papa has told
me all about you, you know. He enjoyed his visit to your
house so much, and he says Exmoor is such a very lovely
town."

She told them to sit down, saying her sister, Mrs. Saxton, was not quite ready to appear. She seated herself in
a very big chair, whose sitting surface was very deep. She
did not talk much. The secretary rattled out common-

places and his society funniness, in that way relieving the tenseness in the situation of a beautiful small witch-girl, first meeting a decidedly interesting young fellow.

Vivian lolled on her seat, her little feet just touching the floor with their outstretched toes. She had a feline grace of movement, and curled herself into comfort, like an old cat before the fire. Each garment seemed so minutely exquisite. The sleeves looked chubby and infantile, and the bracelets round the plump wrists were of so reduced a circumference. The whole impression was that Worth had made an outfit for a big doll, only the doll was alive. To Julian with his Italian feelers thrown out like the sensitive hair-spirals of a plant, to feel and to writhe at any incongruity, any break in beauty, this artificial perfection was exquisite, because it was altogether harmonious with itself, its very conventionality forbidding "gaucherie;" thus to him it was more seductive than a proud and regal beauty, or any charm of genius even, because all natural heats by their very force verge on vulgarity or bad taste, and a touch tips them into offence.

They had not been seated five minutes before Mrs. Saxton came in.

Julian was struck with Mrs. Saxton's resemblance to her father—the same commanding height, the same chiselled implacable countenance, the same finished mould to all the features. There were the same straight imperious brows, decisive nose and long face, pasted over with a woman's soft skin, and scarred by no battles.

Mr. Gay was away, driving his fast horse supposably, but no one really knew. Mr. Saxton would be in soon. These were explained.

Mrs. Saxton talked with the secretary. He sat with his forearms on his knees, his body leant forward. He spoke to her with an intimate's air. Julian stood with Vivian before some pictures. The little beauty entertained him easiest this way. She told him where in Europe they had picked up this picture or that trifle this last summer, and then she would turn her big innocent eyes on him, like batteries unmasked on unarmored ships; she enjoyed the evident effect of her volleys.

Presently the secretary asked Vivian to get him that thing she promised him two days ago.

"It's a present from Paris, I believe. Just like you to pick it up for me." Vivian and he drew aside together, chaffing.

Mrs. Saxton approached Julian.

Perhaps Mancutt had given her the cue. At any rate, she sat down by the young man's side and smiled over him, looked pleased and interested and so won him—as any rich and powerful woman can win any crude young fellow whose lot is struggle and aspiration for the future. She was just sufficiently matronly and good-looking and patronizing, and he found himself telling her how he came to New York and what he wanted to do.

"I think you were wise, very wise, in coming to New York," said Mrs. Saxton, after Julian had hinted at his hesitation in essaying practical life. "Especially if one is ambitious, this city is the place for him. I think sedentary pursuits always leave a man discontented; he must feel as if he had not done all or lived wholly. I know how it is, you see, for my own husband has the scholarly drift; but now he is with papa and he is much happier."

"And after all," said Julian, philosophically, "one had best go with his generation. The thinker has no place in this generation; they don't want him. So, you know, if a man exhausts half his force in resisting the tide and in embanking his position so that the world will allow him to think, he hasn't got much left to think with. It is not worth the game."

"True," assented Mrs. Saxton, as if she were endorsing

an opinion long ago thought out by her. She did not exactly know what he meant; nevertheless, " It is most true," she repeated, in the oracular tone of the infallible society goddess.

Julian was flattered with her graciousness and that his own ideas were so intelligible to a "grande dame." He was about to say some more, but she interrupted: "And then, such men get such miserably wretched little salaries. Bah!" and she poked up her plutocratic nose in infinite scorn of the meagre possibilities in that infinitesimal pay. Julian felt that a life of ideas was contemptible.

He said, "After all, a fellow likes consideration and money. That is the first thing, after all canting is laid aside."

Mrs. Saxton understood him now; he spoke her own world's vernacular. "Good! That is excellently said. Ambition is splendid; if I were a man, I should go far, far as effort and ambition would put me. And then, you know, as you grow older your needs multiply, and you want more and more money. New York will cure you of all feeling like yours, in a very short time. You will get into the rush, and that costs. You will want a great deal in a few years."

A gentleman of thirty-five, perhaps, came over the carpet with noiseless tread and stood for a moment behind Mrs. Saxton's chair, unperceived by her. He touched her shoulder. She started. "Oh, it's you," she said indifferently, and introduced him as her husband. He bowed silently to Julian and passed to an easy chair, dropping just the slightest recognition to the secretary. The latter looked cool. Somehow there was a deprecatory tone about Mrs. Saxton's husband, Julian thought.

Lunch was served by two servants; it was elegant, and Julian liked good things. The conversation became general; they were all quite gay, and they laughed heartily at the secretary's droll stories. Julian enjoyed himself; he always hated Sunday evenings in New York, it was the time he missed Exmoor and his old circle up there. But this was different.

The secretary and his protégé left about nine o'clock. The door closed behind them, suddenly substituting for warmth and ease the grim walls of the house-fronts and the wet granite of the avenue. The mist had sprinkled into rain.

On the lowest step of the entrance-stairs a huddle of thin garments and shivering flesh implored the elegantly attired men who emerged. Julian looked into the battered face of the hag. This vision of bleared, red eyes and scrofulous, scrawny vulture-neck, twisting out of stained and tattered rags of shawl, introduced a sudden cataclysm into the serenity of happy digestion and pretty memories, made up of beautiful rooms, delicious lunch, and lovely women. It was a shock of ice liquid dashed over roseate shoulders, the cloven foot of the unpleasant thrust from beneath the robes of innocent happiness. When Julian walked on, all the avenue seemed full of two faces, whose cheeks jostled each other,—the doll-face with its violet eyes, and the haggard skull, outlined beneath the livid skin drawn tight as a drum-head.

Beneath the palace marble of the democratic rich squats the pauper of free society. That stone street of impregnable fortunes, miles in length, slabbed with dollars, without precedent in history, the illumined page America holds up to Europe as proof of our success—this, the embodied goal of the fortunate in a land where fortune is his who can grasp with fingers of steel, has its vermin, its lice, flattened on the pavements and clinging to its stairs, which emerge mysteriously from the slums that make black the city on either hand. O Democracy, O Millennium for very tired humanity! human nature has followed hard upon you, not to be exorcised by chantings of blatant-mouthed optimists, not to be shaken off over seas, and left in the Old World, nor yet to be made as it ought. Passion of man's heart, selfishness of his head, hunger derived from law, and pain imposed by God—these exist, and New York has but repeated Paris and London, as democratic man retains the nature of much-governed man, and cannot fight loose of it.

And yet, in this new land the presence of this old-world poverty has a peculiar pathos, all its own. America promised so much and believed so much; she held out her hands to the poor of all nations, to the oppressed of the earth. Out from this new soil a new society was to grow, made novel by the absence of the curse of hunger and oppression. Oh, we were so well favored, the events of history had conspired together to give us a fair show! What has followed? We, that began the race so well, are we winded? Are we too staggering around the ring, as all have done before us? Does the Cape Horn, around which lies peace, stretch its rugged length out into storms, impassable, treacherous, menacing? Shall a Cape of Good Hope never arise out of the Atlantic of years for us? Can Democracy not resist those social vices that attack the others? Ah! if the hundred years' history of the American Republic teach anything, the old lesson is proclaimed, that there is no perfection under the sun, that government and its function are limited, and that nomenclature is wind, that humanity carries itself on its own back and its salvation depends on its inner self.

Hidden within the high walls of the Gay house, separated by a stone partition from all the significance of that street, its construction, its walkers, its vermin, its imposing magnificence,—a frivolous girl chatted in her boudoir to her maid. To her slight existence what were nature, humanity, the city, the Avenue, the huddle upon her steps, or the destiny of the young soul that trod the pavements homeward from her doors? Vivian was only interested in the curl of her hair, in her chubby soft feet couched upon the cushion, in her plump white shoulders. Is not imagination the differential that divides individuals into groups? Vivian was amiable, she was sweet and not very selfish; but society was an atmosphere about herself, not an organism, distinct and importunate with its needs and pains. Imagination never lifted the contented creature's eyes above the level of the walls of her ego. That poor hag was a thing to slip a quarter to, when she descended from her carriage; but whence the haggard face or the why of its existence or the conditions that spawned it—the daughter of John Gay never got a gleam of the idea that she and the parasite were the two poles of a social sphere, that the laws of social economy bound them together, each the cause and effect of the other.

Jeannette, the maid, brushed the long hair of her mistress. This was the hour of confidence, when Vivian confessed to her maid all her vanities, her fancies and her frivolous plans of pleasure. Jeannette knew how to handle the reins; she flattered the conceit of the small beauty.

Vivian was half extended in a long chair, her shoulders and feet naked. She held a hand-glass and surveyed her face microscopically. In the intervals of admiring her face's reflection, she drew up her foot and patted her "cute" toes.

"Now, Jeannette, did you really see him? Wasn't he handsome, though? Such symmetrical limbs! I do hate an ill-shaped man." Vivian spoke with her mouth close to the mirror and the breath obscured its surface.

"He was a very nice-lookin' gentleman, I am sure, Miss Vivy. I seen him as Dolph went in with the tea. I looked over Dolph's back, it is so big," answered the maid, in an unctuous tone, imparting a long, soothing sweep to her brush. She had made a study of brushing Vivian's hair and got the effect of each variety of stroke down to a science. Now that her mistress felt romantic and ruminating, she used prolonged brushings, soft and dexterous.

"Don't you think him quite as handsome as I told you he was that time I saw him on the Avenue?" asked Vivian, still looking into the glass and pushing her nose a little bit to the right with her forefinger to see the effect.

"Oh, Miss Vivy, he is more handsome than that. He's just beautiful like a girl, if he only weren't so tall. Why, if I were a girl I should go wild over him," replied the maid, ceasing her brushing, and striking the back of the brush on one hand.

"Well, Jeannette, he certainly is good-looking," said Vivian with a drawl. "What if I should marry *him* —what would you say?" The possible husband was frequently suggested between them.

"Say! I shouldn't be astonished, though the young gentleman in question is not a millionare. You'd show your taste anyway, and the girls who marry the rich uglies would be mad about your husband's good looks, wouldn't they, now?"

"Husband!" cried Vivian, in assumed alarm, "husband! Oh, Jeannette! don't it seem queer?" Vivian giggled.

"You've got to get one some day, Miss Vivy; and as for looks, you will have to go a long way to strike his match."

"Well, I suppose it is true. Any way I intend to suit myself in the man. I don't care a cent for titles, and that bow-legged Lord St. Edmonds may as well get out, for I'll never have him. I am rich enough to do as I please, and if I want to buy a husband, I shall please myself, just as I do about another new gown or a ball-dress."

"You may as well, Miss Vivy. One buys candies as suits them, and diamonds and dresses. Now there's more enjoyment in the proper kind of a husband than in any of them others, and I don't see why you shouldn't suit your-

self, as much about one as the other." Jeannette chimed
in with her mistress's sentiments on all occasions.

She always did. That was the reason of her favorable
fortune. When she was chambermaid back in the old
house on Lexington Avenue, she had flattered Miss Vivian,
she had used every little opportunity to gain the good
graces of this millionaire's princess. As a result a year after
Mrs. Gay's death, Vivian had advanced her to the position
of maid over all French candidates. She had increased in
favor from thence afterwards.

"I do intend to suit myself," announced Vivian with
emphasis. "How I'd like to kiss him once!" she added
impulsively.

"Oh, Miss Vivian?"

"It isn't shocking at all, so you needn't 'Oh' me. You
would like to yourself, you know you would," cried Vivian,
blushing in her glass.

"Mebbe I would, and mebbe you would let me!" said
Jeannette, sententiously.

"I couldn't interfere. I don't own him."

"Perhaps you don't, but you could to-morrow," rejoined
the maid. "You could buy him up, and he'd be bought
easy, you're so beautiful."

"Let me see, let me see," mused Vivian. "Mrs. Julian
Clyde, Vivian Gay Clyde—it does sound *distingué,* and
then—I'm so rich and he would be so aristocratic-looking.
Mrs. Julian Clyde would dazzle New York. Do you know,
Jeannette?" she said to her maid, who stroked her hair with
caressing touches, "I think I'll marry him. He's got a
swell name and he is so crushingly handsome. Then I
like New York better than Europe. Women are so restrained there; and then, you know he'd be dependent on
me, and I'd rather have a man dependent. I'm rich, and
that means to do as one chooses. When I get a little sick
of him, I could just go off, push him out of the way and

have a good time. I think I'll get married—a girl has more liberty than when she hasn't got a husband to lend her a Mrs."

And this patrician of the New Babylon went to bed.

CHAPTER II.

BUSINESS—IDEALS.

WHEN the master of realism wished to represent one of his young men as grown hard, as crystallized into evil, he plunged Philippe Bridau into New York, as a blacksmith plunges his horseshoe into water to temper it. There in that community, "the most individualistic on earth," as Balzac says, all the selfish instincts of the young Frenchman were drawn out by force, as a magnet selects the iron and leaves the gold. The great modern delineator of humanity divined the American Babylon aright. Here, where commerce is concentrated and bargain has her temple, where is archetyped, as it were, the energy and shrewd calculation of the American people, where ambitious young men throng from the extent of a continent, where are no citizens and only fortune-hunters and money-spenders, where is little or no interest in the community, where people roost but do not dwell, where the tide brings up new faces every day and carries them out to all sides on every train,—the self is enormously enforced.

We are all strangers in New York, every other man is an alien; and we are fighters, not neighbors. "Love of city" has a strange ring about it to us who regard our town as an

immense stock-exchange with telegraphs to all the world,
or as a huge caravansary, where we tarry a while for pleasure or for gain.   But obligation or affection for the city's
self—bah!   We let a lot of immigrants run it and debauch
it, and we stumble over the vilest paving in the world to
the inside of our palaces.   Don't let us be such hyprocites
as to pretend to any civic sense.   Each for himself, and
don't mask!   The very configuration of the narrow island
encourages this tendency.   Shut up between two deep sea-
arms, buildings are crushed on a strip of earth and rear
themselves high up, as in geology a plain is forced up into
jagged peaks by the lateral pressure.   This tallest of towns
has grown in one direction, north, and the immense addi-
tions to her bulk of late years have all been erected on a
three-mile-wide strait of earth.   New York has built a
tower on her head and every year increases the congestion
of the lower quarters.   Thus moderate building is banished
into Long Island and New Jersey, and toppling business-
blocks crowd tenements and brownstone residences.

Balzac wrote fifty years ago, and since then the spirit he
discerned has become emphasized into a peculiarity and
developed into distinctive character.

The stragglers and their yawning appetites, the adven-
turers and their freedom, the millionaires and their expen-
diture, have drained into this sink from the arteries of a
continent, and are clotted here together.   New York pre-
cedes the age and the country lags after her.   She is the
prophecy of the materialism to come, the prototype of the
future, the Americanization of America, the funnel of the
whole whirlpool of commercial and individualistic civilization.

The immigration is filling up America's interstices, and
slowly wearing down the old community of English habit
and Puritan tone which made us a nation and is the foundation of the continental civilization to come.   Here and

there are spots like Exmoor, untouched as yet. But for the most part the masses are foreign or extracted from thence, and to be purely American is getting to be an accomplishment in these days. The influx of plebeian Europe has flowed under us and lifted us, as a flood does a wooden village, above its own level, the sooner to swallow us. New York, it is the future, that radical which is to overcome us.

When he first met Vivian, Julian Clyde had been in her father's office for over a year. A year of New York had surged over him, and left its residuum on his soul. That spirit which gave itself generously, persuaded that there was much to learn, had had its ductile metal shapen as with a moulder's instruments.

He never forgot his first day of business. Trepidation sat in his knees, and yet an elation like wine coursed his veins, when he entered the elevated train with a sense of his destination as Wall Street. He read his newspaper, ranged with the *other* brokers and big business men in the car. The speed, the faces, the portentous hours ahead excited him, used as he was to the empty Exmoor days. To dive out of Broadway down that narrow alley of commerce, how delightful! And the giant blocks above him, story above story,—to feel that he belonged there, that this was to be his familiar environment, gave him a pride in himself. He was a Wall Street man, in the whirl, where the orchestra of the world boomed fastest. How had he ever stagnated there in Exmoor for so long a time?

The great office amazed him. The succession of rooms, the precision of movement, the subdued intensity, the counters and desks and books—a labyrinth of labor, an intricacy, before which he sat helpless. He trembled before this spider-web of commerce, where flies were sucked dry and Gay himself was the monster hidden in the midst and bastioned by bald-headed, incisive clerks. A fellow of less imagination would not have been stunned like Julian, he would have only been eager to go ahead. But for Julian the immensity, the intricacy of affairs struck home. Could his mind ever master it?

He was given a desk, where he sat for two hours with nothing to do. In that time he learned the carelessness of power and the indifference of the world. He was made to realize the mathematical implacability of the machine that dumped baskets of gold at Gay's feet. The secluded scholar, who had all his life dreamed vain dreams and dissipated in great thoughts of other men, understood in reality how futile he was and how mechanism subjected mind. When a clerk came, looking respectful, to say Mr. Gay wished to see him, Julian felt faint, his knees shook. Mr. Gay was quite another personage from the taciturn and courteous guest of his father.

"Sit down," a bass voice with an imperious note in it demanded. "Young man, I am glad to have you in my office. A word or two. If you are a genius, we don't want you. We want a man of head, cool and common-sensed. We business men dislike the literary fellows quite as much as do the politicians. I intend to give you a chance, you take it. Look out for your own. Let no man take you in. Take nothing for granted, and get there. Good-morning."

Gay oppressed the youth's imagination. The image of the speculator haunted him. This stern taciturn man, who controlled fortune and broke men across the counters of his banking-house, who sat ensconced in the midst of turmoil and held a hundred reins, who drove his chariot of success skilfully and boldly where most men blanched pale—in the course of the year Julian saw him impassive in the thick of business rout, marble where others shivered or turned hot with desire—ever the same; cold as fate, never out of patience, possessed of Italian subtlety; a man who could

wait the revolution of the wheel of luck, who could bend
to every storm and play a weak part, who could descend a
pitiless shock at the very moment when a sudden blow
would shatter. He had something of the Bismarck in him,
with a little Disraelian leaven. No one knew him inti-
mately, and his friends were always inferiors. His person
was almost unknown to the public, and thus rumor made
its legends. This invisible sovereign of finance was like
the shadow of a bird of prey, for his victims first knew him
by the darkness beneath his wings as he settled for the
final swoop.

In Julian's estimation he was a great man, much more
than a mere business instinct. As the young man became
better acquainted with the office and the operations on
foot therein, and became able to properly estimate them
by the laws of business, he waxed in respect for John Gay.
There was a largeness about the man and a gigantic stature
about his schemes. They were woven about a continent,
and his agents were sown up and down all Christendom.
He evolved from his brain a transcendental geometry of
finance, as Napoleon raised war to incarnate science of
offence. Logic was here applied to commerce, and the law
of cause animated the pulse in the body of his success. In
Minnesota he lightened on a timber tract, in Missouri he
wrecked a railroad, on Lake Superior he throttled the
copper-mines, in Nebraska he grasped two counties in his
hand, in New England he operated the fall of breadstuffs,
and he dictated in England the price of cotton. His eye
was upon everything, and by massing of capital and supreme
nerve he broke into a hoarded wealth, or stunned a prosperous industry, or shattered an opposing syndicate, as
Marlborough drove over the French at Ramillies. Surely
he was great. Every quality of mind which pedestalled on
celebrity such men as John Churchill or Augustus Cæsar,
he had displayed, and over magnitudes as great as theirs

in some ways; for a hundred millions in America means the power of a great captain of things, as they of men and armies. And his motives were not the Jew's, but rather the gambler's. He played for the game's sake, and his passion was the strain, not the gold that rewarded success.

Was the man conscious of his stupendous power? Or did he but play with it, as a child plays with a cannon-shell and knows not the pregnancy of his toy? Julian often asked himself which. Perhaps it attends on all genius not to recognize the potency of its own acts, to march over Europe and think it a picnic, to subvert an empire and think it an act in a stage-drama, to promulgate an earth-shaking book and smile at men's credulity of wonder. Can any man, however great and ruthless, be presented with the full responsibility of his acts and not be unnerved? Have not many changers of history imagined they were only playing at dominoes?

The millionaire occupies the imagination of our people, not only because he is the fortunate possessor of what a trading civilization conceives to be the best good, but also because he is picturesque. The world has never seen such gigantic massings of wealth, and the owner cannot spend its income for himself. After baptizing himself in indulgence, still he must necessarily constitute himself trustee of the larger part for the benefit of others. There is a mean in wealth at which a possessor can most selfishly live for himself, but beyond it the ratio of burdens increases, and at a point the possessor actually becomes a mere public servant to run manufactures for his employees and railroads for the people. It is the American solution of those general social functions the old governments assume or manage themselves. Thus our millionaires are sovereigns, despots, in a way. They are interesting, and not envy nor money-lust alone makes us admire them. We have the worship for them Europe gives to her kings. But every admiration involves a reflection of its object on the soul which worships. Thus we, who have substituted the millionaire for the old ideals of a great statesman or a great genius, have taken an influence from those royal riches. Wealth is not so much our desire as our ideal. And it is this veneration for capital itself, not our eagerness after money, nor our national restlessness, that is so tragic, so hopeless, so barren for the future. We all feel it, the best of us are shadowed by it, this universal adoration of the millionaire. That wealth is so huge, so enormous, it staggers our comprehension, and we view it much as we do the extent of our country and the perfection of our liberty. It is a canto in our national lyric in praise of bigness.

And the admiration and awe Julian had for Mr. Gay produced its effect. The youth was not conscious how great was the gulf between this esteem for the operator and that spiritual idealism on which he had hitherto been nourished. To be open to all impressions, grand and puerile; to be docile and ductile; to see the sweetness of others and to hate the limitations of self-sufficiency; to endeavor to understand and feel all natures and all moods; to be no fixed and frozen uniformity, solidly casting off influences, as the turret of a monitor casts off bullets, but to be able to think with each period of history and to slip at will into the feeling and thought of opposite personalities—that was the maiden-passion of his intellect, the ideal of the poets and the seers. But this latest attitude was different. To be powerful and inflict our personalities on men, to cut and not to be cut, to be a hammer of bronze and pound events to a shape to suit us—that was the type for which Gay stood. And as the successful millionaire had profited by contrast with the thinkers of Exmoor, having those apparent qualities which the young love, so his personality and his ambition to Julian's eyes seemed stable and massive, something to console a proud man; while, on the other hand, the illusive and difficult purpose of his college days grew unreal, sentimental, a little mawkish. It was Bonaparte outtopping Goethe, fact ahead of fiction, deeds majestic over thought, Fortinbras with blare of trumpets. erect and gallant beside the pitiful Hamlet dead.

Then, too, his ideals had another assailant, a negative force, as his admiration for Gay and able men was the positive. To the curiosity of the new which occupied his first weeks, succeeded depression. The country youths who suffer loneliness and despondency, we have all seen them alone on the streets at night; with the hunger in their eyes and desperation in their faces. The indifference of a great city can be properly borne only by one who is careless of self or concentrated self. But for the young soul, tender of life and its fond ideals, who has not yet stepped over the threshold of absolute egotism, nor yet learned to renounce, the face of an unknown crowd is like death.

"To carve out a success." At home, in Exmoor, the words had a noble ring. They meant the fairest things, honor and truth and courage. Here, in New York, they were hollow like vain clatter. His rooms on Thirty-eighth Street offered a meagre asylum, and the business office grew daily more dolorous. There are two indifferences— that of nature, that of men; but the latter comes to us first, when we love humanity, and the other remains for middle age to welcome as a refuge and a peace. "Success" —stuff! The huge machine, named Society, ground out relentlessly and its iron crunched over vibrant nerves, over goodness and over genius, as over commoner metal. Success was impersonal, unmoral, absolutely impartial, and force, sheer force, be it evil or noble, or contemptible, or pharisaical, was its only master.

The colossal buildings, the miles of the avenues, cut straight through cliffs of brick and mortared stone, the crush of the crowd and its mad stride, the millions swarming and clustering and dissolving—before the multitudinous manifestations of sheer material existence, in the face of this infinite will to live, this resolve to survive—Julian cowed; a lethargy sat upon his buoyant enthusiasm, analogous to that powerless feeling of the biologist before the history of physical Nature. This so great world, this overwhelming life, whose narrowness had not yet had time to come to him—the young, ardent, reverent spirit bowed before it, struck tame with humility.

This "taking the conceit" out of a young cub is done more thoroughly in America than elsewhere, because in old countries birth and the acknowledgment given to intellect interpose artificial barriers, behind which the few can protect themselves, while in America the disproportion between man and society is greater, something like what it is in China, and the very vastness of the State keeps down the personality. Verily in America the majority rules, and every young fellow who comes up to the barriers of the career is exposed to all the assaults, the sneer of the average ideal and the ridicule of the dominant mediocrity.

While thus subdued, Julian hit on a friend. Russell P. Andrus was a partner of Gay's in many operations. He had come up from the bottom himself, and so, perhaps, was led to notice the young fellow, introduced by Gay, and now treading the wine-press alone. He stopped at Julian's desk one morning and asked how his "young friend" was getting along.

"Fairly," answered the fledgling in a wan way.

Andrus saw his distress, and so out of the warmth of his heart sat down on the opposite side of the table.

"Let me give you a few points, my dear boy," he began in his bland, sympathetic manner. "Don't get discouraged; you'll get along."

"I'm not discouraged," put in Julian.

"Well, you're not, that's good; a young fellow like you has no business to be discouraged or downhearted. I've been through the same thing myself. It's hard, but it makes a man. It made *me*."

"You mean those who survive, survive," interrupted Julian, with a forlorn laugh.

"I mean, young man, that those who are men are made more of men. It's good for 'em—knocks the nonsense out of them. If you are a man with a man's qualities, strength and gumption, you're all right," continued this genial optimist, whose own success was established. "I've been through it all and it did me good. It will make you, too, my young friend. You ought to be glad you have no fortune. Your need is your future; remember that, remember that."

Success would be defined by Russell P. Andrus as resolution to follow out one's best, to foster one's natural instinct for respectability and position. Success involved no limitations, was coupled with no degenerations from higher aspirations. The scroll of life lay out plain, and as one marked out a short route from New York to Chicago, so with equal facility a young man should mark down a straight road, whose ties were hard work, whose rails were ability, whose spikes were honest determination, from impecuniousness into wealth and weight. To be honorable, to have his word as good as his bond, to be bowed to and sought out, to possess the wherewithal to gratify his domestic tastes, his love of good dinners, of fine turnouts, to dress his daughters as they wished and to have his sons behind no other man's, to subscribe his part to charity and to look distinguished in his church-pew—such was his conception of life, which he shared with the majority of the able in America. And what a splendid fellow he was!—able, good, genial, kindly, a basketful of homely, comfortable, sincere, virtues. This western civilization has plenty such as he, they are her peculiar fruit; she is planned and upholstered for them and she loves them. Admirable men; any country with such men is stable. May we preserve the species! Very good! But it's hard on the other fellows, the Julians.

"Now, my dear fellow," urged Andrus, laying his hand in good-fellowship on Julian's coat-sleeve, " you must not estimate this world too hugely. Just you grasp it boldly and get your grip right and you can wrestle a fall with it easily enough. It don't require such a tremendous head; I've seen lots of big-headed man fall down. You be attentive and industrious, that's the most. Now Gay, in there, passes for a man of miraculous intelligence. Of course he is a brainy man, but between you and me, and for your encouragement, it's the ordinary qualities of night and day at it, persistence, patience, detail, attention, that makes him. This world is none too great, boy, and so don't be afraid."

Julian, being a strong young fellow with plenty of spring, got speedily hoisted out of the slough of despond in which his sense of insignificance had immersed him. He found the world opening up, the office untangling and becoming intelligible. His daily orbit included many fixed stations, and in a short time he looked for certain men and things as known out of all that horse and human route of Broadway and the business peninsula.

Mancutt showed him the town, or some of it. He was enjoying life in a way. The longer he lived in New York the more complete the objective existence became, the superficial rising and drowning thought and meditation. Business, dinners, club talks, drives, chats with women about inconsequentials, elbowed the inner man out of doors. At the end of a year, the self-communing student was half an animal of the surface. Even his walks on the streets were absorbed in observation of the life jostling against him; thus his whole speculation, and a mind like his speculates always, was on the common forms of existence, which throng the city, the beggar, the proud man, the prostitute, the rich woman. He developed, as it were, a "Zolaistic" knowledge, and that science of the lower forms evicted the lofty abstractions of youth. The influence of New York in this way is inconceivable; that dry atmosphere of practicality and naturalism furnace-heats the soul, sucks up her juices, desiccates the blood, and leaves a heap of powder for a beating heart.

With the dust rising from the streets an immaterial dryness ascends; the used air of the city contains a subtle atmosphere which the soul breathes and stiffens in, as does flesh soaked in alcohol. There are emanations of spirit as of matter, and as the gases of the gutters go up to the nostrils of the passer-by, so the ether that rises from a crowd bathes the bystanders. In the New Babylon where men clash together like the swords of duellists, and where schemes break lances in the lists of competition, an electricity is generated which permeates the inhabitants and drives them to a frantic pace. There surges up from those narrow high-walled streets, where a continent's commerce is planned and manœuvred, a wave of calculation, of daring, of cool selfishness and utter materialism.

The spectacular theatre so adorned and so tasteless for the most part; the splendid gleam of restaurants and cafés, blazing at night, where one imagines New York is but a stomach; the fashionable streets of impossible architecture; the materialism of the women, who marry for wealth as the men do in Europe—these pander to the sense-life and excite to ostentation and flare: and in a city, too, where intellect is neglected or misunderstood, where art and music is imported and made a false fad, where there are no virile influences to make towards beauty or truth for their own sake, there necessarily results a great conspiracy of forces against the soul, and that money becomes the standard weight and the only goal for the runners is the inevitable decree.

By the end of the year Julian was deep in schemes with Mancutt, and the two talked late into the night about how to advance their fortunes. Then, too, the awe Julian had conceived of Gay had become transformed into a desire to imitate him. *To be able*—magical words, that startle the blood. To do and to dare project ourselves into effort, to mould some portion of void into form and utility. We Americans have the English inheritance and our fathers' education of toil, so that our genius is all practical, and it lies in every man of us. Words are such vapid gaseous globules; and as for thought, it never walked. Theory will never raise us a roof between our heads and the weather, nor will it drain our sewage or make us comfortable. As Julian walked the streets that year and mingled with men, his goal of life gradually swung around and the East stood in the place of West. He derived a satisfaction from doing a piece of business deftly, greatly in contrast to the carping discontent he used to suck out from a paper in metaphysics or a speculation in history. To write a business letter or negotiate a sale was to despatch a neat clean-cut work—to write an essay was to despair over the abyss between the ideal and the accomplishment. What did literary criticism amount to, anyway? The Lord and the vain only knew. That "Blougram's Apology" of Browning's presented the matter rightly; the man of power and sane ability over against "Gigadibs, the literary man." But to this negative, this scorn of borrowed plumes, of parasitism, came a positive judgment. To ceaselessly attain and to grow in power with the years, to grapple problems and to break them, to grasp money, men, circumstances, and wield them; to be a force and hurl one's self impact upon facts and change them—how massive such a success

besides any other, some shifting puny reputation of letters
or science, which but exposed the possessor to controversy
and criticism ! At least, men never insulted. Gay, never
doubted his power, never belittled his career ; even the
literary fellows cajoled him, and the world admired him.
He was the man of the age, and all other genius ran counter
to its drift. Intellect—men called it folly or left it
to grow moss in a corner! Genius—men said "another
crank," and went to the memorial services after its de-
cease ! But Gay—a cannon opening on a mob, a visible
force that hammered an acknowledgment into men's
heads.

The Monday night after the Sunday of the lunch at the
Gay house, Mancutt sat in his rooms with Julian, each
lounging sumptuously in great chairs, smoking before the
open fire. They were ending a long talk. The secretary
had been telling a good deal about himself, his situation
and its prospects. Even this man's life had its pathos, and
Julian divined it in a half manner. The struggle to hold
his head above water had been a bold fight. Julian saw,
as it were, the long years of persistent effort, the lonely
days of labor and discouragement, in which the man had
walked. With all his barbarism and his concealed hardness, he too had need of compassion. After all, the quan-
tity of sorrow is measured out in equal quarts to every man,
it only differs in quality and sort.

They had spoken of this man and that, known in the
world. Mancutt had thrown round each name that unap-
preciable air of detraction, stabbing each nobility under
the doublet. The two stripped down every reverence and
vied with each other in explaining every seeming eminence
on low grounds. That politician of to-day's fame had won
by shrewd unscrupulousness; that successful railroad president was in reality a commonplace man of luck and genial
tact, but no such genius and wit as he was given credit for.

Love, it was a bore, and women were fools and of facile consistency.   As to the church cant—fah!

They were silent some minutes, on Mancutt's face a shrewd smile, in Julian's heart the dull ache of disenchantment.   The secretary shifted his position, so that he could see Julian.   He began:

"My philosophy is just this, after all's said and done: money is the only good, the foundation of everything else, and I'm after it, neck or nothing.   A man can get it if he's only determined.   The ornamentals are nice things, perhaps; yet at bottom what difference does people's opinion make to me, anyway?   They always accept the moneyed man finally; shekels count.   And the question is, how am I satisfied with myself, do I enjoy myself?   Suppose I am an ass; if I have a good time out of life, I'll never know it."

Both laughed.   Americans so enjoy the humor of a thing, for, at bottom, they understand that the other does not tell all he believes.

"Now, I regard myself as fitted to enjoy myself.   No man has a better digestion for good dinners and a better constitution to stand the racket.   I've worked for ten years and have just got a start; in my humble opinion it's time I was 'razzle-dazzling' it.   The short-cut is to marry it rich, and I intend so much.   Love's another one of those ornamentals, all well enough when you can afford it, but it don't contain the solid things.   Religious sacrament is played out.   Marriage is a contract, and I'm up for the first woman who'll exchange place and shekels for my illustrious self."

Julian laughed again at the secretary's ridiculous gestures.

"What else can a man do in this country but go in for money?"   Julian burst out.

"He might preach," suggested Mancutt.

"Politics are barred.   There's no question up worthy an

intellect's attention. People won't listen to good literature, and I can't see a sacrifice or any other hifalutin hysteric that wouldn't be ridiculous. What's a man to do?"

"Go in for himself and make coin. The only text I know is, 'To him who hath, it shall be given, and to him who hath not, it shall be taken away even that which he hath,'" leered Mancutt.

"But it's all so damned commonplace," growled the other.

"What, commonplace? What more do you want? The earth and the fulness thereof? An heiress interested in you, Gay to back you, the fun of the fight and a hundred horse-races and theatre-parties in prospect! You're the damnedest ideal fool I ever met."

"You're right; it's all disgusting, and the only thing is money. I think I'm in love with Miss Vivian," replied Julian.

Their eyes met and they laughed outright. The two men went on, turning the comic light on everything, and the bitter cynicism of the younger man equalled the genial cynicism of the other.

Did Julian believe what he said? The outer man, which handled the world, no doubt did. But within, covered over with sense-desires, worldly ambitions and instinct for comfort, existed the idealist and dreamer, who believed in the tender and gentle things, who shivered at the tremulous white throat of a girl, who stored up for contemplation images of vulgar happiness, of pure affection, of simplicity and integrity. At this desecration of the reverences of life and the flowers of human nature, the inner man sickened. Yet it was an irritation to feel like the stupid people. One could not take arms like any Methodist parson, or country deacon, or middle-class animal, against the smart proverbs of the worldling.

Pierce the American deep enough and nine times out

of ten you will strike a well of human candor and sweetness of soul.

So the year went over the young man's head.

Business and ambition, self and money! New York is the furnace into which America throws her sensitive and potential spirits, to bake them into bricks to line her chimney of industry, or else to harden them into earthen pots to hold mere gold.

CHAPTER III.

A MONEY-PRINCESS.

JULIAN was seen on the Avenue, in the Park, driven by Miss Gay. His acquaintance among the few young men of pretension was much influenced by the event, and the son of the Hegel of Exmoor was proud of his apparent conquest. His intimacy with the heiress was taken for granted down-town, and he became the recipient of much consideration—bows prefixed to greetings, unexpected invitations to lunch, and cordial hand-shakes on the street.

These results all came about in the following way.

Thursday, after the momentous Sunday of the lunch, a note came to him at the office. It ran:

" MY DEAR MR. CLYDE:

" Will you pardon my hurry after you, and come up at four o'clock? I wish to take you driving if you will consent. I have a beautiful new black horse with a white nose, as saucy as he can be, and you will have the honor of first ride. So think yourself an honored man, and don't disappoint me.

"Yours cordially,

"VIVIAN GAY."

The blood flushed his cheeks in elation. Was it true, as Mancutt said, he had made a "crush"? The great John Gay's daughter, who figured in society journals and was one of the richest heiresses in New York—that she should succumb to him, after no campaign at all, thrilled the nerves of his vanity.

They thumped over the granite of Fifth Avenue, her little hands firm on the reins and the short arms filled with muscles that curbed the young horse.

Julian posed for the street and the impassive footman behind. Rich women stared at him curiously as they passed in their carriages, and he bowed with Vivian to distinguished-looking men in tall hats. Vivian was proud of her companion's natural air of hauteur, while his handsome face at the same time stirred the woman in her. And, then, such delicate little compliments on her driving and other things, and such naïve admirations he expressed! The lack of self-assertion in Julian, which permitted him to wonder at this brilliant creature and to make bows to all the little superiorities she chose to assume, worked to his advantage. Vivian was a true Gay, in that she loved her dominion in feminine ways, as her father in larger things. So the implied flattery of Julian's boyish awe enchanted the little marshal and reinforced his physical attraction. She was exceedingly vivacious, and as lovely as she had ever been.

The talk of two young and beautiful people—how repeat it? It is trash unless you are one of them and meet the tilt of the lips and flame of the eyes that pack eloquence into silly speeches. Julian uttered commonplaces and

looked at her little, gloved hands or into her glowing face
with eyes that carried gratification to the foolish heart, that
her feminine vanities, her position, her self and her flesh
were fine things to this young and handsome fellow.

They drove in the line of ostentation that files through
the Park every day. The lust of life was strong in him,
and he was swept off his feet by the seductions of riches
and vanity and feminine beauty.

He looked everything with his Italian eyes, and she did
not grow angry. When she gave him her hand to alight,
she said, "Come this evening. I have an invitation
out; but I shall be sick, and you and I will be alone. Can
you grant me so much?" She looked very arch, and Julian
could only mutter an effusive acceptation and move away.

Eight o'clock that evening found Clyde on the Avenue.
He was dressed to perfection, and had spent the last quarter of an hour in his rooms arranging the part of his hair,
and the hang of it over his forehead. His heart pumped
excitement, as he came under the huge portal. This was a
crisis! Was he to increase his hold upon Miss Gay; or, by
one of those incongruities of action that suddenly provoke
disgust in a woman awakening into love, was he to lose all
at a touch? Station, wealth, power, all in a dazzling mirage to be solidified and made his, or to dissolve away before his thirsting eyes, as the whim of a small, egotistical
girl!—he could have choked her at the moment. He was
calculating, like a worldling; and when the servant admitted him, he entered her home with the sinister purpose,
cold and brutal, of subduing her and her riches. And to
this problem of love and money, of passion and the world's
consideration, he concentrated the powers of no mean mind.
He entered the room where she sat, pretending to muse
before the blazing fire, with ambition in his blood and
geometry the dictator in the citadal of his brain.

The lights were low in the chandelier, and the leaping

flames cast momentary glares over the luxury of the apartment—a half-light here upon silken drapings, a sudden
light that freed the lustre of the gold-hued furniture from
the shadow, or revealed for an instant, as through a
veil rent midways, the marble limbs of the old-world sirens.

"This is my own particular property, this room—my
very own boudoir. Do you not think it pretty?" So the
charming thing greeted him, challenging his admiration.
He saw her, the manufactured product of luxury, gloriously backed by the golden tints of the splendid upholstery,
and he answered as if half smothered by the novel wealth
of the apartment. She was charmed that her power seemed
so great, even while he stumbled into a chair, feeling that
he was a fool and had missed his stroke. Every woman has
a touch of the Egyptian, and to dazzle a strong man into
stupidity is the frankincense of intoxication to their
coward souls. Clyde in his confusion had committed a
master-stroke. Vivian conceived a great pity for this boy-
admirer whom her resplendence crushed. She was inclined
to push her fingers through his fine hair and see if it was
really floss of ruddy gold. She was swept unexpectedly
out on the wind of a longing to kiss the full lids of dark
eyes and to possess herself of him, as she would of a child.
Poor boy! Well, she would be good to him; she would
take him into society under her patronage and make him
have a nice time. It was such a pity he must slave for his
living!—so handsome was he with his Italian complexion,
his Titian hair and the girl-refinement of his face.

He got up to take off his overcoat, which he had forgotten in his nervousness and which was now too warm. She
proffered her services and made him lay it on the piano.
His height surprised her, when she stood close to him.
After all, he had a manly figure and he looked so strong!
They went back to their chairs before the fire, each too conscious of the other. They talked of their ride; it afforded

them a past together, and they used it, as if it had been ten years of intimacy. They had passed the first period, that of measurement, and had come to the second, that of confidence.

Gradually they rid themselves of embarrassment and talked "I" and "you;" making piecemeal confessions of tastes and hopes, and even the mutual charms of each to the other.

The fire played, crawling up the black coal-battlements and issuing out of red-glowing abysses in tongues that shot green and blue and crimson and orange. The subtle magnetism of flesh bound them in single coil; the flush deepened beneath Clyde's olive skin, and the undisciplined girl looked at him and secretly pictured out the rapture of a touch.

This rich girl, motherless and accustomed to every gratification, had precociously anticipated in imagination the passions of womanhood. That is one of the ways we pay for emancipating the American young lady.

Julian had regained his control; and all the forces of his speech and of his beauty were swept in grand, effective charges that melted away the squares of her resistance, and were directed by cool reason even in the midst of desire. For he understood that this woman was to be won by no high-stepping heroics nor renunciating soul-gushes. He knew that to her he was simply the physical. And physically he supplemented her; he had the opposite traits. Everything combined, both blood and stature and tints, backed her compassion and her complaisance for him. The electric currents were turned on and there needed but one swift conjunction to flash combustion out. The strain was tense. Vivian broke it with a deep inward drawing of the breath. "I want to poke that fire," she said.

The black iron sunk into the heart of a red fissure in a huge coal. The wedge broke the lump and a conflagration issued and enveloped the dark mass. "Here, let me help !" cried Julian, starting from his chair.

" No, no. I want to do it, you sha'n't," and one plump arm waved him off.

Inspired by the divine boldness of youth, Julian caught her outstretched hand, and flinging his other arm around her shoulders, he seized the poker; clasping his man's hand over the little fingers clinging round the bar. A shock wrenched their nerves; the girl shuddered, as if in fright, and dropped a pathetic " Oh !" prolonged and even sad. The blonde face turned up to his, overhanging. A pitiful little *moue* was couched on the scarlet lips ; a look in the blue eyes lent a child's weakness and appeal to the small features and the dimpled cheek.

The poker fell with a bang on the floor !

Was this love ? Julian was not deceived. He made no extravagant speeches; he did not say he adored her, nor did he suggest marriage. He knew she would have laughed at such proposals. This was but the prologue to the piece; or, at best, but the first act of the drama. It established a hold. He had got standing-room. But such manifestations are not usually the finale in America, they are only the salute with which we open the campaign against the independent young lady.

When she let him go at twelve, she guided him along the darkened hall herself, and opened the ponderous door for him to slip through the crack. Just as he was about to go, she put her two arms about his neck and drew down his face and kissed him over with her perfumed breath, as if he were really her lover. It takes so little to deceive a man !

He conceived a tenderness for the little thing, and he mentally styled this pinch of egoism " poor little girl."

As he looked into her doll-face, he vowed he would make up by devotion what he had gained from her by mathematics.

The Avenue was less sinister to him that night. He defied the lordly piles and all their wealth. He was their equal, the favorite of one of their princesses. He almost persuaded himself he loved Vivian; for the fumes of vanity are colored like love's, and are more heady, to boot.

That was the Tuesday night of this eventful week: Wednesday was ordinary; Thursday evening came, the night of Mrs. Van Vooster's grand ball, the opening event of the season, the first profound salaam of society to the gayety of the winter.

Clyde hove up underneath the great house of the Van Voosters with far greater *esprit* than on any previous hail of his with the magnates of wealth. All that fine scorn of his for mere money had wilted down, like a tallow candle, in the fierce heat of New York life, and his comparative poverty had seemed a shameful thing. But to-night he faced house and blazing lights and footmen, and elegantly attired worldlings with their sneer-veneer, and literary dowagers who patronized him as the son of an impecunious New England celebrity. He advanced into their midst with confidence, and dared the splendor and ostentation of it all. For was not he preferred of Vivian Gay? And he caught the glint of her glance on him as he entered to greet the hostess, and he saw that slight beckon of her fan. So Clyde stood up straight to Mrs. Van Vooster and the two blonde and thin-skinned Misses Van Vooster. He minded not their perceptible condescension; but he imaged to himself the day when the husband of Vivian Gay should bow with hauteur to his meek guests, the pink pigeons of Van Vooster, that shrewd and stupid financier.

Miss Eleanor Van Vooster detained him a moment.

"Have you read Obermann, Mr. Clyde? Ah! I can see you have. You New Englanders so precede us in artistic matters that we must always seem to you sadly ignorant. But Obermann!—mamma and I think it delightful. It is so elegant and cultured, you know. It just paints my inner feelings ; and it is such a boon to have one's secret sorrows relieved by utterance."

She was a made figure of silk, lace, jewels, wire and cotton. Julian looked at her, at a loss where in that bony fabric to find a soul that cried for utterance. He surveyed the mother and wondered if these culture-throes were not the yearning of a beer-keg for relief at the bung-hole. "No," he answered hotly, "I think Senancour a pretty tall fool. It's simply that that culture-carpenter over there in England, Matthew Arnold, has set the fashion, nailed up the golden calf, and we of the ' cult,' of course, must follow suit."

He preferred to disown his pearls rather than to nose them with swine.

Miss Eleanor Van Vooster grew red, and then haughty ; and drew back to dismiss him with the frozen bow of the plutocrat, who understands neither the " noblesse oblige," nor possesses the born aristocrat's indifference to an inferior's insult.

Clyde looked down the drawing-rooms, where the most fashionable women, the greatest heiresses and the oldest names of the New Babylon were reared against the walls, or scattered here and there in groups. That unconscious antagonism which lay between him and this world, which but suffered him in obedience to a literary affectation and because of his father's little notoriety, inspired in him the strength to take it by the throat and shake it in pure despite. He strode about very magnificently.

He was alone, leaning against a door-post, scanning the crowd. He had avoided Vivian ; he felt it best policy not to press too hard. A touch on his arm and a jerk at his coat-tail from behind ! He turned about to Vivian. Her small face was puckered, as if she were about to cry.

"Are you not to dance with me ?" The shining eyes

were so child-like. "You have been devoting yourself all
the while to Miss Babel—bad boy!"

Julian protested.

"See my card," she continued; "this is the sixth
dance, and the fourth, the seventh and the ninth I have
kept for you. Why did you not come and take them?"

"But you have so many other men," and he named
four of the richest young bachelors of New York, one the
son of a great Senator.

"Pooh! do you suppose I like them? They are not handsome, nor so awfully rich. I could buy them out, so I am
not setting my nets for them, like the other girls. There
is the music; come with me, Sir Backward." As they
danced, she told him her father was up in Exmoor and that
she was empress at home. "You shall come to-morrow,"
she said.

Julian pranced the dance with her. Somehow, he wondered at her vivacity and her bold front to him after that
evening. Was it a little brazen? He thought of that
Puritan girl and her cold innocence up there in the hills
of Exmoor.

"Come with me. I know a place behind a screen that
no one would guess at. I am tired of dancing; aren't
you?" she commanded, when the notes of the waltz had
ceased.

"But what will you do with your other partners, the
names written there?" he asked, pointing at her card.

"I'll just be out of the way and they won't find me,"
she said saucily, hanging a little more clingingly to her
captive's arm.

Vivian steered their course through several rooms,
until they reached one all empty. The chatter of the
crowd came to them like bundles of small fire-crackers
set off together. She stooped beneath a tall palm, and passing through the narrow space between its pot and the wall,

disappeared. Julian plunged after her. They were behind a great screen set to hide the fireplace. One seat
was visible, a box that had contained flowers. Julian
threw a rug over it, and the girl sat down on the perch.
With the conscious grace of a lover the young fellow threw
himself at her feet, planting his chin in his palm, his elbow
set on the mat very close to her feet.

"Isn't it lovely? Don't you think so? I discovered this
all by myself. I was looking around for some nice corner
to which you were to carry me off, and Spriggs, Eleanor's
little dog, pushed his curls right out at me, there, at the
fern. So I just put my own head in and this is what I
found." So she warbled on in her candid way, appropriat-
ing the young fellow completely, as she had been accustomed to appropriate anything that pleased her, a diamond
in a jeweller's window, a box of candy when she had the
appetite, her Jeannette whom she raised from chambermaid, a caress from any handsome youth.

"What made you like me, Julian?" she asked. Julian
laughed and told her it was much more to the point to ask
why she liked him,—she, who could have any man in New
York, why did she choose to honor him, a mere youth to
fortune and to fame unknown?

"Oh, I—I have my caprices," she answered.

"Then I am a caprice?"

"No, no!" She clasped his head between her two palms.
"No, you exceed a caprice; you are almost a passion, and
I may marry you yet."

"Well, Mademoiselle Cæsar, I may not have you myself," he returned, slightly piqued.

"You may be glad enough I even smiled on you, not to
disdain what I said; for I spoke in no jest. I don't usually pick any one up, you handsome boy! There are lots of
fellows would let me walk on their necks to get half the
show you've had. Do you appreciate your advantages?"

she finished, laughing in his face and patting his cheek tenderly.

" I'm no fiddle-string to respond only to your bow, young lady," he declaimed.

" Now don't get angry ; though you do look handsome with that flush! You know you enjoy this, don't you, now ? And what is the use of raising a row over an idea that don't exist and so spoil the pleasant time you are actually having ? To go back to our subject, shall I tell you why I am so fond of you ? It's your looks mostly. The first time I saw you on the Avenue, you remember, I just wanted to kiss you. Your hair and complexion are beautiful enough for a girl. There! do you like that, ma belle? Now kiss me and don't growl any more, you big beauty !"

Clyde liked it perforce. Vanity of the flesh is an ingredient of most handsome and some ugly people. Julian would be years older before he could utterly disdain this passionate admiration for his looks.

She took him to her carriage, explaining that Mr. Saxton had gone home two hours ago. When he left with Vivian and Mrs. Saxton, Miss Eleanor Van Vooster had forgotten his bad manners.

Mancutt had offered his rooms to Julian that night. The young reveller found the secretary in his dressing-gown, reading a novel and smoking a Turkish cigarette.

" Hello, old man! just lay off your toggery and get into that garment of leisure on that chair there. See it? Had a good time, did you? Enjoy it ?"

" You bet !" answered Julian, laconically, divesting himself of his festive array. "Never had such a jolly time. Tell you it was a swell affair, and such a gale !"

" Ah ! appropriated Vivian and cut out the other fellows ; I see," said Mancutt with affected languor. " Well, tell me about it."

" You ought to have been there," began Julian.

"I couldn't, you know; wasn't admitted; haven't a literary papa," snarled the secretary.

Julian went on in vivid descriptions of the women and noise and expense—and Vivian.

They were just ready to get into bed. Mancutt sat on the edge and pointed his last discharge. "I suppose Saxton was there, expanding himself."

"What are you always kicking at Saxton for, anyway?" asked Julian.

"Me? Nothing. I don't fire at Saxton. Only I can picture his mug at all aristocratic circuses—a mere annex of his wife. Well, he'll ascend soon enough, and then he'll have a successor. His physician told me he would be dead in a year—Bright's disease, deuced thing!"

A shift of gorgeous scenes, a kaleidoscope of brilliant colors, of tinted ices, of vivid violet eyes—the orgy of his brain in swift-revolving fireworks all night, leaving fevered hopes and hard ambitions as legacies for the morning!

The progress we have rehearsed had daily commentaries, delivered in Vivian's dressing-room. The heiress poured out her heart to her tiring-woman, and Jeannette was sufficiently shrewd to invoke confidences and to excite her mistress to deeper enthusiasm over the young impecuniosity, by half-queries and little ejaculations of admiration and innuendoes of the street. It suited the maid that her mistress should wed a poor man whom she could control and own, for then no foreign influence would shut out the maid's own power.

Even while Vivian and her maid raved over his looks, and the maid goaded the girl's passion by every means, possibly at the very hour, Clyde was in his rooms, possessed of haughty pride that he had brought down such noble game. Poor boy! he imagined she was a sort of 'grande dame,' and himself an American expurgated edition of Eugène de Rastignac. Despite her free actions and her hasty surrender, the glamour of gold gilded her, and he prized her as a kind of social "Kohinoor." Yet he never talked with her other than the commonplaces of society and boy-and-girl love; she had no concern with his mind or his aspirations. She simply filled every sense-need full, and satisfied his objective wants—pride, that she was great; comfort, for she invaded his solitude and stole away youth's melancholia; beauty, for she steeped him in her artificial Parisian perfection and smothered in her color, her vivacity, her elaborate toilets, that Greek sense of his for severity and simple truth.

She became necessary to him, and the sense of ownership was developed and satisfied in her. She soothed with her languors and excited with her luxuries; she grasped him by his vanity and made him to bask in the sunlight of her admiration for him. She was the lotus-flower he had not dreamt of, a softness that sucked out altruism. Higher motives decayed in this sweet air. When the downtown world of barter and of matter weighed too heavily, when he felt smitten down in humiliation and impotency before the engines of commerce, smothered by the apotheosis of individualism, he came to her. She resuscitated his bruised self-esteem, she restored him to dignity and vanity, the Gay in her liked this dependence and this power; she hung before him a real hope, a future of consideration and station, more substantial than those dreams of a noble fame or a magnificent manhood.

In the half-light of her boudoir, in an air that breathed perfumes of Indian gums, where the darkened colors glowed with their own inner radiance, and the gleam of marble limbs shone above lustrous cloths, like the steel of a dagger half hid in a sultana's bosom, Vivian thrust him upon the divan, packed him over with cushions, and kneeling, murmured endearments in his ear. The small siren fixed

him, she bought and owned him, she used him in a miniature Cleopatra way, bestowing upon him all but herself.

Was it wonderful the poor fool was seduced into love, or
something like it ?

Was this young innocent who left college vapid with aspirations, to resist the whole armament of modern voluptuousness ?   Was it strange that New York, her materialism
and her women, sapped his soul?

———

CHAPTER IV.

HAMLET IN BABYLON.

ONE night at the Gay house Julian picked up a book
lying on the table.   It was Pascal's " Provincial Letters. "

"Are you the one here who reads Pascal ?" he asked
Vivian, quizzically.

" Who's Pascal ?" she said.   " Oh, I suppose it's one of
Henry's.   You know I am not literary.   I never set up for
being intellectual.   Did you think I did ?"

Her frankness pleased Clyde.   Better admirable Philistine than canting posturer!

" No one ever accused you of the sin, I'm sure, you pretty
little ignoramus !" and he looked at her tenderly, as we
look at an animal we love.

" But I am not stupid," she retorted, facing him squarely.

" That is not one of your crimes, either.   Just see ! you
think me of some importance, so you're absolved from any
taint of blockheadedness, my grande mademoiselle !"

It was true she represented to him all his vigorous passions, the vanity of youth and a man's ambition; but as he took the book of Pascal's from her dimpled hands, there was born the comparison between the woman and the dead great one, between his worldly existence and his inner and true self, between the gay, sun-loving, desiring, ambitious flesh and the toiling, renunciating, ideal-winged soul therein encased. For the first time within the year, there looked forth his old self, which discerned a want, a something not there, in Vivian, in society, in business. He would seek the owner of the book the stranger in the house, the silent man of suppressed look. He felt that keen intellectual thirst for mind-companionship, the old boy-hunger for dialectics and speculation and pure ideas. He had been so long without it, the sympathy of truly cultured and curious minds.

From that time Julian, when he had opportunity, fell in with Saxton, much to Vivian's disdain. What could he find in Henry? Henry was so slow; for her part, she would be too utterly bored.

Clyde's advances were impersonally received. When he suggested a book or a man, Goethe or The Republic, for instance, interest crept into Saxton's dim eyes. And when Julian had proved by his talk that he knew something and had ideas, Gay's son-in-law even broached literature, or a philosophical query voluntarily. Each grew to measure in some degree the intellect of the other; and they obtained pleasure and excitement in the fence of minds to whom nothing of human thought was absolutely unknown. But not once did Saxton shove aside the screen before his personal self, and after a month's constant intellectual intercourse Julian read that sad face no more freely than at first sight. The man apparently was entirely reserved and never let his hopes nor his griefs slip the leash. Yet there was an unconscious bond, for both felt the other to be an understander of what New York either derides or affects, but cannot buy.

Their intimacy became so patent that Mancutt spoke of it, and Mrs. Saxton, as Julian fancied, bestowed upon him a portion of that indifferent hauteur she always wore for her husband.

"What makes you so thick with that fool Saxton? He don't know enough to make his living. Gay set him up in business by himself and he busted, or would have, if the old man had not kicked him out and wound up the affairs himself. After that he came down into the office and tried it on there, until Gay thought it easier to support him than to employ him." So Mancutt sneered, not liking his protégé's new friendship.

"Why, I thought he was rich in his own right," said Julian.

"So he was, I believe, until Gay smashed him. Gay just transferred the fortune to his own pocket for better keeping, that was all. Sort of trustee to a lunatic. Married Isabel when the old man wasn't king of Wall Street; thought it was a great step upwards for Isabel,—the Saxtons are an old family, you know. But Gay always hated him ; he wasn't even good enough to sell tea; so his father-in-law manipulated and broke him and gobbled his fortune. Has him where he wants him, I guess. By the bye, it won't do you any good with Gay to be over-intimate with his son-in-law, I can tell you."

The shaft thus directed had effects the archer little meant. Mancutt appealed to his love of success, the strong-est motive according to the secretary; but his words only struck the scales from Julian's eyes. That Saxton was not able and that the millionaire hated him, that prestige arched no halo about his head, spoke to Julian's deepest compassion. Many coldnesses, manifested by the Gays to-wards the unsuccessful man, were explained. When Clyde saw the husband and wife together and marked the shallow impassive beauty of the woman and her unrestrained contempt for the languid downcast man law decreed her mate, a loathing arose within him, a hatred of her diamonds and her eagle face. In this money-palace the man had lived many years, as if packed in a refrigerator; his sympathies unuttered, his modes of thinking unknown, his possible talents despised, cheated of that success in letters or science which might have been his. This hourly humiliation, this continuous contempt, this inveterate and unswerving ignorance—they were his companions and his intimates. Clyde read the subdued browbeaten countenance, he divined all the despair and the utter indifference and disgust in those wan eyes—eyes he had seen brighten over some pure intellectual theme. The sealed lips he had heard enthusiastic, eloquent even, over Plato or Spinoza—they had the mark of the scoffer's hand smitten across their tense silence.

And then the fatality of it—like a young man he was driven into curses. The man might endure his martyrdom to the end, and these worldlings would never see his superiority. They had not the sight for the high things.

Edwin Booth was acting Hamlet before the New Babylonians that month of December. Vivian had proposed a great lark that should include only those she loved best, as she said. She would have Julian, and Isabel could take whom she might wish and act as chaperone at the same time.

"And whom will Mrs. Saxton select?" asked Julian. "Not some personage before whom we must act the demure, will she?"

"Why, you st-o-opid!" cried Vivian, "don't you know yet the person she'll take? Mr. Mancutt, of course. You, who were so long-headed in getting in with him, can't you see?"

The four had a box. They purposed a private dining-room at Delmonico's after the play.

The great tragedian presented the mind-sick Prince to that audience of practical money-makers and lovely material women. It was a fashionable night and the scenery was magnificent. The mounting itself was a drama, and the mediæval costumes were a study in styles. The manager had conspired to arrange some very effective tableaux with the lights and the dresses and the colors, and Edwin Booth's slate complexion; not that Shakespeare ever viewed their like, but then they tintinnabulated on the senses of these merchant-worldlings. They were applauded—the setting, at least, was understood.

Isabel with her cold eyes surveyed the theatre. "I think the audience, the crowd, the varieties of men, more fascinating than that sixteenth-century egotist and weakling," she announced to her friends.

Mancutt protested loudly. He said Booth's representation was high art, and as much as the ideal sits crowned above the prosaic commonplace, so much the more was this supreme dissection of Shakespeare, blown through such a golden-mouthed trumpet as the great actor's, worthy to be considered, as compared with the people in the pit.

Clyde always remarked it; the indifference of great wealth led the Gays to out-and-out disregard of the usual cants of society, while the secretary, who had as much elective affinity for Hamlet as an ordinary millionaire for the priceless pictures his vanity buys, always sprang foremost to assert the claims of the stage of the Wagnerian opera. There is this much about the Gays, they are frankly themselves.

"Oh!" sighed Vivian, "Oh dear! I do hate tragedies. They're so depressing. Why should that villanously dyspeptic actor spoil my dreams of Delmonico?"

Julian laughed. He wanted to kiss her for the speech;

he knew it expressed so large a share of the real opinion of the house. Mancutt smiled condescendingly on the poor little Philistine, whereupon Vivian and Julian laughed together.

"We're all dyed-in-the-wool Philistines, except you. You represent the culture of the crowd," he gibed at the secretary, whose superficial dogmatism and cock-sure half-knowledge had often galled him.

The four enjoyed the play: Isabel, like Balzac, seeing in the modern crowd of dress-shirts and décolletées on the theatre-seats inchoate tragedies that paled the stage into a puppet-show; Mancutt, alert, on the watch, detecting every mechanical point of the actor's interpretation and carrying a business problem in his head to triumphant conclusion, for lights and people always made his brain unusually clear; Vivian, couched in her chair, half yawning and showing her pearly teeth, with visions of champagne and terrapin to come, a delicious piece of listlessness, of plump, colored flesh and violet eyes; Julian, impressed at four or five different surfaces, his impulses mixing themselves,—to make grimaces at the secretary, to clasp Vivian and press his lips against her throat, while an admiration stole up against his will for the magnificent woman who scanned the house with the frozen light of her father's understanding of men and actual forces in her gray eyes.

But all four enjoyed being the cynosure of the theatre. Vivian bathed her beauty in the public gaze and Mancutt his self-satisfaction in the envy of men, while Julian loved it for vanity's sake and an Italian pleasure in social vivacity, and the rich matron knew she was rich in the eyes of the gold-hunting populace of energetic clerks and earthen women.

So Hamlet was played out: his supersensitive sickliness, his morbidities, and all the deep distrust of existence and doubt of reality, that belonged to the incompetent sceptic-

dreamer, the unpractical, sublime thinking brain,—played
out, laid bare, displayed, stripped nude, before the devour-
ing eyes of New Babylon. What do those worldlings, those
able, unhesitating, executive men, find in Hamlet? What
do the women, beautiful, material, mercenary or sanely
commonplace, seek of Hamlet, the " egotist and weakling,"
as said Gay's daughter? How they attempted to find
some American fun in it, to detect the spice of Mark
Twain's jocularity in the speeches of Polonius,—those
comic-pitched souls of sensational, humorous New York—
who would have been better suited at a minstrel-show,
that one, say, in which Mancutt had been end-man, far
back in the years before he struck upwards and rose with
millionaire Gay.

And when the thing was played out, and the poor Hamlet soul lay quenched forever on the sloping boards of the
stage, the people emptied themselves into the street, some
to eat and some to dalliance, and a few to go home to feel
the words of the great actor in their dreams. Our four
travelled fast in their carriage to the cheer and costly luxury of Delmonico's. Hamlet and the woes of men were
forgotten, as they sat down in a room all mirrors and
beamed upon each other in delicious anticipation of the
miracles of gastronomics prepared. They were four merry
human stomachs:—Mancutt so delighted to order the
waiters around, and Vivian frisking about like a kitten,
purring over her gloves and Julian, and the Roman-coun-
tenanced Italian who stood behind her chair.

"Now, Monsieur Delmonico," she said, addressing the
classic menial—whereat they all laughed—"we expect the
very nicest things you have, and we hope we won't have our
implicitest confidence abused in you."

Augustus Cæsar, *in servante*, received her sally with the
identical unmoved face on the imperial coin, his prototype
in bas-relief.

"Now, then, Leonardi di Vinci, you grave dog! get around and show me your best trot!" cried the secretary, holding out to the abused a five-dollar bill. "That ought to oil the machine," he said to Julian, with his dental grin.

They came on, the oysters and the unpronounceable soup, and the delicate *entrées*, and the gorgeous and garnished salads; and on and on, a tide of fanciful dishes, ticketed with pretentious names. Then the champagne fizzed and bubbled in silver pails set on the floor and filled with chopped ice—fizzed as if no shadow of a possibility of its being Connecticut cider, instead of vintage of French grapes, impeached its veracity.

These were the daughters of John Gay. The obsequious servants faltered before Mrs. Saxton's half-word of want, and the head-waiter himself ascended from below to ask what command he might obey, and if there existed the slightest complaint. The fact crept around the restaurant, communicated itself to the hall-boys and the door-keepers, —that the two richest women of New York, prospectively, were crowding their stomachs with the delicacies and wine of Delmonico.

Julian moved in a golden haze; he had some dim idea of an airy waltz down the apartment, and every whirl brought a vision of a tall youth with loose hair, circling with a dumpy little fairy decked out in Paris fashion. The mirrors flashed by him like waves of clear water. He thought, too, that Mancutt leaned well forward and showered before Mrs. Saxton his whole store of firework wit and Gotham stories, while she sat pleased, a complacent smile on her beautiful, flint face.

Life! He felt that this was life, red-blooded, tingling! that drank one up and left not an unnamed longing, no passionate vacant aches.

Finally it was through, done, completed! All things end, thought Julian, sadly, as the four trooped down the stairs,

flanked and preceded by bows and flourishes of subservience.
The carriage was there, the Gay vehicle of state, with its
two black horses and gold-inlaid harness, its liveried coach-
man and imperturbable high-hatted footman. The ladies
were helped in, the gentlemen followed; a bang of the
door, a wave of white aprons, a sinking of lights into darkness, and off they rolled up the wide granite of Fifth
Avenue.

Then Vivian said impetuously, "Mr. Mancutt, get over
by Isabel; I want to sit next to Julian."

Mrs. Saxton demurred; but Vivian was determined, and
after a moment of high-hat hitting against the roof, the
young lady fell into the seat by Julian. So they rode,
Julian and Vivian, and Mrs. Saxton and the secretary side
by side.

They were silent in the dark there; the grind of the
wheels on the stone made a dull noise that protected whis-
perers. Vivian cuddled up to Clyde; she put her small
soft hand in his and insisted that he take the glove off. The
young man was clearer in his head now, and he slipped an
arm about the soft child and drew her tenderly to him.
He had never felt so tender; he would like to hold her always this way, and protect her from the over-strong world;
and this chivalric notion was altogether oblivious of the
fact that she would have fifty millions to interpose bulwarks
between her virginal weakness and the cruel plebeian world
some day.

The carriage had turned in near the curb to pass a gas-
main-hole, one of those excavations that always obstruct
New York. As the coach swung under a street-lamp, the
flare shot in, for an instant, a little on Julian and full on
the back seat—space sufficient to reveal Mancutt and Mrs.
Saxton and the expression of the man's face. A light
broke in upon Julian ; why, he did not know, but somehow
the momentary gleam on Mancutt's face had poured an un-

derstanding into events, heretofore meaningless. He understood Mancutt and his schemes at last. He knew whence the hatred of Saxton; he remembered the Bright's disease, and he shuddered in the dark that his knees touched the knees of that gambler in death-certificates.

And he felt Vivian! He lifted her from himself and sank back into his corner. And this was the world and the Gays! The glamour of a hundred millions slipped from that household, plucked away by his sickening disgust. Ugh! there was no fighting about this, no Mark Antony in this struggle; only the mean nature of a shopkeeper, using bourgeois tricks. The aristocracy in him, that builds itself unconsciously a code, felt nauseated. He would vomit forth the whole of them, their little lies and contemptible subterfuges. The majestic Miltonic Satan, the Cæsarian duplicity, were impossible in these democratic days of thieving clerks and gossiping good-nature. Better return to goodness and simplicity!

Vivian was piqued. She cuddled in her corner silently; she wasn't used to being set up against the wall in this fashion. When the carriage drew up under the Gay pile, the princess descended with hauteur. She took Clyde's arm and followed the secretary and her sister up the steps. She hated Julian. She bade him good-night coldly. Suddenly the young man took her fingers in his hand and squeezed them. "I may come to-morrow?" he whispered imploringly. She passed in, appeased. It had struck him his mood might be different to-morrow, and then he would kick himself for throwing a moment's temper in the face of fifty millions. A year ago he had not calculated thus; he would have obeyed his impulse and flung it generously to scout an offered crown if need were.

As the two walked down the Avenue, the secretary said, "Congratulations, old boy. I watched you, and you're making progress famously."

Clyde stopped. "Damn your smartness!" he broke out.

"What's the matter now? You're pretty familiar, seems to me," demanded the secretary. Then in his usual genial tone he went on: "You mustn't think you can dispense with me just yet, my young friend; even if your feet are on the top rung of the ladder. You've got to get off yet, and that's the hardest part. Suppose you have got Vivian down fine; the old man comes in, and he'll have to endorse any little arrangement, you know, before it's negotiable."

Julian saw the truth. He must not break with the "kitchen-cabinet." This disgust would blow over by morning, and for its temporal sake he must make no fatal ruptures.

"Besides, it's just possible we'll be brothers-in-law, some time," suggested Maucutt. "Let's shake on the future connection."

Julian shook—not very heartily, however.

"On the whole," concluded the secretary, "we've done a pretty good night's business. It will pan out better than weeks of labor downtown. I hope you'll catch Vivian, instead of some damned stuck-up swell like Bergen Van Vooster. I thought he was in at one time, and I knew that if that kind married Vivian, there was an end to Gay's private secretary; even if he did know all the old man's schemes and was prepared to make fast money. You see, the Gays have some democratic notions left yet; but if Isabel should get a Knickerbocker millionaire for brother-in-law, she might become vaccinated with exclusiveness,—don't you see?"

"Yes, I'm on. And that's why you backed me for Vivian?" said Julian.

"Certainly; didn't think me a fool-philanthropist, did you?"

"Responsibility! I bear Cæsar and his fortunes," laughed Clyde, with an ugly guttural.

CHAPTER V.

THE PLACE OF THE UNPRACTICAL GENTLEMAN IN SOCIETY ON THE AMERICAN PLAN.

ISABEL GAY SAXTON was strikingly handsome; that hard brilliant beauty that strikes across the vision with a severe impression. She was altogether unlike her sister, who was suggestive of all comfortable things, of cushions and soft luxuries. She always wore diamonds, great brilliants as large as pebbles and shining a hard light like herself.

Isabel Gay had had the career of a professional beauty, although her father's money was insufficient to garnish her girlhood with the halo of his later success. That clear face, chiselled and cut into an impassive mask of marble, haunted men's memories, and there yet live gray-haired plodders, whose youth has dropped in ashes into the cinderpan of every-day regularity, who, if any dream still shadows them, retain a blurred picture of her carven shoulders and moulded throat.

She had drawn most largely from her father. He had given her his temperament and his tints, gray complexion and steel-blue eyes, to be worked into softer expression by the blonde loveliness of the pretty little school-teacher John Gay had wedded in his youth. From her the daughter had received the firm flesh of her magnificent figure and the buoyant animal vivacity which gave her enjoyments from every incident of living.

She had first met Saxton in Homburg, at the Kursaal, one summer evening.

The lights shone on the marble and the wide glistening floors. Women of the street brushed the chaste robes of Georgianas who had bargained their charms for an establishment. Gamblers shot fiery glances on mothers of families, and daughters like Isabel Gay drank the admiration of the mixed assemblage with no discrimination between the lusty glance of the devotee of sensation and the conventional homage of the non-vitalized gentleman. The young man fixed her, out of all that modern crowd, as an artist turns to the Greek head in a gallery of inferior sculpture. He was rich, richer than her father; he was a Knickerbocker, his grandfather had been a Cabinet secretary, and his grandmother had brought the strain of Washington Irving into his family. She married him, for it was a brilliant match; and he was a gentleman, with the manners and appearance of distinction.

As we approach the middle of life the fundamental inheritance emerges and crushes those equalities which youth shares with every youth, even as shore-lines which at first rise from the sea in uniform levels break into hill-ranges and slope into undulations as the ship draws landward. So Isabel Saxton gradually put away her girl-qualities of tenderness and admiration and amiabilities, as the woman-character crystallized into its real proportions. The father in her gained year by year, the tinted face marbled into eagle-features, the woman-eyes sharpened into glints of steel, the moist girl-mouth curved into haughty form. At thirty a great French sculptor had wished to model the head of his " Justice" after hers.

Power and possession became the foci of her ellipse of life. She developed the ability of a financier; she divined a commercial situation in an instant; she speculated with her own money and it was growing her single passion.

She developed the hard contempt of the successful Wall Street man for everything except energy and shrewdness. Her father became her unconscious ideal of masculinity; perfect accord reigned between them. She petted Vivian and despised her. She had never been in sympathy with her husband, and gradually she had acquired a secret contempt for him. She had never made an allowance in her own life for his notions or his desires. She had pursued her own path, perfectly self-sufficient, without friction, altogether unhindered; when she wished to come home to live, she announced her intention, and brought him along with her wardrobe and maid. He was a student, a dilettante, a cultured impracticable gentleman, who had his ornamental uses; but he was without capacity and she classified him among her other chattels. She knew enough of her father's affairs to recognize the secretary's importance in them, and she respected him for his adroitness and his great executive and financial ability. She was too cold for romance, and too unimaginative to swerve from the respectable line of conduct, for Mancutt ever to attempt the "affectionate racket," as he termed it. He simply grew indispensable to her father, gave her hints in her business operations, made himself a constant and pleasing attendant, and waited until death should play third hand before he trumped the trick.

Mr. and Mrs. Saxton lived with each other for ten years, absolutely apart, however. There were no tempests. He made no protests against her conduct, and if she winged a sneering aside to him, he simply winced and went out of the room. He had no cause for offence, no excuse given him to interfere. And then the enfeebled will of the man, baffled in its every desire since his embarkation on the huge steamer of Gay success, still clung to his wife in a mute admiration of her splendid energy. He obeyed her slightest whim; he fetched her a bank-book from her safe upstairs, or set the stool beneath her feet when she so intimated. That wide mind of his, that sweet nature, were in her thrall. But Isabel Saxton had judgment and she demeaned herself with high decorum, so that her tyranny was never blatant. She loved power and not its show. And she had liked Saxton a great deal a decade ago, and at this time she liked him still.

Perhaps the semi-pitying glances Julian Clyde shot at him were observed and stung the pitied into pride. Perhaps the growing contemptuous stare of the secretary and his little overlookings of the husband, as of a straw-man, drove into passionate action the pride of the self-despiser, the purest pride under heaven. At any rate, Mrs. Saxton had a prelude to her theater-party and Delmonico refreshment that was just the bitter to rightly tincture the after-pleasure.

She had dismissed her maid, and stood gazing at her superb reflection in the pier-glass. She had already begun the movement to turn and go downstairs to greet the secretary and Julian, when her husband's slender frame slid uncertainly into her presence.

"You here, Henry. Why, what is it?" she asked, a note of surprise in her voice.

"Could you think of taking me with your party? I— I should like to go with you."

His wife had been smoothing her glove on her hand. She looked up quickly.

"All the arrangements are made; we can't very well break into them," she said indifferently.

"Please, I should like to go—" he began.

When had he been so persistent?

"You see enough of me at home. I don't understand your desire."

She caught up her dress and prepared to sail majestically before him down the great stairs and on into the room where the three awaited. She moved to the door. She had already forgotten him.

A passionate anger assailed him, such as his quenched spirit had not stirred under for years. He was powerless to direct it, for it was novel, and we always go down before a new sin or an original passion.

He stepped before her quickly, so that her head, flung back haughtily at his opposition, almost touched him. He felt her close to him, and he looked into her great inscrutable gray eyes.

"Isabel, I intend to go with you," he said, his face flushed.

"You are misinformed, my dear; let me pass, please."

The coolness exasperated him.

"You sha'n't go with that Mancutt alone. You're too intimate, anyway."

Her eyes blazed two inches from his nose. It was the wrath of John Gay over again; and before that anger of a strong will, the fierceness of his weaker temper quailed.

"What do you mean, sir?" she said, in low tones. "Is it insult you dare direct against me? Do you for a moment forget I am Isabel Gay, that I never stoop? Ah! you are contemptible to believe me capable of a letting down, and if you had spirit you would seek the man, not your wife." She gave him one stab of a look that broke his thin skin and pierced into his self-respect with a poisoned taunt. He sank out of her path, and she paraded down before his eyes, a living triumph over his insignificance. She soon forgot the incident, she was so taken up with real things.

But another had heard and had smiled grimly over his daughter's masterfulness. "The puppy! how came it that she ever married such a watery creature, anyhow? That idea about Mancutt, though, is not bad; queer I never thought of it. He knows a good deal about me, and there ought to be some one to hold the reins when I'm gone. I suppose

Vivy'll marry a fool, and then who is to handle things? For no ordinary man can drive my team. If that fellow would get out, Mancutt's the exact man to a dot."

·Saxton sat down with his head in his hands, after his wife's exit. What a miserable affair he was! He asked himself if he had any reason for being. What did he supply to the world, of evil or of good, that it owed him of woe ,or of happiness? Nothing. He had been a piece of furniture in Gay's house for a decade, one of his wife's luxuries, wherefor her father paid some ten thousand a year—clothes, horses, clubs, dinners, and the non-necessities of a leisured man. And his vanished youth came up to him—how different! Those lost ideals of his, those smothered aspirations, that desire to know and understand, and his young contempt for the "average sensual man !" He had become that loathsome thing; for he buried his old nature and distracted his uneasiness with champagne-dinners with a few of his old chums, and he chatted away the time which was to have brought him learning and attainment. He asked himself why, wherefore this degeneration? The cold Gay faces rose up and surrounded him, even as the bergs tilt up against the Arctic explorer's doomed ship and wall it round with Polar desolation. Those acquisitive, unfeeling countenances, that had chilled him every day, had drawn the zest of life and left it flaccid; a term of years consumed with groceries and dresses and stocks and traffickings. This young fellow who played now about Vivian's candle, eager to get his wings singed, how like to himself in those gone days! Julian recalled to him his old happier, better self. Yes, yes, so it was. But what to do, what to do now? Will he slip down this present ignoble path, trodden on by his wife, despised by the man who aspired to his empty shoes, furnished by the old man with the wherewithal for a Sybarite existence? Was there a possible freedom for him? If he made an effort, and a bold one, could he cut these millionaire-meshes and get to be a man? His first ambitions came from their grave, and all the hopes and prophecies of those early friends, his friendship with Agassiz and his worship for Emerson.

Across the hallway the millionaire paced his padded feet. He came within and faced his brooding son-in-law. Saxton looked up, and the confronting face of coolness and clear eyes seemed to evaporate the mist about him. He felt the genius of common-sense would stab his romantic notions. Ten minutes from now he would wonder he could have dreamed there was a realm outside the world of sordid fact. Mr. Gay dropped into an easy chair and arranged his limbs easily.

" Well," he said, fixing his shadowless eyes on Saxton, —" Well, what's this row about?"

" You probably understand sufficiently to need no explanation."

" You imply something," said the millionaire, in his dangerous tone.

" Not at all. I merely remarked, sir, that you knew what it was, and need not feign ignorance to draw me out."

"Humph !" exclaimed Gay.

" For I won't be drawn out," pettishly.

" Won't, eh ?"

" She's my wife, and if you choose to overhear my private conversation with her, it is not your concern." The blue light of anger, caused by questioned authority, sprang into Gay's eyes.

The millionaire divined where the sting was, and he lashed out.

" So you wish to define my right of protection over my daughter, when I hear her good name attacked, as an intrusion, eh? Strikes me it's like a puppy, one picks out of the gutter, occupying your own bed and defying trespass."

The victim writhed.

"I'm no dependant of yours," gasped Saxton.

"No, no; nothing leechy about you, as all the world knows. You have not sucked your sustenance out of your father-in-law, oh no!"

"I tell you I brought as much as I have taken, and you know it too. Besides, I gave you and your parvenues an entrance into society and a standing other than mere money."

"Ah, no doubt, you're quite the leaven of the lump, with your damned blood and culture and your prowling ideas at night."

"You're a brute!"

"You're a gentleman, a scholar to boot, and a son of both."

Saxton was silenced. All his violent anger seemed so senseless against this cynical, smiling money-despot. As well let a battle-ship batter the basalt Palisades. It was so absurdly ineffectual.

The millionaire rose and stood over him.

"I'm an illiterate old cuss, according to your standard, I know. A little vulgar too. You are the sixth generation of culture and damned literary and all that. But I've got the whip-hand ; I hold the coin, and don't you fight me ! - I can down you every time, and you know it. You couldn't earn your salt to-morrow. Dare to speak to Belle again the way you did to-night, or interpose one objection to her friendship with Mr. Mancutt, who is ten times more a man than you, and you can walk your cultured carcass out of my house."

He eyed Saxton for a minute to see if any signs of rebellion appeared in that cowering figure. Then he went out. The millionaire enjoyed this crushing a man into a nonentity. This was the reverse of the Gay coin, the opposite face to that of that great business capability, which

was seen of the world. Such was the last stage of the unpractical ; let us see what his first had promised.

In the year 187–, in London, two famous literary people
had talked together at an afternoon reception.

The man was an American, known as a novelist, and for
his criticisms on American society and his revolt against the
great ruling Philistine ideals of his countrymen. He had
a fine face, in which everything but intellectual perception seemed worn away, like a shell one picks up on the
seashore with all the glutinous substance dissolved out
of its lime framework. There was so much fineness and
delicacy about the whole man that, beside the solidly
built woman he talked with, his figure had a want of
strength. The Englishwoman had the deep chest and the
sturdy neck of the middle classes, and her features were
heavy in repose, but a passionate lightning flamed over
them frequently. She, too, was a portrayer of human life;
but she stormed the soul and had won the world's heart ;
she had wept over the world's story, before she set it forth
in ink.

"What does your America with such men?" she asked
the novelist. She pointed to a young man whom some
one had just introduced to a neighbor as an American.
"I can discern his type at a glance, and I ask you, does
the American economy consider it ? What will your gigantic, utilitarian, material, individualistic, humorous, petty
America do with him ?"

A bitter curl of the bearded lips, born of the smart of
experience,—"For the most part, we let his kind rot," answered the American, abruptly.

The woman felt she had struck the strained chord of her
companion's life, and with artistic curiosity she struck it
again. "If that type is repudiated in America, how is it
you produce them ? I see so many such, young fellows,
with heads flung high in the air, parading Europe by the

score ; and they are platonists, all of them.   How do you explain it ?"

The novelist set about the required explanation with an abstract air, as if analyzing a chemical compound.   He put one index-finger in the palm of the other hand.

" He is one of many, as you say.   And he looks typical, don't you think ? all ideal and very little of the trader or practical fittest-survivor about him.   America is so strong, she produces or imports everything.   Now, we have New England and a remainder of the old spirit, which exists apart from the present American life.   It is clustered mainly about our college-towns and old conservative places. Then we model our universities on the schools of Europe. We shape our curriculum after European models; our professors have studied in Berlin and Paris.   Thus the conception of education is European, and the views of life that prevail there are European.   I urge no protest against that fact, but only contend that it accounts for such products, such metaphysical alien Americanizations, as this young fellow.   Our young men of mind imbibe the spirit of European society and non-utilitarian ideals.   We rear our youth in the purest and highest atmosphere, and then, after college, after a year of travel, we set him down with an emphatic jolt on a high stool and give him his creed, ' God is on the side of the almighty dollar, and success declares the man.'   Thus you may often strike against a transcendentalist under the garb of an insurance-clerk, or a poetical dilettante prancing the Stock Exchange. Such is the fifth act to Goethe—strivings, and high disinterestedness."

" Oh, the pity of it, the pity of it!" the woman broke out.   " Look at the boy with his German head, and the black locks, and the understanding of the face.   Ah! your America will strangle all that out of him, will sneer down his ideals and bring out his common-sense.   It was bad enough when you had New England, and now, you tell me, even that is swamped beneath the tide of the Western spirit and your immigrant pauperism."

The American listened without sign of disapproval to this British and literary verdict of America; for, at bottom, he felt he owed his country a grudge in that she was his undoubted mother, and he, despite his English beard and sympathies, considered that he still held the impress of her deformity.

"That is it," he said, pulling his long mustache. "I remember my own youth and how I crossed back the sea with an enthusiasm for my great new land, how I exalted her hegemony in material prosperity and bound up my own ambitions with her intellectual future! Ah! thirty years ago we were not all trade, and New York was not yet a bourgeois Paris. We had then a great struggle ahead, and in its shadow we were spiritualized."

The young fellow who excited this conversation of twenty years ago was Henry Saxton, just returned from Paris, where he had studied.

In that same year Mancutt gathered together his profits of five years' minstrelsy and embarked in business. He had no antecedents; he sprang from a blank past. He had been educated in the streets, and necessity had quickened his wits; he could see the opening in the crowd through which to slip and wriggle to success. He had no arrows in his quiver, save his alert sense, his genial hardness, his engaging immorality. He prided himself on his generosity and, indeed, he was not mean. He had known no world save that of business; he had learned his social precepts from the Bohemia of second-rate actors and sporting managers.

These two men came to the lists together with these diverse preparations and different conceptions.

It was perhaps a week after the theatre-night that Mr.

Saxton invited Clyde to dine with him at the "Belshazzar Club." Of course Julian went joyfully to dine at that swell club of millionairedom. He was glad, too, to meet Saxton privately, for he experienced more and more the thirst for intellectual communion and understanding. How many feel that thirst in New York! If only for a moment the pleasure and business crowds would dissolve around one and admit a single sympathetic ray, to which might be revealed the unpractical questions which never accrue to one's profit, and the poetic desires that are incompatible with common-sense limitations!

They dined splendidly in a much decorated-room set with little tables. Men in couples and singly, were dispersed up and down, eating, and talking over their wine.

The two conversed, in the French sense of the word—quick touches, lively remarks, of literature, of society, of politics, of affairs in Europe. Both were happy, feeling that they were understood. Round about them the New York talk went on, made up of sporting news, business and the inevitable stories. Men laughed perforce, out of convention. Is not humor our one social talent? They spoke of the war-scare in Europe and the chances of a future fight. Mr. Saxton had read in the evening paper a long article on the condition of the German working-people, in which Bismarck was condemned.

"As for that, I believe the German masses are happier than ours. They have not the restlessness and the continued longing for better material position that poisons the content of our working people. And they have ten amusements to our laborer's one. They inherit the distinctive modes of pleasure which have belonged to them as a class for generations, while our toilers have nothing peculiar to themselves except their toil. They are composed of all people and ranks, they have the ambition of Americans and the tastes of freemen. It would be all very well, but that ninety-and-nine out of every hundred are doomed to disappointment and so to unhappiness. A civilization which permits its average citizen to drink beer and delight in music and work contentedly is not so bad as our newspapers make out."

"I'm with you," Clyde answered. "I go farther. The German system itself has merits, and the army is worth all it costs. Von Moltke is right. War and its manhood, the military and its discipline, the continual pressure of enemies and the consequent feeling of nationality, are worth blood and tears and miserable shekels. That is better than being besotted with the money-curse *à la* Tennyson's 'Maud.' " Julian forgot that Saxton belonged to the millionaire order.

Saxton smiled approvingly, as if the sentiments were those he had long wanted to hear but had not dared to utter.

Julian went on.

"They may scorn Herr Bismarck all they choose, but he has done what philanthropists and politicians couldn't even conceive. He has presented to the young men of Germany, to all Germany, an ennobling principle, something to live for other than mere personal gain."

"That Germany," said Saxton, wistfully, as if addressing a dream of his mind,—"That Germany, whose men are noble and strong, whose ideal is not Commodore Vanderbilt, under whose eagles the thinker is not despised and the doer of valiant deeds for the many's sake is not sneered at! If royalty by divine right, and blood-and-iron Chancellors, and tremendous armaments, make her what she is,—why then, Bismarck is right and the normal condition for a nation is a strenuous resistance to outward foes, thereby engendering within wholesome sacrifice to public good and other motives than selfish comfort."

"It's better than commonplaceness and Carthaginian

barter, at the least. They're always telling how the army service draws young men in the prime of life from trade. That's an advantage. It improves them physically and teaches them to a certain degree the heroic qualities; it lifts them above the stomach and the personal needs for a little while and at the very entrance of life."

"Oh, we needn't talk!" Saxton responded. "Our pensions cost us about as much as Germany's army costs her. And after all, our Anglo-Saxon individualism and *laissez-faire* has based us on a poverty such as no other age can present. Germany has no East End London pauperism, nor such as we ourselves are fast growing, here in the Eastern cities."

"But the main point is the type of manhood the two civilizations create," urged Julian, impetuously,—"whether the Crown Prince Frederick and the old Kaiser and Bismarck and Moltke are not nobler than that young man there, for instance, eating his dinner and talking to the waiter." Julian tossed his head in the direction of Russell P. Andrus, Junior.

They both regarded him.

Russell P. Andrus, Jr., was a youth of twenty-five, of full habit and plump, pink face. He resembled a fat capon, his favorite dinner-prey. He had nothing to inherit from his father, save the money; for the energy and business sagacity born out of struggle and meagre New England the elder Andrus possessed merely as a life-estate, which he could not devise to his heirs. The younger Andrus ate his sumptuous dinner and spoke to the waiter between times. "Emile, what's this salad? I'm extremely interested in its composition. I wish you would write its recipe out for me, so I can preserve it."

"I will do so, sir, with pleasure, sir."

"You can get me a pint of Madeira. This is my day for

that wine. You see, I never drink Madeira except when I dine alone."

When the waiter had brought the Madeira,

"I have a wine for every occasion. Depends on how I dine, whether alone or with other gentlemen, and I always consider what I purpose to do in the evening as well."

The waiter murmured his appreciation and poured out the liquid.

"Now this morning I took a light breakfast. I never partake of an American breakfast after a night of late amusement. So I just had coffee and two of the delicate rolls of the 'Sybarite Club.' I always breakfast at the Sybarite. Then I had a vermouth cocktail. Don't you think one needs a vermouth, or something of that order of a morning? Lunch was delayed to three, for I could not enjoy it, after so late a breakfast, until that hour. Then I had oysters, a salad, a shred of quail, and a taste of veal truffled, some vegetables, of course, and for dessert some rum-cakes and English plum-pudding. I flanked it with a pint of Pontet-Canet,—always confine myself to claret at lunch. Now, let me see: you must get me a Victoria Regina—I always smoke that cigar here and the Henry Clay Specials at the 'Sybarite;' you excel in that brand here. Let me see: do I want anything more? Just go over with me what I have had and let me see if anything else suggests itself as necessary to the harmony, so to speak."

The two listeners rose from the table, and bowed to the club-man as they passed out.

"He is Lucullus without elegance or wit, a prosaic gentleman, with plenty of money and nothing to do, who treats himself as if he were a boiler," said Saxton.

"He is a man of fashion who decrees conventions and marshals germans," sneered Julian.

They passed upstairs through a parlor where three men, two of them lawyers, were talking. One said, "I understand he makes his living out of his books, and so, I suppose, we can forgive him his high music."

Another responded, " Well, yes, only a man hates to have a fellow pose, when he's after the coin as much as any one of the other vulgar."

A third insinuated,—"Hump! it is the same old game of the loaves and fishes. There isn't any romance in reality."

The two passed on. In all that great club-house, whose members embraced New York's wealthiest, were heard but business and chat and the practical aspect of life. Where elegance and fashion gather in New York, little of wit or art or dialectics passes. It is always affairs, affairs, deals and chaff.

Later in the evening, the secretary met Julian by appointment at the Hoffman House bar. Julian was glum. " What's the matter, old man ?"

" Nothing; only I am sick of things. I have half a notion to give it up."

" No, you won't either, my friend. You're not discouraged. You are getting along in splendid shape. Just look at that last promotion of yours. Why, Gay intends to do a lot for you." Mancutt looked astonished.

" But I am not cut out for a business man," responded Clyde.

" What's the matter with you now? Vivian and you had a crack? See here: don't you know enough to recognize a good thing? Just see how swimmingly you have got along so far."

The secretary had the genuine good-nature of a New Yorker. He was determined to pull Julian out of this fit of blues.

" That isn't it," interposed Julian.

"Gay your well-wisher, an heiress gone on you, and rapid promotion! Do you want the earth? If you'd had my hard climb, you might complain."

" I'm not complaining ; I only mean, I don't believe I've got the requisite qualities."

" Qualities !" echoed Mancutt. " All that's required is force and good-nature, and you've got both. Why, man, I had to have perseverance; I can remember the time when I entered a broker's office only to get edged out politely. I just took it good-naturedly, and finally, by taking things with a smile and always bobbing up serenely again, I was first permitted and then welcomed. What have you got to make you down-hearted, when every door in New York is open to you and every office is graciousness itself?"

The picture of the secretary's cringing and eating dust in order to profit, Julian compared with that military bearing and self-respectful dignity he had talked about with Saxton as so admirable. He drank his cocktail in a loathing of the secretary. The splendid saloon, its tapestries and its paintings, its glare of light and the hum of conver-sation, the clashing of tankards and the movement of the crowd,—all drove a disgust into his soul. Verily in this democratic age, when power was bestowed by the suffrages of the many, wheedling and humiliation were the wheels of success. Bah! how he hated the multitude ! The face of Roscoe Conkling looked down upon him, that proud man's face, imperious and haughty, who had gone down because he would not bend. Even abilities such as his could not afford to dispense with complaisance to that commonplace average which tyrannized the age.

CHAPTER VI.

REACTION.

UP in Exmoor for the last year the widow Ballard had reigned sovereign by grace of the favor of Mr. Gay. The millionaire had bought the faculty by his promissory note of three millions of dollars, and Mrs. Ballard was the regent through whom he acted. Everybody in Exmoor, except the critic Keyes, bowed their necks to the New York man, and the professors who had disliked her, the leaders of provincial fashion who had underrated her, made little manifestations of regard, extending those slight courtesies to her which are tokens of the world's consideration. The widow sat in her house and they came to her. She discussed the new plans with President Pompes and suggested novelties for the curriculum to Doctor Ponder. Every wish of Mr. Gay's passed through her mouth. The millionaire was delighted to exalt her and to think of those cultured men quivering at her nod. He clothed her with power as other men clothe their mistresses with rich garments and jewelry. He understood that he best pleased her so, and he had an exorbitant pride that he could give her that costly trinket.

Perhaps her influence, more than any merit of his own, conspired to gain for Julian quick promotion in the Wall Street office. Gay himself saw to the young man; he pushed him through the approaches and had lately dragged him into the very citadel of his own private office. Julian felt the clerks were exceedingly respectful. He was sitting in the sun of the world's regard, and, as the secretary intimated, any man of horse-sense should have blessed his stars and felt happy.

Nevertheless the December morning after his dinner with ' Saxton, Julian rose with a tired feeling. As he dressed, life seemed to him bare, made up of disjointed, minute fragments, wretched details with which one must occupy himself; but he had a feeling that they were beneath his best self. He ate his breakfast sullenly, he ascended the Elevated stairs to the train with a dogged resolution to pursue the barren day's existence, face the gruesomeness of its flat hours of uninteresting minutes, and fling himself through them and be done with them, as speedily as might be. The deeds counted by the many as great seemed to him trivial in essence, so utterly without lasting significance, so merely temporary.

The train sped down the streets making for the business city.

Was this all of life? Were there no moments of supreme being, no instances when passion, or triumph, or love, or heroism, packed all of sense and mind and soul into one immediate point? This monotonous round of mediocre days—nine hours of solid sleep and three meals of taste-gratification, eight hours of close attention to figures and papers and bargains, a slice of social chit-chat or of dancing, with a slim slip of unspeculative convention between the work and the slumber,—such was the unvarying time-wheel. And not a faculty other than care and attention, and the usual sociability of the social animal, brought into play or needed for success! Bah! it was stupid. A clean-faced, portly gentleman opposite him—would he not have smiled a superior smile and laughed at the young fool's "transcendent asininity"? Julian thought so. But what did it matter? Must he come down, then, to this bread-and-butter conception of life? How he loathed it! Was it true that poetry and nobility and rhetoric and disinteresteducss were fantasies? everything unreal and crossed with silliness and affectation, except business? He looked down the car along the two ranges of well-dressed, sleek, smart merchants and lawyers and men of the commercial world, and it seemed likely enough.

The hours of office-work crept. He bent over his figures, striving to find in them that interest they had once contained when he deemed them the piers of the bridge to the great things. What trivialities they were, and how they absorbed a man and left no room for thought upon the verities! He despised the continual strain of the mind on the mere means of livelihood. Was he never to concern himself with those basal truths in which his self and his gain had no place, but which were the realities after all?

Russell P. Andrus and another successful gentleman had a little conversation in Julian's room. They were awaiting Gay, and they easily dropped into that American talk concerning the news of the day. A disastrous accident had occurred in mid-ocean and the morning papers were columned with it.

"It shows the progress of civilization," began Andrus, in the meditative-complacent-congratulatory strain of the nineteenth century, "that the whole world should know of it within twenty-four hours; and certainly men were never so united in brotherhood as now, when the news sends a sympathetic thrill through every community."

"How true! Twenty years ago it would have been impossible. The world is advancing. I tell you, Andrus, our sons will see Europe with American ideas, and they'll do business with the Congo niggers, as we do with India," responded the stranger.

"Yes, yes," laughed Andrus, "the Prince of Wales will have to earn his living yet, and we'll see such progress as'll make good business-men out of the dukes and counts."

All the New England in Julian that made possible Concord and her mode of life, all the artistic and intellectual nature of the man, rose in protest against this commercial, this bourgeois (for bourgeois it was, even if lacquered with millionaire-wash) idea of the universe and of society. To these great merchants, the business-men of Wall Street, history and law and war and great men meant but a preparation of the world, in order that they might trade. Trade was the standard of civilization to these modern Carthaginians. Humanity—its infinite toil, its divine genius, its passion and its pathetic mistakes, its inordinate vanity, its sublime resignations, its fateful story, were but a preliminary consecration to the high calling of exchange; and all else was to be considered as folly, except willingness and condition to engage in commerce. To the young man at his desk the two business-men shrunk up, crumpled like burnt paper before this withering thought. And Gay, his old ideal! For a moment there in the Wall Street office, in the presence of these two generous livers and successful business-men, over his financial papers, in that dry and calculating atmosphere, there rose before the youth a picture of the race, its momentous history, the rise and fall of social orders, the sovereignty and decay of divers ideals, religions and their grandeur, art and its beauty, poetries and their passion, truth and its half-seen visions—all that is grand and terrible and lovely in humanity, in its heart and its abortive progress. He caught a glimpse of that, and the blinding conviction smote him that thought alone was worthy man, the only thing that should consume a *man*, the one thing great and everlasting. These men about him, what contemptible manikins, mere phenomena, mere little concentrations of force! He asked himself how Gay could have ever seemed to him extraordinary or godlike. He wondered that this city had oppressed him. Bah! what rattletoys of *The Supreme Thought* were they!

He left the office at four o'clock. There was a dinner

that night, at which he was expected. He must go to his rooms and dress.

A light snow lay on the pavements, covering the dirt of the city, as an angel's garment might clothe a leper's disease. The dim December light lent a bluish tinge to everything and added to the very purity of the snow. The Street was unusually silent, and the young man walked up it in a half dream. All his old ideals had come back to him. Trinity, its snowy buttresses and its white-capped tombstones, seemed set there to mock at men and their works. He emerged from Wall Street, and he felt happy to throw off the sinister shadows of her cliff-like buildings. He made for the Elevated station.

He walked up and down the platform among the waiting crowd; he was unconscious of any bodily motion. He stopped mechanically before the illustrated newspapers tacked up about the news-stand. There was one picture, the holiday first page of a weekly paper. A winter background of white snow and sombre evergreens, a figure of a Puritan girl, tall, draped in the severe simple dress of her times, a wide bonnet shading the face, a bare white hand holding a sprig of holly-berries—that was all; but it was a poet's thought, an artist's study. The pure, pale, passionless face, the sad, great, meek eyes that looked and looked, the peace of it and the rest in it, a soul and its veil!

What a slight cause works an effect in a susceptible nature! The beauty of Puritanism, of the North, of austerity, and of rest, were in that engraving. It spoke to him of Exmoor. He thought of Milton, of the beautiful Elizabeth, wife of the great Protector, of Miles Standish, and the love of John Alden. The snow-shrouded hills of New England and the stately mistress of his father's house, the quiet church under the blue-toned sky, and the tranquil Margaret—these came back to him.

He looked at the picture again; he turned to buy the

paper—but no, that would be a desecration. He carried her image into the cars with him. In imagination he re-created her as she had lived in her time, in Plymouth or in Salem. He saw her at home, driving her spinning-wheel, with white deft fingers in motion. He saw her bending over a psalm in the great Bible in the flickering blaze of the huge fireplace. He saw her in her room under the great beams of the roof, unclasping her waist-band and gazing half across her shoulder out into the still winter night, the soft neck curved half away. Somehow, it seemed to him beautiful, the cold of the north country, and the comfort of her simple living with her dogmas and dearth of excitement, but after all, with her spiritual peace, such as he had not found in the stress and crush, in the crowds that urge each other up and down the streets of the city of desire and sensation.'

*　　*　　*　　*　　*　　*

Julian sat down to the luxurious dinner-table. The servants glided about noiselessly; without friction, without any of the little jars that grate on fastidious tastes, things proceeded. Elegant dress-shirts, sumptuous toilets, lined the board; jewels blazed from breasts and shone on the white fingers of the ladies. He drank scented wines from thin glasses light as eggshells, brittle and brilliant.

The lights, the low tones, the perfumes, the high-backed chair in which he sat—he experienced that elegant sense of superiority, of aristocracy, of a marshalled luxury, which tickles the palate of our self-consciousness and would genialize John Knox.

As he grew accustomed to the novelty; his sensation gave place to perception, and coming, as he did, from the contemplation of a moral beauty, he began, in the pauses of his conversation, to make observations and draw distinctions, like one steeped all his life in such luxury, and hardly such as he a month ago, the country youth of high thinking and low living, plunged suddenly into Capuan pleasures and blinded by the glamours of wealth, would have retained enough of coolness to make.

The very commonplace and stupid interchange of vocabularies—for it was not conversation—with his right-hand dowager duchess and his left-hand débutante, left him room to survey the table.

In some way there was no mirage created by the broadcloth and fastidious linen of the gentlemen, by the jewels and heavy tapestry gowns of the women, by the plate scintillating under the glowing light. The true features of each person, distinct and apart from clothes, stood out to him; the naked animals, with the primal passions and bottom nature, peeped out of high collars and flowered out of *décolleté* waists.

Gold, china, glass, clothes, gems, perfumes, toilets, soft inflections, little ton-affectations, the distinctive manners of the snob and the plutocrat—what were they? Nothing but encasements, accidentals; nothing but formulas, shells, husks, taken on to attire the bareness, to be stripped off in a score of years to become the habiliments of their successors. The young man in that hour of his life fought himself free from his generation's idea of what follows on a man, its subserviency to the tag attached; he sought again for the man, the real man, the true thing. He parted the clothes from the body, flesh from the bones, the carcass from the soul.

He looked at the dowager duchess on his right hand. White, leathery, wrinkled skin; a plebeian complexion inherited from some hard-working mother and bleached by indoor life of no exercise and an infinitude of laziness; a great burly frame suggestive of a complete establishment of such feminine charms as solidity implies, and plenty at that; big false puffs of powdered gray hair, battlementing the vacant crown. She breathed hard and pirouetted

her thick neck with difficulty, to stare at one with blank
fish-eyes that excited curiosity as to whether they had any
light in them. Aside from her dress and her shape and
her snobbishness, what aristocratic flavor had this white
leather bag, such a one as might be seen any day in Fulton
Market ?

He turned to his left-hand slim débutante. Straight
American features that might suit equally well a servant-girl
or a princess, so little personality dwelt in them; the bright
complexion of a blonde; the yellow hair of insignificance
and inoffensiveness—by dint of her father's dollars she
passed for a beauty. He noticed the hands that held her
knife and fork were red, as if swollen with a rush of blood;
but he did not know her maid had supported her arms
aloft for half an hour that afternoon, though the feat had
not the success of Moses'; nor did he know that at last she
had flopped them down disconsolately, and snapped to her
maid, "Get out, you stupid beast! my hands are lobsters,
born boiled at that." Even without such knowledge, Julian
saw in her mouth but a food-receptacle, and in her figure
a fashion-scaffolding to lay rich dresses on. He glanced
across the table beyond the cold, high face of Saxton.
His eyes followed the line of white shirt-bosoms, placarded
between the ornamental busts, like panels between flower-
pots. He observed Colonel Hughes, a great overfed blonde,
whose tender flesh oozed out over his stiff collar; the round,
florid face with the little deep-set eyes and their piggish-
ness, the broad crown with the stiff bristles sticking up as
in a field the glebe stands, each separate hair detached and
exact.

Next the Colonel sat a little tremulous lady. When
addressed, she turned to her interlocutor with a miniature
flutter of nervousness and alarm. Her husband had left
her a great fortune, even according to New York measure;
but rumor whispered in the streets that she had suffered tor-

tures in her married life. She was given to little feminine
stories about the men of note who had gathered twenty
years ago at her celebrated father's hospitable board. She
was fond of ministers and would snuggle up close to some
young divine, as she was doing now, with diminutive patronizing insinuations, and repeat how Seward had folded
his napkin in such wise and how she had once seen Lincoln
lift his knife to his lantern jaws. The verdict of the
woman of society upon great originals is microscopic—wit-
ness Marie Antoinette's on Mirabeau, and Mme. de Remu-
sat's on Napoleon.

Verily the Puritans had arisen out of the grave, and the
moral spirit of his New England ancestors looked out
through his eyes on that night and took note of the
world.

The flaunt of the dresses, the blaze of crimsons, the delicate mauves, the imperial blues, the magnificent circle of
color and gorgeous fronts, the sweet-scented air and the
renaissance urns bursting into flowers, rare orchids and
tropical blooms—all the wine and glory of life, the tingling sense-effects and exquisite harmonies of hue and
form, which appealed to the Venice in him, passed him by
as an idle smoke. The glint of the delicate glasses, the
gleam of the satins, the soft fall of intricate laces, masses
of ruddy-tinted or raven hair thrust through with gold and
diamonds, the countless folds of heavy draperies—all were
but properties, adjuncts, tissue of matter.

And matter, the transient, the garment, the sheath, fell
away from those sumptuous women and those sensualistic
worldlings. He pierced to the centre, to their shrivelled
souls. A dress was a dress. Gold was a metal. Beauty
was flesh, and goes with years. A wealthy man was a man
with a long tail and a great lot of stuff attached. A fashionable woman was a woman with the world's halo nailed
above her head. What was the wealth of that man?

That which he is. And what the halo of that woman? The crystallized effulgence of her tenderness and of her heart.

And Vivian sparkled across the board, keeping a general in a roar by her winning sallies. Half the men at that table had their eyes on her. The miniature and exquisite creature was like a bird that plants itself on the rim of a stone basin after its bath, and plumes itself with a sense of its brilliant plumage, cocking its conceited little head on one side and then on the other, the better to exhibit itself to itself. The dainty bit of animate flesh with smooth, rounded, short arms, her soft, short neck, her kissable cheeks and rosy mouth,—the limited little thing had a supreme satisfaction in herself, and she laughed and showed her white teeth to the men; she amused her neighbors with her infantile caprices. Was not she herself lovely and the world altogether delicious? But Julian hated her self-sufficiency. He hated the limitations her egoism imposed; he hated her narrow judgments on men and the world, on Saxton, on the end of life. He writhed under the knowledge of her certain contempt, if she could but discern the real nature in him, the Senancour and the *amor intellectualis*, which he had concealed from her. And this was the woman he had desired to mate! It would have been a second tyranny, something like her sister's. All the natural independence of his spirit burst into hate of her, her artificial type of beauty, her narrow brain, her insufferable conceit. "Damn her!" he muttered. Then to his hate there came a scorn. After all, how insignificant she and her kind were! And all the riches of human thought, the treasures of literature, the profound joys and sorrows of the imaginative free spirit dwarfed her and money. Bah! She was immensely stupid, so dense, so utterly little.

He went to his rooms and laid off his evening dress. "To

be free," that was the constant beat in Julian's mind. As
Keyes had said, that was the height and climax of manhood. He put on his business suit and packed his bag. It
was Saturday night, and there was a late train for New
England. He could get into Exmoor Sunday morning.

He sat down in the car, with his elbow on the window-
sill and his chin in his hand. The moon was going down,
but its last hour made the night a radiant tissue, that
half revealed the landscape. How beautiful it was! As
with Mrs. Ballard years before on that night of her travel
Bostonwards to meet her dead, so the train unloosed
Julian from the immediate, and flung him out of his
accustomed orbit to the contemplation of life in the
aggregate. The revolving dance of the wheels on the rail,
the rush of dim landscape past the train, the projectile
speed of the vehicle which carried him, forced upon him
the universal as against his own individuality.

America rose up, the continent between two oceans. He
pictured her aspect, as she lay beneath the orb of the all-
seeing moon, half veiled in the shadow of night. Her
great lakes shone like immense plates of liquid silver; her
rivers poured along in tawny strings, meandering through
the basins; her mountains sat based in broad glooms with
white summits gleaming in the moonlight, like the up-
lifted sabre-points of charging cavalry. The desolate hills
of New England and their waste winter barrenness; the
Appalachian valleys clogged with furnace-smoke and lurid
with tongues of flaming chimneys; the broad expanse of
the central basin, its farms, its gleaming wells of natural
gas, its mighty Mississippi; the plains of the high plateau,
its droves of shuddering cattle driven before the polar
cyclone, like ships with sails before a tempest, on to death
and awful hunger; the South, its warmth, its fields of
cotton, its oranges and its primeval trees, cypresses and
disconsolate pines; the California slope, its grand Sierras

and the landlocked Bay of San Francisco—all this extent under the high heavens and cold stars of infinite space! And on that map were points of lurid light that struck up as through a dust-cloud, and these were cities; he counted them, New York, and Boston, and Cleveland, and Chicago, and St. Louis, and Minneapolis and San Francisco, and New Orleans and Cincinnati and Washington and Baltimore and Philadelphia; under those luminous sheets of their own dust and light, men and women slept or revelled or cursed or prayed, or schemed, or sinned. He saw trails of shooting lights and illumined smoke; they were trains, the many shuttles that shot in and out the woof of this continental nation; he saw them making across the mountains and the plains, piercing into towering towns and connecting pyramidal furnaces; lacing together that girdle of smoking piles men call cities; thundering through the night. He pictured the humanity under and within it all, swarms asleep and awake, toiling and squandering, beautiful and horrible; some of them living statues, cleansed and polished and painted fair, and some, the rats of the human sewer, big, brown, brawny, ill-smelling, with carrion appetites and sinful eyes.

It was grand, America and her folk, and he was glad that he could feel it in some measure; he felt that it was worthy a man's effort and his time to endeavor to understand it in some part. He repeated Arnold's stanza,—

> " He who hath watched, not shared, the strife
> Knows how the day hath gone;
> He only lives with the world's life
> Who hath renounced his own."

The moon descended; the darkness drew her robes more closely round the earth; the car hurled on at increasing pace, making for the Massachusetts hills. Manhattan smouldered far in the rear. Julian Clyde was glad of it;

he had the joy of a prisoner escaped, and he loathed that Babylon where life had beat so high for him and the wave of his fate had seemed to kiss the pediments of success.

CHAPTER VIII.

THE MORAL *FAR NIENTE.*

IN the library of the Exmoor house, father and son talked over the young man's home-coming.

"I regret that you have determined upon this course," Professor Clyde said, in conclusion. "It goes against all my plans, to tell you the whole truth."

There was a touch of remonstrance in his voice.

"Plans! I never supposed you had any plans," Julian darted back, an unconscious sarcasm in his manner.

"You are right to accuse me of drifting, for I have been dead to the world, seemingly, for years. Still I cherished the hope you would carry my name into the ranks of the living some day. Learning in itself is a vanity and a weariness to the flesh, after all. I am disappointed. You will not reconsider your decision?"

The scholar urged his wish with wistful eyes, as if he could not bear to have it as Julian declared.

"So you feel this way," said Julian. "I didn't suppose you cared a rap. You say this was always your desire. Well, if it was, if you wanted an active man of me, why didn't you put me into the swim earlier? Why did you turn me loose among your books and drop Plato and the Germans in my way? You were always insisting on character and the personality of the man, as opposed to mere material success. I unconsciously formed an ideal of manhood, with a good deal of Goethe in it and the literary conceptions. Why did you permit the growth of this ideal, or any ideals, indeed, if you meant me for an adroit bargainer, an astute manipulator, like Mr. Gay? As a man, in intellect, in scope of passion and sympathies, he is a mere nothing. If you wanted me that, why did you give me so much?"

He spoke calmly, nay, coldly and solidly, as if repeating a legal argument; but a depth of bitterness bubbled up underneath the crust of restraint.

Professor Clyde turned on his son with a wonder, and, perhaps, a horror too, in his face. He surveyed Julian long.

"Is there a conflict in you too?" the scholar gasped. "Ah, I had hoped the double demon was laid to rest. I thought your generation was homogeneous at last. And yet why not, why not?"

He looked the young man's face over again, and he said, "Yes, yes, it's the world and the spirit, the desire against the intellect. You want happiness and glory, the world's sunshine and the cold light of the thinker's truth. They are irreconcilables. Well, you can but suffer."

Mrs. Lancaster came in and the three talked till dinnertime, the gossip of Exmoor and its affairs. Julian learned Mrs. Harris had got a new baby; that Doctor Ponder's health was giving way; that Elaine Browning had found her Launcelot, who had won her and jilted her. All the little minutiæ of provincial life came up and rather annoyed him than otherwise. They told him about the new buildings and the increase of students; a new hotel had started, some new stores had opened and the railroad were to build a commodious station. He learned of Mrs. Ballard, how she had governed President Pompes and how she had enjoyed her sway. Had it been rumored him that she was to marry Mr. Gay? And did he know that she had not been seen by any one for over a month, since the millionaire's last run to Exmoor? She had those dreadful stupors. Poor Margaret goes round so pale, with such sad eyes; the girl actually bears the whole burden of the house and guards her mother. The physician had whispered there were symptoms of softening of the brain, or some waste of brain-tissue. Mrs. Lancaster dwelt perhaps a little lingeringly on the gossip about the fall of the widow Ballard.

*   *   *   *   *   *

The snow fell silently down, weaving in the gray twilight the white shroud of the earth. Lights gleamed through the flakes with wan glimmers. Gradually the covering was woven, and so softly that the work seemed uncanny, weird, as if a host of swift persistent spirits of perversity, with incessant motion, were swathing the corpse of a barren world, and anon would heave it into its grave, out into the unfathomable spaces. The flakes fell, but one could only see them fall. They fell and builded themselves, and yet one could only note their presence; they fitted atop of each other without sound, without friction, like the great stones of Solomon's Temple.

Julian sat in the library without light, his chin supported on his hand, the hair of the Venetian painters thrown back from his brow. He gazed out at the impending night. He had been reading all that Sunday afternoon, in his old way, reading and thinking, or rather feeling, letting his mind drift in revery, as a weed drifts in the sea. The despair of the struggle was upon him now, and in proportion as a life of gain grew gruesome to him, so the ideals of his boyhood started back from his grasp, swung off over the gulf of unattainability, and jeered at him from the vacant air.

Somehow the quiet of that day in his father's house had

thrown the colors of his last ambitions into flaring, inde-
cent light. The harmony and peace of this simple existence brought out the discord in the other; the rooms with
their refined tone and their humble height seemed truer and
more sincere than the great, crowded chambers of the Gay
house, with the millionaire profusion. The opium of peace,
of Arcadia, of mild melancholy; the irresponsibility of
drifting on the tides, of a few settled dogmas for a good
self-directing boat, of innocent animal pleasures, of domestic affection, and the timid steal of Priscilla-hands about
the temples—they seemed delicious, choice treasures peculiar to Exmoor existence and not to be lightly laid aside.
Their imagined beauty floated in upon his soul and possessed it. And if he thus surrendered himself and longed
no more to obtrude himself upon the world, and sank all
the lust for action and power and the vanity of a Vivian-
love in the curbed well of quiet and revery and home, his
ideals and the struggle for their attainment dissolved like-
wise. They, too, entailed suffering and anguish on the
possessor. He would let them slip. They were as costly
as the world. Let them go! He entertained regret for
them, a regret whose experience was a melancholy pleasure,
a lotus-eater's incense of sorrow. Ethereal things passing
like clouds above him, beautiful, evasive, impossible to
touch, most futile the attempt to cage them! They were
like the smiles of dead women, like the kisses one would
fain shower on the lips of Titian's grandest dames. No, he
would lie upon the sands of this sombre tranquil Exmoor
shore, and nurse his indolence and ideality, avoiding the
disgusting things, wishing at times that he might have been
more energetic, more brutal; but yet believing in the bottom of his soul that ideals are better dreamed of than
precipitated into reality; content to watch the signal-sky
which tells how the distant battle goes.

The gray deepened into black and still he gazed unseeing,

out upon the snow. Let him succumb to the opium, this
man of giant forces. Let him nod his head in the fumes
of this delicate melancholy—this intellect, predetermined,
by the law of its being, to probing for the reality. Let him
wrap himself gently and lave his limbs with the ointments
of repose—this ambition with its gaunt eyes and untiring
verve. Let him steep his heart in simples and box his infinite pulses of desire with some virgin soul, pure and un-
aspiring—this heart with its genius-fire, with its bounding
aspirations, its intolerant impetuosity. The lotus-fruit
was not for Ulysses, nor yet for this man.

The church-bell rang within the falling snow; the long
swing sent the sound across the house-roofs; the air-waves
trembled above the clear ice of the brook, stole amid the
spired fir-trees in the yard, smote upon the dulled senses of
the dreamer. His native energy waked sufficiently to urge
him to go out; he thought to seek the church, where he
went as a boy. Rebellion was all gone out to-night, and he
remembered the beautiful things about the Sunday-night
meeting, and a deep yearning came upon him to experience
it all again. He would drain the opiate to the dregs and
drown the numb pain at the heart. He would soak his being in tranquillity, in that sweet religious melancholy; he
would cling to his faith in the old things.

The man was half in dream. His overcoat seemed shadowy
to him, and he put on his hat as if it were a shape of air.
He sauntered from the door. The earth his foot struck
seemed impalpable. He did not feel the outer things. He
almost reeled down the walk. All wore the aspect of a
dream, for he suffused every object with his mood. A
melancholy, sweet and stupefying, hung an atmosphere
about the great tree-trunks, seemed instinct in every soft
pattering flake that settled on his face.

Down the street where the leafless trees crossed their
arms like fleshless wicker-work of bones he went. The

sombre houses with their one light half darkened by the clustering snow upon the window-panes, the wan flicker of the street-lamps, the silent street and the enveloping damp, that made the air thick and a protection, a fluid rather than a gas—all had effect on his tranced nerves. The thought of death came to him as a quiet consummation, a gradual slipping away into a Nirvana of unconsciousness and rest.

Yet underneath this death-in-life mood of the nature so ardent but yesterday, like the eyes of a demon in a shroud, lay in wait himself watching for himself. He was conscious that it was a mood even while he lived in it, for that deeper self within had watched the birth and growth of this languor, understood and pampered it, and silently awaited till its consummation should approach. It divined the result. The subtle consciousness, deftly buried within our unconsciousness, weighs the hair-weight of our glooms and joys and has estimated, when we ourselves are in suit at the feet of destiny, the final force and consequence of our passions.

The doleful chant of a hymn came to him from the church. "Good," he muttered, "they're singing; I can slip in under the cover." He opened the door softly and stole to his old boy-seat far back, where he had sat so many evenings in line with Margaret's face, the pure face that had filled his strange boyhood's need of devotion. He put his head within his hands and opened the gates of his spirit to the influences of the place. He did not listen to the words of the minister or clearly distinguish the prayers of the suppliants; he only heard the monotony of the voices and felt the human contact, and his tired, much-fought-over soul drank from the place its peace, as a dusty battle-field greedily drinks the rain the thunder of its cannon has gathered together. Charity seemed a good thing, the only possible thing; righteousness burned before him a holy

flame; he felt a yearning to throw himself back on the great
idea of a Saviour, a Comforter. He would loose himself from
responsibility, from self-reproach; he would heap upon the
shoulders of Christ the queries and dissatisfactions and
shortcomings of his life. He had tried struggle, and he was
through with it. He felt like reposing on the spirit that
emanated from this prayer-room, just as one lies down upon
a bed. He was in that mood that makes fine natures con-
verts to the Catholic Church.

All the while his inner monitor apprehended the futil-
ity of his emotion. To-morrow the intellect would regain
its dominance, to-morrow the senses would pulse with passionate blood, and desire and effort would be reborn. No
man can carry my responsibilities, and Palestine and its
sacrifice cannot be vicarious. Between me and the future
stands an empty space, which I am to fill by myself. I
only am the artisan.

He looked up at last at the familiar place: the same girl-
profile was there. A tide of pure affection and perfect
trust went out to her. He regarded that face for a long
time; he saw in it sure love, steady virtue, domestic ease,
happiness, perhaps. His mind ran out along the rails of
his future. Quiet work, lowly unambitious motives, moderate joys—they hold their charm, they are the ideal dream
of many in this electric generation. Mornings welcomed
as advents of an even and not unnatural duty, afternoons
of revery and reading, the long winter evenings in the
great colonial house, a mother's serenity and nobility,—the
picture soothed.

Underneath the protest still ! He knew this girl; his
mind had followed up all the lines of her being ; he knew
the forces that made up her nature ; he knew the mould
into which her plastic youth had been crushed ; he knew
the compressions her mother had laid upon her and the de-
formities of her education. Said the inner self,

"You wish to burn your bridge of retreat, for you are weary of deciding; you long for repose, even if it is found in stagnation. You would make a bolt at fate, because choice is intolerable. Yet at bottom you understand your destiny; you know that if you cage your spirit and your action within the frail lathe-work of a mouldering existence, thwarted powers would make reprisals."

To which replied the desire of his mood,

"Disgust of turmoil and of effort, a sickening of responsibility, a horror of action, assail me. Why expend myself on details; why struggle towards the gloom, the sooner to embrace it? Here is peace offered, here is the purity of holy love, the comfort of a mediocre career, the soft joys of revery, the sweet distillations of a torpid existence, of melancholy shadows. Take it—decide your fate—seize with an effort, and there shall be an end of effort forever."

Then the inner man responded,

"Fool, to cajole your imagination in this way! Ennui lurks within the simple things, and the monotony of such existence would press your tortured nerves. You have already known such a life, its train of interminable small evils and trivial inconveniences, the failing of the furnace-fire, a hole in your stocking, the smell of the laundry in the dining-room—things more formidable than the great breakers of human strength! You could wrestle more willingly against despair, against the despotism of the Philistine, against the indifference and heat of a great city, than endure the gnat-bites of mean pains crowded into a monotonous life. Rebellion, disgust would follow; you would learn to regret the Puritan character of your wife and her devoted maternity. The conception is an anachronism, it comes from the state of your nerves."

Some one whom he could not see was up speaking; a classic phrase caught the dreamer's ear. He heard a voice in clear tones saying, "There is the Hellenic mythus we all know, if not by book, then by experience. For the Sirens have chanted to us all of pleasure and of the sweetness of sin. And the ancients tell us two men alone escaped them, the one by craft, the other by conquering song. The ship crawled upon its oars past the enchanted isles. The songs of the sisters, ravishing, beautiful, floated across the floor of the sea, kissing the waves and caressing the ears of the sailors. But not a rower leapt from his bench and the steady sweep of the great oars was maintained. Only upon the deck, bound to the mast, the master Ulysses, the weaver of wiles, writhed in his bonds. He had stuffed the ears of his companions with wax and they had tied him fast, so that he could not go. This is the other story. The Argo bears down upon the isles with flashing blades. High on the stern stands a man with golden hair and the laurel crown about his head. The enchanted siren-song comes over the waters, sensuous, evasive, suggesting all desires and the fairest sins. Boötes, the fairest of men, leaps into the golden sea, crying, "Fair sisters, I come." Then Orpheus crashed his cunning hand across the lyre, his great sweet voice gushed out and rang across the decks. Of high endeavor and loyal courage, of the glory of battle, of the splendor of endurance, he sang. He poured noble great-hearted purpose into his hearers, for he told of a purer ideal and a loftier beauty than that of the sisters. They drive the oars down deep and hurl the quivering Argo out across the sea, and the islands sink down in the horizon and go out in the ocean.

"In that old pagan tale (as we style it) lies truth. It is nobler, manlier, greater, to disdain the world and conquer its seductions by devotion to a supreme beauty than to block our ears with selfish prudence and eschew temptation, because it endangers our gain."

Was it Keyes? He had been known to speak oracularly in prayer-meeting once in ten years.

Julian waited for Margaret outside the church-door, as he had used to do in his boy-days. She stepped out upon the stone alone and hesitated a moment before walking into the dark. He came close to her.

"Margaret."

She started and cried, "Oh, you! What, you Julian, here!"

They moved off together.

"And how long do you stay, Julian? I never thought to see you again. Mr. Gay told us how splendidly you were doing."

"Your mother, Mrs. Ballard?" Julian queried.

"Oh, mamma is not—she is sick, so sick," faltered the girl.

After a pause she went on,

"But Mrs. Lancaster was glad to see you, I can imagine it. You haven't told me yet how long you will stay."

"Indefinitely."

"Indefinitely?"

"I am back to stay, to remain."

"Come back to stay! What do you mean? You are joking."

"No, Margaret, I have come back to Exmoor, and I ought never to have gone out," he answered.

"Julian, I had hoped you had gotten over your foolish fancies. Why have you come?"

"Because, because—you know the reasons. Books and study and things."

He could not tell her the why, she wouldn't understand. It suddenly came to him, her practical temper and her limited sympathies.

"Julian, you'll never get over charging the windmills. You're a Don Quixote."

With which last sentiment Margaret Ballard vanishes from our story, carrying with her a fund of womanly qualities, a sound faith, and heroic loyalty. Only, if she had been some other, another than her admirable self, she might have grasped this man's fate and set it straight on its pedestal.

CHAPTER VIII.

"LET US HEAR THE CONCLUSION OF THE WHOLE MATTER."

MONDAY morning—a world of disillusion. The smell of the laundry pervasive, a breakfast of meagre living, Professor Clyde in a brown study impatient to be gone to his lecture, Mrs. Lancaster in an every-day countrywoman's attire, the cold fog curtaining the windows, the insufficient heat of the low furnace-fire—disagreeables.

Ah, what a fool he was, what a perfect ass! As if it were for him to plant himself firmly on his instincts, as Emerson entreated, and let the huge world swing round to him! for him to essay—the uncertain fluctuating nature never decided on anything, never sure in deed or faith, never ready to acknowledge any instinct as paramount over his life; always a donkey between hay and straw and deliberating forever! Pshaw! what possessed him to imagine life packed with great contents, or he himself as worthy to be aught but a breadwinner with the others? Let him not deceive himself with wind, or delight his eye with vain reflections and unsubstantial rainbows. He was no genius, in the first place, though there was great doubt if anything more than successes ever existed in reality. Common-sense and practical reason told him to come off his high horse, get down to reality, drudgery and dollars ; desist from fool-ideals and Don Quioxte windmill-hammering.

After breakfast he went into the library. It was filled with a numb warmth, that curdled the chill blood and provoked a dull discomfort. What should he do to pass the morning? The sensation of empty time ahead of him was unusual and not agreeable. New York had for a year and a half crowded his hours with work and enjoyment. He had forgotten how to meditate as of old. He flung himself down with a book, then he flung the book down. He looked out on the forbidding winter and then he strode about. He kicked the waste-basket under the table and cursed. He demanded sensation of some sort to make him act, to make him think. He was no longer the Julian Clyde of Exmoor monastery. He was like the habitual coffee-drinker, who is stupid until he drinks his morning cup. He needed the streets of New York, the pressure of men, the tide of business, the whirl of life. Pure contemplation was forever lost to him; he demanded excess.

He had been baptized in his age. He had acquired its genius. He denied all things, all things save money. He desired all things, he enjoyed none. He had the imperious necessity to feel, but he could have no feeling. This morning in Exmoor he descended into scepticism as far as yesterday he had ascended into belief and love. He turned upon everything the Mephistophelian eye, and it was all ridiculous or windy, veriest vanity. He came to the window, pressing his forehead against a pane. What should he do in the world? There was nothing to fight for; liberty was won and crowns were out of the question, religion was a relic, and honor laurelled mouthers and praters, demagogues and jolly good fellows. Learning,—ah, he knew enough to know what a four-pronged skeleton of dry bones it was. As for culture, everybody was cultured, even Mancutt. There wasn't a single ideal to defend or proclaim, nor a single glory worthy a man's life. The only possible career was the gold-maker's; that came back to him with intense significance. America had so constituted society as to erect barriers across the entrance to every noble career; in politics, in art, in everything, save money-winning. *She had an almighty partiality for the commonplace.*

And was he worth anything more than to pursue the commonplace? He felt an utter doubt of his own capacity for higher things. Bah! were there any higher things? Of course not. All worth a man's while was to go in, fight, grasp the hard substantials, and enjoy the real sense-realities, success, women, dinners, ostentation, pride. He was altogether sceptical about the grounds for the existence of beauty or truth. Phenomena, things, facts, were the only existences.

He felt tremendously bored. He wanted Wall Street.

In the afternoon he went out and walked about the Hill and down through the town. How desolate was that winter landscape, and how forlorn the great barren bulks of hills! They had cut down the great oaks Keyes and he had talked under so often; they were setting the cellar of Gay Theological Hall where the old roots had twisted. He discovered new paths about the college and new faces on them. The change made him impatient. He found a transformation in the village. There were new Queen Anne and other modern fantastic gimcracks of houses, breaking in the old severe and stately range. Rich farmers had moved in and Philistine manufacturers had floated in, with the boom. Gay himself was building a summer-palace on a wooded knoll just below the college—for Mrs. Ballard's occupancy, gossip had whispered three months ago. Two new streets had been cut through, looking like raw wounds. There was a bustle in the business end and more stores. New flaunting grocery-wagons paraded the streets. The town was being awakened, revived, and all owing to one man's energy. Julian heard that the town-council seriously discussed a change of name to Gayville or Gayburgh. Would not Keyes curse and proclaim that the Vandals had at last broken in? How the critic must hate the millionaire!

Julian went to the critic's house. He saw Mrs. Keyes, as placid and portentous as of old, who said Mr. Keyes was not at home. Would Julian come in? Hardly had he seated himself, before the critic's slouching figure in great-coat, and seal cap set like a Cossack's, slipped in. He circled all about Julian, tiptoeing a dance of welcome and delight, as it were. They talked of commonplace things. Julian said he should go back in a few days. He liked Keyes, but the critic was certainly more peculiar than ever. But then he was not a New Yorker.

Julian left shortly.

On the way home he met President Pompes, who was cordiality incarnate. Was it true, as rumor had it, that Julian was back for good? Julian detected the glint of satisfaction in the President's eye. "He thinks I've failed and have come back."

"Oh, no indeed. I go back to-morrow, or Wednesday. Mr. Gay could not spare me longer. I don't think I could ever be content to leave New York."

The President acquiesced, a little discomfited, and, after many words, passed on.

Julian went up the hill. A telegram awaited him:

"Saxton died this morning. Come at once. MANCUTT."

He ate his supper, packed his bag and sat with his father and Mrs. Lancaster until eleven o'clock. He meant to leave on the midnight accommodation for Springfield.

Saxton dead! Poor fellow!—but he was a weakly sort of man.

The charm of Exmoor had gone. Her people seemed different and Gay was tearing open her countenance. Mrs

Ballard was stricken—a fitting end. Let the candle of her unhappy fate go out. It would have been better if she had not been caged.

He never would be caged.

A sullen anger at the order of Fate, at the world and its way, at God and his decrees, smouldered within him. He would avenge his slain ideals on the world that sneered them out. He hated it all. He would go down to New York and flatter Mancutt and fool him ; model himself on the millionaire and get out of him all he could. He would capture Vivian, marry her money and crush her self-con gratulation.

For it all became clear to him. Man is set in a world of time which he must somehow fill up—he eats, he sleeps, he loves, the coarser sort get drunk, the more virile plunge into work, but all avoid the reflection of the truth; they would cheat themselves and think themselves beautiful and powerful, not the unvailing Yahoos that they are. He understood why Keyes grasped at all people to talk to and would not let them go; he wished to fill up time. The moonlight of sentiment and romance and beauty had shifted off the world for him and he saw it as it was, ugly, stale, unprofitable, flat.

He was relieved when train-time came. It was prosaic work to sit there with an old-fogy professor and a strait-laced widow.

Julian Clyde returned to New York disenchanted and "settled down," determined to plough to success and achieve the only American distinction, millionairedom.

He had left his ideals in the house of his boyhood.

THE END.

www.ingramcontent.com/pod-product-compliance
Lightning Source LLC
Chambersburg PA
CBHW030118030726
47498CB00007B/2439